G000058716

The Curse of Minerva

by

William Nicoll

Read & Enjoy!

The Curse of Minerva

This book is published by Gladman Publishing and printed by ImprintDigital.com

This book is a work of fiction. Any resemblance to people or events, past or present, is purely coincidental.

A CIP record for this book is available from the British Library

ISBN 978-1-3999-3640-8

Author's Acknowledgements

A big thank you to David Unite for taking on the laborious task of editing my work. I struggle to find words to describe his endeavours although the ones I would use are: efficient, tireless and cheap! (I can't remember, was it one or two bottles of wine I paid you?).

The book cover is the hand of the exceptionally talented and highly creative - Darren Trenchard. It is a unique piece of colourful art, portraying some of the many characters within my shambolic tale and adroitly depicts the ethos in which the book has been written. Surely, the cover is worth the purchase price alone?

For enquiries about further commissions by Darren please contact darrentrenchard@gmail.com

The Curse of Minerva

Chapter 1 - The Greek Bureau of Culture

Gladios Fatiakos was sitting at his desk within the suite of rooms occupied by his department - Lost Cultural Heritage - at Galaneo Street in the heart of Athens old town. Irritatingly, sweat dripped from his chin as the ineffective overhead fan clattered round and round, thrusting warm air over his tubby frame and ruffling his dark, wavy hair. His clammy hands left smudges on the paperwork.

Running his right index finger down the new menu of the Sarcophagus Tavern past the entrees: Tzatziki, Dolmades, Souvlaki and then the mains: Moussaka, Barbouni, Gyro… Gladios paused staring at the Chef's special - *Skewered Mongolian Lamb*. Mongolian Lamb? What was wrong with Greek lamb? The Kolonos Hills were swarming with feral unkempt sheep and goats, so were the Cyclades Isles; where he and his comfortably rotund wife had stayed only last summer. His thoughts returned to the smelly, old billy which had resided at nights on the patio of their small two-bedroom villa. Baa, baa, baa it had bleated every ruddy morning just after sunrise. Why couldn't the new Turkish chef at the Sarcophagus Tavern have skewered that wretched goat and left the indigenous people of the Mongolian Steppes to enjoy their own lamb, pondered Gladios.

The door burst open and in strode Helena Tattius, the most attractive and youngest member of his ageing team at just twenty-eight.

'Look at this – *The Curse of Minerva* - by Lusieri.' She thrust forward a printout of page thirty-nine from an electronic copy of the Forbes and McKillop auction catalogue.

'Lusieri?' questioned Gladios.

'Yes, Lusieri,' repeated Helena forcefully...'Giovanni Battista Lusieri.' Gladios looked puzzled, his brow furrowing while he stood up. 'Elgin's man,' continued Helena, 'The Earl Elgin's Italian skivvy who plundered our heritage.'

'Oh, that Lusieri,' said Gladios, regaining his composure as the furrows across his brow dissipated. He broke out into a gentle smile. Taking hold of the printout he stared at the watercolour of highland cattle sipping from a loch under the backdrop of the Parthenon Temple situated on a wind-swept island. 'It doesn't look much like... errr?' observed Gladios, peering at Helena through his narrowing eyes, watching her subtle moves and her shoulders slump in exasperation.

'It's not in Greece. Read the title – The Curse of Minerva, Loch Leven by Giovanni Battista Lusieri 1812. Loch Leven... it's in Scotland!' Gladios' brow furrowed again while staring at the picture in silence.

'What do you propose?'

'Buy it!' said Helena decisively. 'I searched the internet earlier and Loch Leven is close to the Earl of Elgin's ancestral home. It's a long shot, but the painting may harbour a lost secret, something which could help us locate a frieze, a metope or even a pediment from our beloved Temple. It's never been fully recovered.' Gladios remained remarkably nonplussed, looking at Helen while contemplating further before he spoke.

'Estimate of £50,000, that's about €60,000. Money's tight at the Bureau. It will need to go to committee for approval.'

'I know, but... the Parthenon Temple painted on a Scottish Island by Lusieri. It's... it's part of our heritage. I mean, what do we exist for if not to try and recover our national treasures, lost through pilfering Turks during the Ottoman Empire and then that wretched Lord Elgin who flogged our wares to his own Government for a tidy profit. The indignity of having to visit the British Museum in London to see Phidias' exquisite work.' Gladios knew Helena was right.

'Okay, okay. Prepare the committee papers and I will warn Prodius Polopidus to expect an application.

'Thanks,' replied Helena, smiling sweetly and then triumphantly leaving the room with a skip to her step and a twinkle in her eye.

*

Gladios waddled through the small entrance of the Sarcophagus Tavern, nodding to the receptionist, who barely looked up from behind her desk, while she held her head cocked with the phone resting on her shoulder. Past the fish tank, with the owner's pet octopus resting on the gravel floor, and then to his usual table where his wife Fatima was sitting, gazing out of the window across the street at some teenagers kissing on the corner. Gladios made eye contact and sat down.

'Good day at the office?' Nodding, he picked up the menu and started flicking through the pages. 'I've already ordered,' said Fatima with a smile. Hesitating, Gladios looked up before summoning the courage to ask...

'Mongolian Lamb?' Fatima smiled...

'How did you guess?'

Chapter 2 - Ranald and Elspeth at home in Glasgow

Up the stairs of 19 Huntly Gardens clambered Ranald Milngavie (pronounced 'Mulguy'), holding onto the stair rail while bent over, still huffing and puffing from his early morning run around the Botanic Gardens. Straightening, to place the key in the lock, his face reflected crimson red in the landing mirror which he instinctively glanced towards, vainly enjoying his athletic physique and brown wavy hair. He entered the maisonette, on the top two floors, which he shared with his delightful wife, Elspeth, who was still in bed reading a romantic novel set on the Greek Isles. Not wishing to disturb her Ranald went for a shower. A quiet time in the seclusion of the bathroom, a time in which to reflect on how his life had moved forwards at a frenetic pace.

Married! Who would have thought, the eternal bachelor, tamed at last and settled down with his beloved Elspeth. And what a catch she had been; quite the toast of the Glasgow art scene and successful owner of Hutchinson's Gallery in the heart of the Merchant City. He recalled their wedding ceremony in mid-April, only last year. The day had been kind, the sun had shone; a wonderful occasion when the minister pronounced them husband and wife on the terraced lawn at Fykle Lodge, the Argyllshire estate of his uncle, Sir Hector Munro-Fordyce. And how they enjoyed the ceilidh in the marquee once dinner had been cleared and the speeches made. Quick step, slow step, spin and heel – a lovely start to their life together!

Now living in Ranald's West End flat, which they had made their marital home, life had galloped onwards in a social whirl. Dinner parties, drinks parties, weekends away, barely still for long enough to catch their breath… but that was all about to change because Elspeth was now into her third trimester. She was beginning to glow, vitality sweeping through her body with the gentle swell of her tummy on show.

*

Within five minutes Ranald was changed and sitting down for breakfast, the usual, a bowl of porridge. Elspeth joined him in her dressing gown.

'Will you be going to work this morning?' he enquired tentatively.

'Later Darling, later. Once I have been for my check-up with the midwife.' Hutchinson's Gallery had remained open although Elspeth had decided to take some time off in preparation of their new arrivals. Yes arrivals... plural – more than one! Twins, who had initially caused havoc with her body; swollen ankles, hot flushes and an horrendous bout of morning sickness. It had been impossible to keep a semblance of normality at the Gallery so sensibly Elspeth had recruited some assistance in the form of her younger cousin; the rather attractive and occasionally air headed, Iona McKinty, who had just graduated from Glasgow University with a degree in archaeology.

Three days a week, sparkling eyes and an innocent smile could be found sitting at Elspeth's large mahogany desk in the reception area. Iona would fiddle with her iPhone, Facetiming her friends, WhatsApping her social groups and old university chums. Barrow loads of flowers arrived from admirers, lunch dates galore and a whole host of business cards left by smitten visitors. But unfortunately, without Elspeth's subtle charm, sales began to flag. There was only one thing for it; Ranald, the aspiring artist, had to lay down his paint brushes and get a proper job!

*

'See you later,' he muttered, standing to kiss Elspeth who remained sitting at the kitchen table, eating marmalade on toast and perusing her book.

'Have a good day now.'

Within five minutes Ranald was behind the wheel of the Forbes and McKillop van, with *Auctioneers of Fine Art and Curiosities* emblazoned down the sides, negotiating his way through the west end of Glasgow, heading towards the M8 and Edinburgh beyond.

Chapter 3 - The Kawatachi Distillery

Along the winding road drove Tadashi Ohno in his battered Toyota Sedan, past the snow gates, narrowly missing a sika deer. He pushed his heavy bottle bottomed glasses up his nose while squinting out of the window, fleetingly enjoying the panoramic views of the Akaishi Mountains in the Japanese Alps. Around the bend before sweeping between the towering pillars and the monstrously large sign, cast in metal - Kawatachi Distillery 1924.

'Good morning, Ohno-san,' said the attentive receptionist, bowing to welcome the wise old man who had a faced shrivelled like dried prunes. Mumbling an acknowledgement, Tadashi pottered down the oak panelled corridor with his head bowed, straining his eyes through the thick lenses, until he reached the eighth doorway on his right. At last he looked up, squinting at the plaque: Doctor Tadashi Ohno - Chief Distiller, a king within the Kawatachi Empire.

*

Cask 264 was on its way for bottling when Tadashi stepped into the enormous maturation warehouse with old sherry barrels lining the walls, rows upon rows in regimented stands, towering upwards to the eaves of the old wooden buildings. At the top hung signs fastened to the ceiling joists with the years clearly marked: 1998, 1999 ...

Minions carefully placed the fine old cask on the draining stand and then Tadashi stepped forward and with an old wooden mallet struck the cork gently downwards. It popped out, landing on the floor as a river of crisp amber nectar began to flow into the large stainless steel holding tank. Eyes sparkling, Tadashi thrust a small beaker under the surge of whisky gushing from the cask and then wandered off to the small laboratory in the corner of the warehouse. He carefully dropped in the hydrometer. ABV - 80%! Brrrrrrrrriiiiiiing went Tadashi's phone.

'Ah, so.'

'Ah, so,' replied his wife. Calamari and bream from the fishmongers, prawn crackers, noodles and soy sauce from the cash and carry, sake from the wine merchants. Tadashi was in a muddle trying to scribble down his wife, Yukola's, shopping list while carefully removing the hydrometer and shaking it dry. Weary from the intrusion, he sat on the plastic chair beside the desk and sighed.

'Ah, so. Ah, so indeed. Arsehole more like,' he muttered to himself while reaching with distaste for the paperwork and removing a fountain pen from his top pocket. Squinting at the hydrometer he began to write: Cask 264 - ABV 40%, no dilution, straight for shipment. Within 24 hours a sizeable batch of Kawatachi premium ten-year-old single malt whisky left the distillery bound for Europe.

Chapter 4 - The British Museum, London

James Fortescue-Fortescue strode down the main path within Russell Square, admiring the delphiniums; ah, such gentle fragrances on this crisp May morning, teasing the senses, lingering, seducing, pleasing - achoooooooooooooo! Fortescue sneezed uncontrollably, showering the proud petals which swayed in the early morning breeze.

Grinding to a halt and glancing towards the stainless-steel sculpture, which reflected his noble stature and dashing good looks, the distinguished Cambridge graduate's mouth began to curl with a conceited smile breaking out over his smug face. Fortescue swept his floppy hair from his face, allowing the frames of his tortoiseshell glasses to glint in the sunlight, while admiring the loud check of his jacket, bright crimson handkerchief hanging from the top pocket, neat drainpipe skinny jeans and polished brown brogues – irresistible!

On went Fortescue, past the tramp sleeping on the bench, a loving couple ambling hand in hand, through the gates at the bottom and on towards the British Museum. His chest was swelling with pride as he looked towards the towering stone pillars of the wonderful ancient Greek styled building. He could be Aristotle – the great polymath - sweeping up in a chariot pulled by fiery sea dragons to rapturous applause. Worshippers everywhere and scantily clad, nubile young women wrapping garlands of flowers around his neck and paving the way up the steps with rose petals. Fortescue-Fortescue, god of all he surveyed, entered the Museum.

'Hiya James.'

Hiya James. Hiya James. Who was addressing the great philosopher in such casual terms? A mere mortal deigning the greats with an insubordinate Irish accent.

'Good weekend?' asked Shona O'Leary, his attractive colleague in the New Acquisitions Department. They swiped their passes and slipped through the security entrance before making their way to the lift.

*

On the sixth floor Professor Don Donavan, the eminent American historian, took his seat at the head of the table ready to convene the Monday morning meeting. The rest of the New Acquisitions team continued helping themselves to coffee and chattering casually amongst themselves.

Shona smiled teasingly while delicately easing her well sculptured figure into a chair then sipping her coffee she slurped noisily. It was all a facade. She had a first class honours degree in Classics from the Open University and was more than equal to the so-called great academics who were sitting around the table and none more so than the highly opinionated and bumptious Fortescue-Fortescue. He took a seat opposite her and smiled piously.

'Are we all ready?' asked Don. The hubbub of background chatter fell away and the committee looked expectantly towards the head of the table where he was sprawled, elbows resting on some files while he chewed a pen. His attentive PA, the diminutive although ever reliable Miss Jones, sat prim and proper to his side, peering through her oblong framed glasses. Raising a hand to her mouth she coughed politely, indicating the meeting was about to begin.

'Any news on the Greek urns to be auctioned next week?' asked Don, looking towards Andrew Johnstone, the Ancient Egyptian and Greek Curator.

*

Shona looked down at her fingernails. Elegant, delicate, immaculately manicured and painted; high gloss which dazzled under the chrome central light pendant. Nails were Shona's thing, recalling her apprenticeship at Pink Lilly's Nail Salon in Wickham Street, Liverpool.

'File and paint chuck, file and paint,' were the only words of guidance barked out by the fiery red head, who ran the establishment for a Mr Singh who was seldom there. And after months of slaving for up to twelve hours a day to return home to the suburban semi-detached house she shared with her parents, three sisters and a parrot called Ketchup, Shona sought solitude in books. It was her escapism, a magic carpet through time, leading to faraway lands; excitement, love, jealousy, all manner of emotions stirred and learnings gained. The genie was out, Pink Lilly's was binned and within six months Shona was signed up at the Open University studying classics. So-called academic jobs followed before she made her way south to London, where, at the tender age of thirty-two, she now found herself within the New Acquisitions Department of the British Museum.

Andrew Johnstone droned on and Shona glanced towards Don who seemed pre-occupied, staring at Fortescue.

Splendid young man, Oxbridge graduate, obviously. Poor degree, but of course that was to be expected from someone of his class. And, oh boy, did he have class, mused Don, recalling the time when he had met his mother, the fragrant and sublime Lady Fortescue-Fortescue. The whole family had class, they reeked of English deference; the ability to sneer at underlings, putting them in their place with a well quipped remark about summer holidays in the south of France, ski trips to the Alps and an effortless lifestyle of cocktail parties with old school chums.

Young Fortescue doodled on the Museum notebook while contemplating what he should do about his current girlfriend Miranda Hedgerly, who was becoming increasingly keen to settle down. Lady Fortescue approved - *Charming young girl, nice family, went to Dashwoods Ladies College.* But despite being in his mid-forties Fortescue was still unsure about marriage, just yet. Play the field and all that. He looked over longingly at Shona, admiring her fiery emerald eyes and striking auburn hair.

*

'And the urns are coming to auction on the 16th of June, guided at £25,000 for the pair,' finished Johnstone. Silence pervaded the room.

Miss Jones coughed delicately, and Don shifted his bulk uneasily in his chair, before picking up the catalogue and looking at the wide bottomed shapes. His thoughts turned to his devoted wife as he began to speak.

'They are not unattractive.' Fortescue nodded with ambivalence although otherwise there was quiet.

'We have a lot of Greek urns,' chipped in Shona. Johnstone looked indignant. 'We already have many urns from the Hellenistic Period. Do our visitors really want to see yet more?'

'But they have exquisite staining, very rare,' riposted Johnstone firmly. Don sighed and his shoulders fell. They had an acquisition budget to spend and were well behind target. Who cares if the wretched urns remained in the storeroom collecting dust so long as their fiscal targets were met?

'I found something else which may be of interest to the Museum,' said Shona, breaking the impasse and reaching for a catalogue from inside her bag. Placing the Forbes and McKillop brochure, open at page thirty-nine, on the desk, she thrust it towards the top of the table.

'The Curse of Minerva by Giovanni Battista Lusieri.' There was stunned silence.

'Giovanni who?' questioned Don, rather too forcefully for a Monday morning meeting. 'Giovanni Battista Lusieri,' repeated Shona. 'Elgin's man. Lusieri was the 7th Earl of Elgin's curator and largely responsible for the Greek treasures we hold today; selecting, cataloguing, he even dealt with the Turks, who granted the firman, allowing the Marbles to be exported.'

Don looked again at the image of the Parthenon Temple on a windswept island with highland cattle in the foreground. Glancing around the table he hoped someone else would pick up the verbal baton with this fiery Irish girl. But no help arrived.

'£50,000 is not an insignificant sum,' he posed.

'Peanuts,' retorted Shona firmly. She sensed the pendulum was swinging in her direction and subtly changed tact, becoming all coy. Smiling sweetly her pupils dilated. 'Surely anything which expands the historical context of our great collection and helps inform our visitors of how the Elgin Marbles come to be here is worth pursuing?' Don was won over. He sighed.

'What about my urns?' piped up Johnstone, with a sense of urgency in his voice. But before Don could reply, Fortescue intervened.

'Why don't we buy both? We are behind on expenditure and you know what accounts are like.

'That's right, use it or lose it,' interjected Miss Jones, helpfully. Don needed no more persuading.

'Muffin idea Fortescue. Andrew, can you prepare the committee papers for the urns and Shona, you lead on the painting.' Mighty fine guy that Fortescue, Don mused before standing up and waddling to the sideboard to replenish his coffee cup.

Chapter 5 - Forbes and McKillop

Hamish Augusta Forbes left the Black Dog at 11 o'clock. That being 11 o'clock in the morning, as he always did, every weekday after seeing the hospitable landlady Agnes McKillop for his mid-morning coffee; Brazilian beans ground to dust, percolated, through the finest Egyptian cotton linen, a dash of milk, a double shot of whisky and a whacking great slug of Baileys Irish Cream.

'Oh Hamish you're a wicked man,' Agnes would protest, running her garish purple fingernails through his greasy thinning hair while weaselly old Hamish stroked her ample thighs.

'Aye you're right, there's no denying it,' Hamish replied with a wizened smile on his old weather-beaten face, revealing nicotine-stained teeth. His pungent breath drifted over poor old Agnes. A quick kiss on the lips and he was off!

*

Through the gates of Forbes and McKillop marched Hamish with a little spring in his step, the ageing sixty-eight-year-old crossing the forecourt and entering the office where he met a generous bottom straining within a tightly fitting tweed skirt. His long-suffering secretary, Brenda, was bent over retrieving a file from the bottom drawer. Oh, Hamish was naughty, outrageous in fact, as before dearest Brenda could stand up the lecherous old man slapped her firmly on the derrière so that she leapt forward in fright and banged her head against the cabinet.

'Get your filthy hands off me you dirty old man.' Hamish cackled, entered his office and sat down at the old oak desk which had been his great grandfather's, Munro Forbes', the founder of the business in 1872 with his partner Henry McKillop; the pair of them standing proudly, shoulder to shoulder, in the black and white framed photograph which hung on the wall. For three generations both families had been selling antiques and antiquities at the rather run-down sale room on the east side of Edinburgh in Corphistine Road. Agnes now held the McKillop shares, a *sleeping partner* as Hamish affectionately referred to her with a twinkle in his eye. After pouring a Crabbie's and whisky from the drinks tray he kept in the bottom right drawer of the old desk, Hamish raised his glass toward his predecessors and nodded in respect. Where would he be without the legacy of Forbes and McKillop? Destitute probably.

*

'Ranald, pass the Daily Record will you?' asked Kenny, sitting in the staff room with Heather from accounts who was having a mid-morning snack - drop scones heated in the microwave with butter and jam.

'They smell good,' said Ranald, rather hoping to be offered one.

'Does that wee wifie of yours not feed you properly?' replied Heather, teasingly. With a gentle smile she buttered and jammed a couple of scones and then slid them across the table.

'Help yourself.'

'Thanks,' replied Ranald. Kenny's hand appeared from behind the paper and grabbed one while muttering something unintelligible. Heather looked on dis-approvingly and shook her head.

Whoosh... the door burst open and Brenda entered, standing with her hands on her hips.

'What's this, break time already?

'Some of us started at eight,' riposted Heather with a defiant tone in her voice.

'Those scones smell good,' said Brenda, not rising to the bait.

'Aye they do,' replied Heather, taking a bite although, otherwise, not shifting an inch from her chair.

'Ranald, come with me. His lordship wants a word, ' said Brenda while spinning on her heels and leading him down the corridor to the Guvnor's office.

*

'Take a seat Milngavie, take a seat,' said Hamish rather too congenially for Ranald's liking. This was the usual schmoozing approach he deployed, the prerequisite to the asking of a favour.

'And will you be having a tipple?' asked Hamish softly while retrieving a whisky glass and some bottles from the bottom right drawer of his desk and placing them on the table.

'Not this morning,' replied Ranald with a wry smile. Hamish nodded. He never really expected his offer to be accepted.

'Now, I presume you are aware of the prestigious auction we have coming up next month, the estate of the late Lady McManus? She was an aunt of Lord Elgin, a fine lady, an up-standing pillar of her community in Grantown-on-Spey, where she lived for the latter part of her life. My father knew her of course. Splendid woman.'

'Yes,' replied Ranald in a monosyllabic tone, not engaging in idle chatter. Hamish looked a little irked. He was not sure how to deal with Ranald whom he had only taken on six months earlier.

'Yes, splendid,' he repeated with an air of suspicion while taking yet another sip from his whisky tumbler and running a hand through his greasy hair before continuing. 'There are some valuable pieces to be sold. We've had a lot of interest in the collection of Chinese ceramics; some are from the great kilns of the Ming dynasty. They shouldn't be difficult to shift. Then there's pieces of furniture by Chippendale, a rare clock by William Watkins - highly collectable, a Landseer painting, a couple of early works by the Glasgow Boys, fine silver cutlery, art deco pieces, a stained-glass lampshade by Mackintosh, early Chopard Swiss watches, knick-knacks galore and we even had an enquiry from the Greek Bureau of Culture about some watercolour. What was the name? The Curse of Minerva by Lusieri? Yes, Lusieri, Giovanni Battista Lusieri. Aye, that was the fellow,' said Hamish, working himself up into a mild laver of excitement. Ranald looked nonplussed while Hamish paused for breath and took yet another sip of whisky. 'You see I don't want all that expensive clobber lying around the premises under our insurance policy. It's been such a bother getting cover after the claim, the excess is stratospheric, may as well not bother with it in my view, but Agnes insists. What was it her late Grandfather used to say...errr, never mind I can never remember.'

Ranald knew all about the fire from Heather's mutterings in the staff room. 'Cause unsubstantiated,' she would whisper, leaning forward and raising her eyebrows. 'No one really believed Hamish's theory about the rats chewing the electrical wiring. Completely implausible, not a rat to be seen anywhere, nothing for a poor old rat to eat around here. And then there was the pay-out... six figures, apparently! Those fine old paintings accredited to Cadell, according to the Guvnor. And who was going to say otherwise? The senior partner of Forbes and McKillop established in 1872, the finest auction house in Scotland. The underwriters never had a chance.'

Hamish's chesty cough took hold as he spluttered with his hand raised to his mouth.

'You see Ranald, I thought that, perhaps, you could take young Kenny and the large removal van to collect the more valuable pieces the weekend before the auction on Tuesday morning? Time and a half?'

Pausing to consider the proposal Ranald instinctively thought of Elspeth's reaction to him working a weekend. A little shudder ran down his spine. Weekends were their time, a chance to loll around, enjoy each other's company and prepare for the arrival of the twins. Braehead shopping centre to look at prams, cots and baby clothing. What colour to paint the nursery? What if they were both boys? What if they were girls? What if there was one of each? Perhaps they should paint half the nursery blue and half pink, just in case.

'Double time?' replied Ranald. Old Hamish paused. Double time. He had only ever paid double time once - 29th July 1981, the day of the Royal wedding. Minimum wage was up. Double time indeed. 'It's a Sunday after all,' continued Ranald. 'God's day, a day of rest and worship,' he suggested, looking to bolster his negotiating stance. Hamish nodded but remained silent contemplating while he thought of his local Minister and the Scottish Episcopal Church service which he attended nearly every week with his wife and seven children. *And go forth to do God's work,* resonated within him and momentarily his normally steadfast resolve, now well lubricated by the whisky, began to waiver. Another sip of the amber liquid and Hamish was beaten.

'Okay then, since it's the Sabbath, double time it is.'

Ranald nodded with a victorious smile enveloping his face before he stood up and left. He still had Elspeth to placate!

Chapter 6 - The Greek Bureau of Culture Meet

The warm early summer weather continued to engulf Greece, sapping the energy of even the most seasoned of Greeks. Not as bad as the 1987 killer wave but surely as hot as 2007 and much worse than 2015. Bush fires ravaged the hills north of Athens, the air remaining heavy with dust filled particles and drifting smoke. Gladios coughed while the futile overhead fan continued to clatter round and round as Helena cursorily knocked on his open door and entered the grubby little office on the second floor.

'You ready?' Nodding Gladios looked up at Helena's fine and sublime classical curves, standing like a Goddess of mythical stature in the doorway. Fitting for Athens, fitting for the Acropolis.

'Yes, Helena, yes,' replied Gladios with his usual bluster while casually stacking a collection of papers and slipping them into his folder. They left the building and headed to the Sarcophagus Tavern.

*

Prodius Polopidus, the Head of the Greek Bureau of Culture, was sitting at the top of the table beside the fish tank admiring the restaurant's pet octopus which was draped over a model shipwreck and waving its tentacles defiantly at the diners.

'Please take a seat,' said Prodius, rising to greet his work colleagues before ushering them to the spare chairs around the little table. Helena smiled sweetly, all manners and meek, belying her tempestuous nature. Gladios nodded before allowing his beady eyes to fall on the octopus.

'I've ordered a plate of Mongolian lamb, very popular according to the maître d,' continued Prodius before taking a sip of the house rosé.

'What's wrong with Greek lamb?' asked Gladios innocently. Helena intervened before he got carried away.

'And how are you coping with the heat?'

'Not so bad. I'm old, you see, I have been through hot times before. The grass scorches, the fruit on the peach trees shrivels so do the nectarines and apricots but the figs fare much better. Could be a bumper year for figs.' The young waitress coughed to make her presence known before placing a large salver of lamb chops on the table with some plates. 'Mrs Polopidus is not enjoying the heat', continued Prodius while filling their wine glasses. 'The air conditioning is struggling to keep our bedroom cool and she hasn't slept well. Seems to have picked up a summer cold, can you believe it? The hottest weather in ages and Mrs Polopidus is coughing like an old donkey with a carrot stuck in its throat. Eey-ore, eey-ore all night.' He paused; he was looking tired.

'And what are your thoughts on the painting?' asked Helena eagerly.

'I've read the application. Interesting! Of course, Giovanni Battista Lusieri wasn't a Greek but there is no denying he's connected to our heritage, albeit through that rogue the Earl of Elgin.' Helena detected a little reluctance from Prodius. Breathing in she raised her ample frame which distracted him sufficiently for her to interrupt.

'He's more than connected to our heritage. Lusieri is entwined with the Elgin Marbles. He's part of our history.'

'True,' replied Prodius, casually. 'However, the real issue for the Finance Committee is that anything which reminds them of the Lost Marbles is a little unpalatable, particularly when the guide price is £50,000. What's that in Euros?

'After Brexit about the same,' replied Gladios, placing a gnawed Mongolian lamb bone on his plate and wiping his hands on the tablecloth. He took a sip of wine and continued. 'We haven't spent our budget in three years. The last item we tried to buy was an old weather-beaten metope of dubious origins which turned up at auction in Istanbul. I bid at the sale, right up to 500,000 lira just to be pipped at the post by the Turkish National Gallery. We were only 10,000 short.' There was ire in his voice.

'Yes, I remember that' replied Prodius sanguinely. 'Austerity at the time, I re- call.'

'It's a lovely painting in its own right,' chipped in Helena as Gladios reached for another lamb chop and took a bite. 'The committee should look at it as an investment not an expense.'

'Ah yes, an investment,' repeated Gladios, through a mouth full of lamb. Grease dripped over his unshaven chin and onto the pastel napkin tucked into his shirt. 'We could hang it in the visitors centre close to the Acropolis beside the old black and white photographs of Elgin and the slides of the... *you know what.*'

'You know what?' questioned Prodius.

'Yes, the *you know what*,' boomed Gladios while discarding yet another stripped lamb bone. Prodius looked puzzled. 'You mean to tell us that you don't know what the, *you know what* is, do you?' The momentary silence answered the question until Helena spoke.

'It's the one thing no one likes to talk about, the so-called elephant in the room.'

'More than elephant,' boomed Gladios after taking a gulp from his wine glass. 'To any self-respecting Greek it's the equivalent to what the House of Beelzebub is to the Greek Orthodox Church. Satan's lair, a den of iniquity, a hot hell hole of purgatory and punishment only fit for, drunks, wasters and sinners,' continued Gladios pompously. Prodius looked perplexed, until Helena decided to put him out of his misery.

'It's the… British Museum.'

'Yes, the British Museum,' repeated Gladios. 'Filthy thieving bunch of British upper-class toffs.' The octopus had moved to the edge of the tank to witness the outburst while letting a couple of tentacles waft freely in the water. Reaching for a piece of Mongolian lamb, Prodius realised he was a beaten man.

'Okay, okay, I will put your request to the Finance Committee and see what they make of it. No guarantees, but I will do my best.'

Helena smiled, Gladios grunted, and the octopus scuttled back into its shipwreck.

Chapter 7 - Married life in Huntly Gardens

Elspeth lay on the chaise longue in the living room of 19 Huntly Gardens, their home; a place of happiness, fulfilment and contentment now that she had put her feminine touch to the old bachelor pad. She had moved some of her furniture in and, of course, some of Ranald's out, redecorated in neutral pastel colours, changed the curtains and added some subtle soft furnishings, a cushion or two. Sipping Earl Grey tea from a pretty little mug she rested her hands on the bump and started to caress it joyfully, down from the midriff, up over her belly button, which was now quite extended, and then letting her hands slide along the sides. Lovely spherical shape. Elspeth gazed out of the French doors, admiring the Glasgow skyline before her eyes were pulled back inside to the array of bright, colourful pictures which adorned the walls.

Since marriage Ranald's painting had taken on a new lease of life. He had re-invented himself. No longer the perfectionist seeking to copy the minutest of detail, no longer restrained by an obsession to be accurate, no longer inhibited. Ranald had let his creative flair go. More than let it go he was now positively flamboyant in his dabbling's. Swathes of colour ladled on with a palette knife, areas smudged with a cloth, splodges applied with a hog's hairbrush. A hot meal every evening and the stability of a good wife had turned Ranald from a middling, half cock amateur into a proper artist; someone who painted with purpose, someone who painted with distinction, someone who caught the imagination, the mood, the ambience and on occasions someone who actually sold the odd picture. Not a landslide of sales, far from it, more of a trickle really, but nevertheless Elspeth had seen the green shoots of his new talents emerge. The start of a new beginning of a man finding fulfilment. With a smile on her face she picked up her book and began to read.

*

Fulfilment was far from Ranald's thoughts as he sat bumper to bumper in traffic on the M8, amidst the river of cars slowly edging forwards, brake lights flashing, exhausts puffing.

'Do you want a crisp?' asked Kenny, scrunching his hand into a packet of cheese and onion. Ranald shook his head while Kenny raised a can of coke to his lips. 'Do you not like crisps?' he persisted, confused as to why anyone should turn down one of his dietary staples. Ranald looked at Kenny, slightly regretting the offer of a lift, enabling him to see his beloved Hibernian lock horns with the towering force of Celtic at Parkhead. Not that Kenny's hopes were diminished at taking on the Scottish Champions in their own back yard. 'If we keep the structure in midfield then we have a good chance,' were the wise words of prophecy, spat out through a mouthful of crisps.

Kenny was much younger than Ranald, a mere loon at the tender age of just twenty-four. He had left school at sixteen to take up a McDonald's apprenticeship only to discover that the intoxicating smells and mouth-watering fayre begin to lose their shine after serving two hundred happy meals a day to demanding customers. But it was at McDonald's where Kenny found himself and discovered his artistic streak in the diners poetry competition - a free Big Mac once a week for a year - to the lucky winner for the best McDonald's poem:

Old McDonald had a cafe ei-ei-o
and in that cafe he had some buns ei-ei-o
with a slap of mayo here, a slap of mustard there
nick nack paddy wack give the customer a...

It was an incomplete composition although Kenny mistakenly entered the children's category and received a *Highly Commended* and enough Big Mac vouchers to sicken him of burger and chips forever. He decided it was time to find employment that was more fitting to his newfound artistic talents. Kenny moved to Forbes and McKillop, Fine Art Auctioneers since 1872, a place surely appreciative of his abilities to recite: Keats, Coleridge, Owen, Dillon and Wordsworth.

'And are you sure your team will win tonight,' asked Ranald, sceptically, while indicating and grinding to a halt on the roadside in Gallowgate close to the ground.

'Aye, of course we will. You'll see 2:1, Hibs grabbing the winner in extra time.'

'Enjoy your evening,' replied Ranald with a smile. Kenny got out and slammed the door shut.

*

Up the stairs of 19 Huntly Gardens clattered Ranald, bounding through the front door where he was met by the soothing tones of Radio Clyde and mouth-watering smells coming from the kitchen.

'Supper's ready,' shouted Elspeth, on hearing her husband arrive. She placed the lasagne on the table beside a generous bowl of salad.

'We've won an important job at work,' said Ranald excitedly after kissing Elspeth on the cheek. She eased herself into a kitchen chair and grasped the spoon ready to serve. 'Lady McManus, aunt of Lord Elgin, passed away recently and we have been appointed by the Executors to sell her belongings. All sorts she has: fancy china, porcelain, even pictures by the Glasgow Boys, Lavery no less.' Elspeth raised her eyebrows.

'Lavery?'

'Yes Lavery,' repeated Ranald. 'One of his early works, but a Lavery is a Lavery and it's not every day we get one of those to sell.'

'Makes a change from handling staid old Victorian furniture and old lady's tea sets,' replied Elspeth, teasingly. Ranald ignored the quip and instead picked up a fork ready to start supper.

'Lovely,' he declared after eating a mouthful. There was quiet. Ranald was collecting his thoughts together. 'Yes, it's a great job… although there is one draw- back!' Elspeth quickly flashed her steely eyes across the table at dear old Ranald. 'I have to be away for a Sunday night in a fortnight's time to help with the packing.' Elspeth breathed in.

Weekends were their time, a chance to be together, a chance to relax and an opportunity to enjoy each other's company before their lives would be disrupted forever when the twins arrived. Elspeth was fastidious about keeping weekends clear, Sundays in particular. No family events, no shopping, no working, nothing but the bare minimum of effort to get by: takeaway meals, casual walks, the browsing of a gallery or museum and drooling over Sunday papers with plenty coffee. Ranald sensed the mood change.

'I know it's not ideal but I will get double time. It's the vagaries of the job I'm afraid.' Elspeth continued to stare at Ranald with pursed lips. 'I hardly ever work weekends,' he continued, justifying himself. Elspeth cleared her throat.

'I am heavily pregnant.'

'Yes,' replied Ranald, not sure where her comments were leading.

'What if something were to happen when you are away,' continued Elspeth letting her hand caress her bump which was on full display. Ranald opened his mouth but hesitated when Elspeth smiled.

'Of course you can go away for a Sunday evening.'

Ranald sighed before taking another forkful of lasagne. The twins kicked.

Chapter 8 - Tadashi Ohno Retires

In the maturation plant at the Kawatachi Distillery there was a row of trestle tables laden with food. Delicacies from the South China Sea, the sacred forest of Yakushima and the Akaishi mountains: dressed spider crabs, sautéed mushrooms and exotic herbs served in neat china dishes. Clusters of balloons hung from the enormous vats with streamers draped in between and there in the centre, amidst a throng of guests, stood Tadashi and his wife, Yukola. Guests bowed respectfully, shaking hands and muttering polite words of thanks.

Kawatachi had been Tadashi's life blood for fifty years. Man and boy at the distillery: bottle washer, clerk of the distillation plant, two years at the Institute of Brewing and Distilling in Fukuoka before returning to take on the pivotal role of Chief Distiller. For fifty years he had driven up the steep mountain road and past the enormous steel sign at the entrance, for fifty years he had parked his car in exactly the same place, nestled under a pretty maple tree, and for fifty years he had greeted the reception staff with a smile before ambling along the oak lined corridor to his place of work. It was hard to let go.

Sunutra, the pretty girl who worked in accounts, arrived with a tray of fine crystal cut glasses and a bottle of Kawatachi ten-year-old malt whisky - cask 264! Overawed with emotion, Tadashi helped himself, downing the generous measure in one. Sunutra refilled his tumbler.

Suddenly, there was tinkling of a silver spoon on glass and a hush swept around the room. The guests looked towards Fuji-Fuji, the slim, grey-haired CEO, who was standing beside the trestle tables from where he intended to say a few words of thanks and gratitude to their most loyal of workers - Tadashi Ohno. Bowing towards the gathering Fuji-Fuji began to speak.

'Just over fifty years ago a teenage boy caught a bus and arrived at the gates of Kawatachi to help out during the summer holidays. Minor errands for the then site manager in and around the storerooms and occasional deliveries. And now, five decades later, the young boy has grown into a man, a husband, a father and become our head distiller...' Fuji-Fuji was starting to hit his stride.

Tadashi felt queer. Hot then cold. Sweating then shivering. His heart was palpitating furiously and he could feel a pulse beat throughout his body, electrifying his nerves and heightening the senses. His soul was moving out of his being and floating upwards, but not to the regimented rafters of the industrial styled building. No, he was moving into a utopia of pink clouds, pretty forests, running water where songbirds sang sweetly. Was this death? Was he dying, moving onto another eternity, his final resting place the great distillery in the big blue sky? He looked at Yukola. No longer in her late sixties, she was now the pretty young girl he had first known, smiling sweetly, invitingly dressed in little more than a silk kimono, which hung delicately off her shoulders and then slipped to the floor. And around her, cows grazed, swishing their tails in contentment with children riding on their backs, smiling, laughing and having fun. It was a happy scene.

'...and finally, I would be grateful if you could all raise your glasses to Tadashi Ohno to thank him for all the years of dedication and wish him a well-deserved retirement.' A hearty cheer rippled around the room and everyone clapped while looking expectantly towards Tadashi.

His eyes were on stalks, his pupils fully dilated. Tadashi was staring at the smiling faces, but they weren't human. Akemi from accounts had the head of a hippopotamus with wide bellowing jaws while Sakura from HR was sitting cross legged on a chair with the neck of a giraffe protruding upwards. The CEO was no longer the smooth grey-haired executive, serenely authoritative, poised with aplomb. He was now walking across the floor on all fours, dragging his huge orangutan arms. And there above Tadashi, on what appeared to be the plains of the Serengeti, was a herd of pink elephants with straw hats and sunglasses accompanied by hyenas in dinner suits. Yukola pushed Tadashi towards the trestle table where he was expected to say a few words and miraculously his jelly like legs moved him forward. He turned and was facing a sea of wild animals making ape like noises, roaring and snorting.

Fuji-Fuji the distinguished CEO stopped clapping and raised his right hand for silence and the audience dutifully obliged. There stood Tadashi all on his own with havoc and weird images ransacking his brain. Instinctively, he reached inside his jacket pocket to retrieve the well-rehearsed speech he had written earlier. Slowly unfolding his carefully composed words Tadashi looked down to see a blur of illegible scrawls, completely indecipherable through his jumbled-up mind. A young, naked Yukola smiled, inspiring Tadashi on. He casually turned towards his CEO and began to speak.

'Fuki-Fuki...

*

Tadashi awoke next morning in the sanitised surrounds of a Fukuoka Hospital ward. He was confused and his head throbbed. Looking up he saw Yukola, no longer the nubile young lady he had met almost forty years ago. Her face was haggard, furrowed with lines running across her brow. She smiled warmly and placed a comforting hand on his arm.

'Quite a retirement party last night,' she mumbled with raised eyebrows.

Chapter 9 - The British Museum Bid

Jasper Cordingwell, the Principal, was sitting at the head of the table within the main conference room at the British Museum, as custom dictated. Not that he was an advocate of custom, far from it. A liberal at heart, Jasper, who had only been in the post for six months, was determined to overhaul the stuffy old establishment and make it into an egalitarian place, welcoming to all comers and no longer the elitist monument of British Imperialism. He had already had secret discussions with the Nigerian Government about returning some of the Benin Masks.

Don Donovan sat down, rather slumped, uncomfortably in a chair which was plainly not big enough for his fuller size. The ever-attentive Miss Jones perched to his right, sitting ram rod straight and occasionally looking adoringly at Don. He moved awkwardly in his chair and smiled at Miss Jones. Everyone was seated, all twenty-four members of the Museum's Council, chatting knowledgeably, piously and conceitedly amongst themselves.

Ms Herschell, a visiting curator from Westerndorf University in Saxonby, was waxing lyrical about the Hellenistic period to a stuffy old professor, dressed in tweeds, who was ambivalent, nodding occasionally while casually drifting off to sleep. He was awoken by the scraping of a chair when the Principal stood to call a start to proceedings.

'Good morning everyone. You all know the form; we have a number of acquisitions to consider,' and then hesitating... he casually looked down the list with his right index figure scrolling through the text while pulling his glasses down from his forehead and peering through the lenses. 'First up, Lionel Borugo with a life size polar bear collected by Landseer.'

Lionel walked to the head of the table and stood behind the lectern with the power point control in his right hand. He flicked to his first slide: an image of the bear standing on its hind legs with its front paws raised and clutching a dwarf dressed in lederhosen!

'Etz enormouz,' said Lionel in his deep guttural Eastern European accent. The Principal looked uneasy, shifting awkwardly in his seat as if afflicted by piles. Don's mouth was open and Ms Herschell exclaimed.

'Das ist ein Zwerg!' Lionel was oblivious to the commotion his slide had caused. He continued, unabashed, describing the bear and how it had been a gift to Landseer by the Arctic Council in 1866.

*

In a small room close by Fortescue and Shona were rehearsing their pitch.

'Luisaarei, was the 7th Earl of Elgin's right-hand man.'

'Lusieri,' piped up Shona. 'Lusieri. He was called Lusieri,' she insisted forcibly.

'Luisaarei, continued Fortescue, 'played a pivotal role in the acquisition of the Elgin Marbles we hold to this day. Responsible for obtaining the firman, enabling the metopes, friezes and other sizeable parts of the Parthenon to be legally exported.'

'Legally exported!' riposted Shona firmly. 'The firman wasn't even granted by the Greeks. It was during the Ottoman Empire when the marbles were taken.'

'No need to get bogged down in the detail,' replied Fortescue with his usual indifference. 'Greeks, Turks they're all the same really. Does it matter who was in charge? The point being, they were taken legally and that's the main issue which the Principal will want addressed.' Shona's chest swelled in anger and she flushed with rage.

'DO IT AGAIN. Go on read it again and this time get it right,' she spat with venom. Fortescue felt a little odd. He hadn't been spoken to like that since his Hungarian Nanny - Henast Itsnigel - used to boss him in the nursery. A tyrant of a woman, a colossus of womanhood, the ex-Hungarian State Circus belly dancer, who was by then more belly than dance, had treated him with disdain throughout his childhood. 'Fortescue, pick up your toys, Fortescue make your bed, Fortescue this, Fortescue that.' And then there had been the smacking! Not rough, nor aggressive, but firm, oh yes certainly firm, in fact… domineering! Fortescue had been bent over Henast's lap and had his tender, pert buttocks spanked, more times than it was proper to do so. Those solid, muscular thighs, oh boy yes, he would clutch onto them with tears of joy running down his face while his delicate little hands tightened their grip and laddered her tights.

Then mysteriously Henast left rather abruptly after being caught caning father. Crikey, there had been eruptions that night when mother burst into the nursery with her usual bustle and impatience, expecting to see her delightful, but on occasion mischievous son, only to find… Fortescue senior bending over the cot with his trousers around his ankles. Henast had flexed her formidable triceps and brought the cane down savagely across his buttocks. Father had whimpered and mother screamed while Henast looked on rather bemused at the sudden furore on the top floor. She was gone the next day, never to be seen again, much to Fortescue Junior's disappointment. He had liked his Hungarian nanny; there was something about her, something he could never quite understand, something, which even at his tender age, Fortescue had succumbed to!

'Read it again,' repeated Shona with conviction. Fortescue whimpered. 'Go on READ IT!' shouted Shona.

'Okay,' mumbled Fortescue meekly, now cowering in his chair with his head bowed shamefully. Shona was surprised, in fact flabbergasted, by the sudden submission. Now standing tall, towering over the poor wretch, she held the upper hand. Slowly Shona raised her shapely boot and dug the heel into the side of his leg. Fortescue winced.

'Lusieri was an important figure, firstly obtaining the firman, during the Ottoman Empire, enabling the Earl of Elgin to legally export much of what we have today...'
Shona smiled.

*

In the main board room Jasper and Big Don were standing over Janet Herschell who had fainted and was now murmuring on the floor while Miss Jones held her head and gently encouraged her to sip from a water bottle. Janet gradually started to come around. Turning towards Lionel Borugo, Jasper shook his head.

'Did you really have to show the slide of the dwarf being eaten by the bear?'

'Eet was funny, no?' replied Lionel in his deep foreign accent.

'Not particularly,' butted in Don.

'The blood was revolting,' added Miss Jones, barely able to make eye contact with the Eastern European professor.

'Est not real. Est a joke. My kinder photo shot this on the internet. Est symbolic of British Imperialism, zee mighty white empire devouring zee little countries for breakfazt.' Janet Herschell opened her eyes slowly and began peering all around. Miss Jones mopped her brow tentatively.

'Est feelingz better?' asked Lionel, bending over and thrusting his bushy moustache into Janet's face. 'Itz not real blood. Ze dwarfz he doezn't die. Est a joke, Funny?' Lionel continued moving his face ever closer and by the time Janet opened her mouth to reply with indignation his filthy moustache was almost brushing her lips. He breathed out, half spitting, half exhaling his pungent tarry breath, polluted from the heavy Soviet Block cigarettes he usually smoked. The doors clattered open when two florescent clad first aiders arrived only to watch Janet Herschell projectile vomit over dear, old Professor Borugo.

'Ezt funny no?' bellowed Don to everyone's amusement. Janet was carried out on a stretcher and Lionel retired to the gents to clean up. Jasper had recovered his composure and was now standing at the head of the table, letting his right index finger scroll down the page.

'Next, Andrew Johnstone with vases from the Hellenistic period.'

*

Shona pushed her pointed heel deeper into Fortescue's thigh, watching him squirm and enjoying the power she now seemed to exert over him.

'Repeat after me, Lusieri.'

'Lusieri.'

*

'Of course, the Hellenistic period is widely recognised as an exemplar of ceramics and the two vases which are coming up for auction are rare specimens, indeed.'

'Do we not already have, what are they?' interrupted the Principal while thumbing through the thick wad of papers. 'Hellenistic vases. Are there not some in the vaults, collecting dust?' Don appeared uneasy, fidgeting uncomfortably in his chair until Miss Jones put a reassuring hand on his knee. Professor Johnstone looked over for moral

32

support. 'Well, what do you say Professor?' continued Jasper, casually leaning back in his chair and putting his arms behind his head.

Johnstone hesitated. He didn't like the tone of the Principal's voice. Chippy, aggressive even, not at all like the demeanour of the previous incumbent, Cannon Boggis. He never cared to scrutinise the merits, or otherwise, of an application. Fortified with rancour Professor Johnstone cleared his throat.

'Indeed there are.'

'Well, why do we want more of these old vase things?' thrust Jasper Cordingwell believing he was gaining the upper hand. But the Professor was not for capitulating, just yet.

'Because we are a museum. We collect old things. That's what museums do.'

*

Shona led Fortescue into the boardroom and stood behind the lectern. Flicking to the first screen shot – Lusieri's water colour - she smiled invitingly at the audience. Again, Don moved uneasily in his chair. Wasn't Fortescue supposed to be leading on the presentation?

'Good morning,' said Shona and waving her hand in the direction of the power point spoke eloquently about the artistic composition which sat before them, extoling its virtues and charm. 'And now I would like to hand over to my assistant, James Fortescue.' She beckoned him forward.

'Assistant!' whispered Miss Jones. Don turned to her with an equal look of surprise. Fortescue-Fortescue of Harthogs Hall, seat of the Fortescue's since time in memorial, social elite; but one step away from the aristocracy, the ruling class, the British establishment. The man who attended Royal Ascot, Glyndebourne and Henley, without fail, every year was now a subservient assistant to - Shona O'Leary!

However, while Fortescue had been sitting, he had reflected more on the indomitable spirit of Henast Itsnigel. Oh yes, he had enjoyed the gentle but firm smacking of his derrière, he had enjoyed the domineering attitude which put a little structure into his otherwise carefree and shambolic life. But he felt cheated. Yes, cheated when she left abruptly without so much as a goodbye. It had scarred his otherwise gentle disposition and probably went some way to explaining why now, at the ripe old age of forty-four, he had grown bashful and arrogant, lording it over all and sundry as Fortescues had done for hundreds of years. Standing at the lectern looking towards the Council of odds and sods the old Fortescue returned. No longer under Shona's spell he rediscovered his mojo and with a rude sneer began to speak.

'Luasaarei was by all accounts a cheap plundering uomo of dubious origins and of limited artistic talent...' Shona cringed as Big Don swelled with pride at the indifference Fortescue was exhibiting with his commanding performance at the lectern!

*

It was almost midday when Jasper started summing up the morning's presentations.

'Unless anyone thinks otherwise, I think we can rule out Landseer's polar bear? I'm afraid it was the image of the dwarf being eaten which finished it for me. Why Lionel should think we would want to display a moth-eaten carnivore... I think I've said enough.' There was muffled agreement throughout the Council. Don piped up.

'It'z out. No, funny?' His comment was met by a cold stare from Jasper.

'What about the vases then? Anyone have any views either way?' The silence answered his question until Professor Mathonus a collector of ceramics coughed timidly.

'As you know I am biased, but the Hellenistic period was hugely important to the evolution of earthenware. Values have increased hugely in recent years; why only last month I was outbid on a late 14th Century Chinese urn in Venice. Used to be able to pick those up for tuppence-ha'penny only a short time ago. Venetian pots have gone through the roof and even Eastern European tat from the Balkans manages to find a home nowadays.'

'We are not an investment house,' interjected Ms Harbottle, the Head Curator, who was in charge of major exhibitions. 'The purpose of the Museum is to promote public awareness, education, enhanced user experience, not stockpile a load of dusty old pots and vases in the vaults.' The nodding of heads appeared to quash Professor Mathonus. He never replied.

Early Roman coins - rejected, 14th century Peruvian cooking utensils - rejected, a tatty collection of Zulu shields - rejected, a Flemish Baroque painting by an unknown artist - rejected. It was almost half past twelve when the final offering was considered by the Council.

Feeling hungry and impatient to wrap up proceedings Jasper Cordingwell began to pull the mornings meeting to a close.

'Finally, the painting by Lusieri or was it Luasaarei?' he posed mockingly.

'The former,' piped up Ms Harbottle, not particularly impressed by the Principal's sense of humour. 'I thought she was rather pleasant.'

'Yes, she was, wasn't she.' agreed Jasper, recalling Shona's sparkling green eyes and bright auburn hair.

'You see, I think the girl had a point about Lusieri,' continued Harbottle. 'The connection through the 7th Earl of Elgin to the Marbles is unmistakable and continues to flesh out our wonderful tale of how they arrived on these green and pleasant lands.' The Principal nodded, obligingly, although was not wholly convinced that they should be acquiring yet more foreign artefacts, especially those which were likely to attract controversy. But it was almost lunchtime, Jasper was hungry and looking to bring matters to a head he quickly decided to put it to the vote.

'All those in favour of acquiring the painting by Lusieri, raise your right hand.'
'One, two, three... fourteen, fifteen. The yes's have it. Approval granted to bid for the picture!'

Chapter 10 - Ranald and Kenny work on the Sabbath

Hamish Forbes was sitting on a hard wooden pew in the second row at the front of the Scottish Episcopal Church, just off Haddington Road, not far from the main street of Musselburgh. Morag Forbes sat down to his left, fending off her husband's groping hand with a firm slap of the wrist and a scolding stare. Would Hamish ever behave himself? Then came the seven children: Rebecca, Sally, Graham, John, Michael, Elizabeth and finally the eldest son, Roderick, the apple of his mother's eye, a fine up standing young man not at all like his roguish father.

There was a shuffling of feet as the congregation stood for the Minister, who was scuttling down the aisle moving towards the front of the Kirk. Norma Campbell, the elderly organist, pumped the foot pedals and tinkled the ivory with her wrinkled old hands. *Lead us heavenly father, lead us,* started to reverberate around the cavernous building. Hamish caught the minister's eye and winked which was returned with a smile and a nod. Extra communion wine for Mr Forbes, the generous benefactor of a stipend, noted the Minister. It was the least he could do for the wretched old fool.

*

Ranald pulled into the service station near Kinross in the Forbes and McKillop van at precisely ten o'clock in the morning for his rendezvous with Kenny. Nowhere to be seen was young Kenny, though. Ranald ambled around the carpark looking for his work colleague, along the rows of parked cars, across to the petrol pumps, the mobile coffee kiosk and finally smoker's corner. Eventually, he glanced through the café window to see Kenny spooning baked beans and the remnants of a fried egg into his gaping mouth.

'You hungry then?' he asked while approaching the table.

'Aye Ranald, aye. Missed my tea last night and old Forbes has agreed to pay me time and a half, so I may as well treat myself.'

'Really,' replied Ranald, sitting down and signalling to the waitress to attract her attention.

*

'The blood of Christ…' muttered the Minster as Hamish's top lip curled over the silver goblet, forcibly tugging it downwards, causing the clergyman to monetarily lose his grip. It slipped forwards and, in a flash, old Hamish quaffed the contents in a single effortless gulp.

'Done it again,' blurted out the Assistant Curate, without even thinking. Wizened old Hamish winked at the Minister as he stood up.

'I'm afraid, we are out of communion wine,' said the Curate glancing down the row of kneeling parishioners.

'What?' questioned Mora McFadden who was stooped over the rail while her elderly husband tried to raise her to her feet, easing the pain on her new artificial hip.

'It's that old scallywag Forbes,' shouted another, only for Hamish to stop in his tracks and swivel towards the altar.

'I simply accept what the good Lord offers me.'

'It was the same last week,' continued the Curate, looking towards the Minister.

'Aye he always guzzles the communion wine,' said Mora, balancing on her two walking sticks and giving the Minister an icy stare.

'Okay, Okay, let me see if I have a spare bottle in the vestry…'

*

It was around half past two in the afternoon when Ranald received a text from Hamish, just as they were approaching Grantown-on-Spey. Ignoring the bleep of his smart phone, he continued along the main street before pulling into Inverurie Drive. He drove slowly while looking for Annabel's, the late Lady McManus' residence, named after the Mayfair Nightclub, which she frequented during the swinging sixties. And, oh my word, did they swing in those days. Lady McManus would recall the hedonistic, drug fuelled parties with fond memories and a twinkle in her eye while serving afternoon tea in her fine Grantown-on-Spey home.

Husbands had come, husbands had gone. The first was much older, but rich. The second much younger and poor. The third, a rock star, was completely unreliable and the fourth, a chartered accountant, need we say anymore? Yes, that's right, he was dull. Golf twice a week and every Saturday morning he would wash the C Class Mercedes Benz which was always parked on the front drive of their suburban home in Purley-on-Thames. Lady McManus had one last roll of the dice and her fifth and final husband was Archie MacDonald, the long serving Head Ghillie on the Auchentroul Estate, who she had met on a Highland trip. The family didn't approve but that was nothing new. They hadn't been overly keen on any of the previous entanglements. However, her trustees were dutiful and provided her with a very comfortable eight bedroomed sandstone villa on the edge of Grantown-on-Spey to while away her later years with dear Archie. Unfortunately, he had passed away a couple of years ago.

*

John Dougal, Lady McManus' lawyer, was there to meet the Forbes and McKillop van when it swung through the entrance gates and ground to a halt on the generous gravel forecourt. Kenny let out a long, high-pitched whistle.

'What a gaff,' he said, raising his eyebrows and looking at Ranald.

'You'll be from the auction house then,' muttered John, leading them through the pretty front door with stained glass windows into the generous hall and onto the kitchen where he put the kettle on.

'Now Lady McManus was very fond of old Hamish, which is why your firm has been instructed although, I must say, I could never quite fathom out why. But then there were many things about Lady McManus I never really understood. She had a colourful life, to put it mildly, but deep down she was a warm-hearted person. Very affable, very friendly, too friendly some might say. No children, of course, so Lord Elgin is the beneficiary and his people have already been to view and catalogue the contents so no funny business - you know what I mean?' continued Mr Dougal while looking pointedly at Kenny.

Ranald nodded in silence and the kettle began to boil. He felt a sudden vibration in his right pocket and after making polite excuses he took the call from Hamish, preferring to deal with the old rogue rather than be lectured by the self-righteous lawyer.

'Okay, okay we will leave everything packed up in the house and nothing in the van overnight.'

'Good, good,' replied Hamish, 'it's the insurance you see.'

'Yes, of course, the insurance,' repeated Ranald. John Dougal was shovelling heaped spoons of sugar into a mug of tea when Ranald returned. Passing the cup to Kenny he started to speak.

'Now, it's been agreed that you can stay here tonight before driving back to Edinburgh in the morning. Here's a key and make sure you lock up if you leave the property. I'll return first thing to make sure everything is shipshape before you depart.' With that, the fastidious John Dougal swivelled on his heels and strode out of the front door back onto Inverurie Drive.

Ranald shook his head while smiling at Kenny.

'Aye he makes a good cup of tea, though, does our lawyer friend.'

*

At eight thirty that evening Ranald and Kenny sat down in the Taj Mahal Indian Restaurant just off the main street in Grantown-on Spey. The kitchen door swung open and another takeaway was delivered to the waiting taxi driver in the reception area.

'Two pints of the house lager,' ordered Kenny before Ranald had even opened the menu.

'Poppadums to start?' asked Mr Sajit who had just arrived to take orders.

'Aye,' replied Kenny, 'and plenty of them. And we'll have some mixed pakoras, onion bhajis, chicken samosas, and even a chaat dahi batata to start.'

'And for your mains gentlemen?' enquired Mr Sajit.

Before Ranald had time to peruse the menu Kenny took it upon himself to order: madras, dupiaza, byriani, pilau rice, boiled rice, fragrant rice, chipatis, nans galore and by the time he had finished he was already halfway through his pint so he ordered a couple more.

'And will that be all?' asked Mr Sajit.

'Yes,' replied Ranald quickly. His smart phone began to vibrate and he saw Elspeth's name flash up on the screen. 'Hello Darling,' he muttered, standing to take the call elsewhere.

*

At ten thirty Ranald and Kenny were still in the Taj Mahal surrounded by a wasteland of half-eaten dishes and empty beer glasses placed on the now badly stained tablecloth which was crumpled at the side. Kenny was lying on the leather bench next to the table while Ranald slumped on an ornate velvet chair with his head in his hands.

'That was quite a meal Ranald,' belched Kenny as Mr Sajit arrived with some hot towels and chocolate mints. 'He'll pay the bill,' continued Kenny, wafting his hands in Ranald's direction who had now sat up and was reaching for his wallet.

*

Along Inverurie Drive they staggered, Kenny occasionally leaning on Ranald to steady himself and Ranald stumbling from time to time. Up to the front door they waltzed, fumbling with the keys and after unlocking the house they both fell into the hallway where their earlier endeavours were neatly stacked. Row upon row of labelled boxes, containing the more precious and valuable items. Crashing into the drawing room they collapsed on the old tartan sofa, sinking into its soft, comfy cushions.

'Good curry Ranald, good curry,' reiterated Kenny in his monosyllabic tones.

'Aye,' replied Ranald in his mocking Hibernian accent. Both giggled and laughed before looking up towards the fireplace and fixing their gaze on the pretty water colour of the Parthenon Temple on Loch Leven island.

'Bestttt not forget to pack the painting,' slurred Ranald, now feeling the effects of eight pints of the Taj Mahal's finest lager.

'Aye, it's a bonnie wee picture,' proclaimed Kenny. 'I thought we may just keep it as a sort of... you know... thank you for all our hard workkk?' Ranald shook his head defiantly before managing to speak.

'Ttttthere's been a lot of interest in that watercolour, inquiries from all over the world according to Brenda in the office.' Both contemplated while enjoying the painting.

'Now, you'll join me for a night cap before we turn in?' insisted Kenny, getting shakily to his feet and stumbling towards the large mahogany dresser near the window with an array of spirit bottles placed on a silver salver. 'Howesss about a whisky Ranald? A Kaw-a-t-achi?' asked Kenny, lifting the half-filled bottle upwards so he could read the label under the central light pendant. 'A Kawwwatachi!' blurted Kenny, struggling to get to grips with the correct pronunciation. 'Kawatachi, finest Japanese ten-year malt − cask 264!' Ranald nodded while standing up and then staggered towards the fireplace to take a closer look at the lovely Lusieri painting. 'You'll take it neat Ranald? There's nee water to hand,' said Kenny, sloshing a generous measure into a couple of crystal whisky tumblers which he found in one of the boxes they had packed earlier.

Ranald admired the subtle water colours of the composition before returning to sit on the sofa beside Kenny and view the painting from afar.

'Why so much interest Kenny? We've had inquiries from across the globe about that picture. Barely an e-mail about the Chippendale furniture, only a few calls for the Rennie Mackintosh piece and even the oil painting by Lavery has hardly generated a torrent of interest. Yet, that little water colour by a lesser-known Italian artist...' Kenny took a sip of the whisky.

'WOTCHA, OH WOTCHA, WOTCHA, WOTCHA ! Cccccrickey that's strong Ranald... bbbbut nice.' He tilted his head backwards and swigged again from his tumbler... 'PHOARRRR,' bellowed Kenny.

Distracted from his musings Ranald sniffed the whisky. Good nose, subtle, mellow not sharp or acrid at all. He sipped gently; nothing remarkable but, gaining in confidence, Ranald buried his nose deep into the glass and bravely opened his mouth, throwing his head backwards and letting the rich amber liquid pass over his taste buds and hit the back of his throat.

'WHOAARRRR, WHOAARRRR,' he shouted, feeling the full force of cask 264.

'You'lllllll be having another,' insisted Kenny, struggling to his feet and taking Ranald's tumbler. He nodded as if in a trance. Swaying, Kenny lumbered towards the bottle which now seemed to be floating. He desperately made a grab for the prize although tripped and stumbled into some boxes.

'Llllet me help you Kkkenny,' stammered Ranald, raising himself to his feet only to trip and fall close to the hearth. Eventually, they made it back to the sofa with replenished glasses.

'He's qqqqquite a well-known artist,' stuttered Kenny. 'I ggggoogled Lusieri the other day and discovered he was responsible for acquiring the Elgin Marbles back in the early 1800's

'Gooo gentlyyy,' slurred Ranald, taking a sip and ignoring Kenny's comments. There were now flames leaping out of the fireplace and the painting was no longer the diminutive watercolour which they had last admired. Now she was a bubbling cauldron of exotic images, flashing up in front of them like a box of fireworks exploding into life. Scrambling their brains, Lusieri's masterpiece cast her enchanting spell on the unsuspecting pair. The Parthenon appeared to be on steroids, flexing its muscular colonnades which were rising from the ground, carrying the elegant shallow pitched roof upwards towards the heavens. And round the great structure circled prancing horses pulling chariots with gladiators dressed in tunics, carrying spears and swords.

'Fffflaming Ffffallgaronis,' spluttered Ranald with his eyes on stalks, pupils dilated and his brow becoming wet with perspiration. 'Cccan you see that Kenny,' he exclaimed pointing to the tantalising scene above the fireplace. Kenny's eyes were transfixed on the painting.

'Iiit's ffflipping magical,' he spat as they were drawn inwards to the centre of the buildings where there appeared a circular image on the tiled floor, shinning like a constellations of stars.

Ranald looked at Kenny and Kenny looked at Ranald before they both simultaneously raised their whisky tumblers and drained the contents… and then their worlds went black. They passed out and slumped to the floor!

Chapter 11 – The Auction

Hamish Augusta Forbes mounted the steps leading to the rostrum within the sale room at their premises in Corphistine Road. The place was packed with buyers, agents, collectors and all sorts of waifs and strays who usually attended their Tuesday auctions. Brenda was sitting in front of a computer screen, ready to take the internet bids, while Melissa and Sandra were poised with their phones waiting for some select buyers to call as certain lots came forward. The large digital display was illuminated with sale items sequentially flashing onto the screen while Hamish surveyed all in front of him before glancing below the rostrum where his *emergency* half bottle of malt whisky was sitting. Not that he had touched a drop this morning. Never did on sale days, well apart from the mid-week auctions of house clearances, bric-a-brac and all sorts of tat collected over a lifetime. Then, of course, there was that time at Meadow Bank when he had a tipple to steady the nerves and not forgetting the quarter bottle of whisky he consumed before the

Craigkannoch House sale when the rostrum began to spin and he slipped from his perch, landing in a jumble on the floor! However, this morning was special. Tapping his gavel to attract everyone's attention, the craggy old auctioneer raised his whiskery moustache towards the microphone and began to speak.

'Ladies and gentlemen, ladies and gentlemen,' then waited for the hubbub of background chatter to die down. 'It gives me great pleasure to welcome you all to the sale of the late Lady McManus' possessions. She was a fine Lady, an upstanding pillar of the community of Grantown-on-Spey and congenial host to anyone who cared to visit her. My father knew her, of course. Splendid Lady.' Lord Elgin, who was seated in the front row beside his wife, rolled his eyes.

'Now without further ado,' continued Hamish, 'let's get the auction underway.' He flicked the control and Lot 1 came onto the screen. 'Now who is going to open the bidding for this lovely garden urn in the classical style? £100 anyone? Barely a scratch on it. £75? Do I hear £75?' repeated Hamish wielding his gavel around the room looking for a bid. 'Okay £50 to get me started. £50 anyone… Thank you madam. £50, £50 any advance on £50?'

*

'Thanking you,' said the cheery taxi driver as Shona paid the fare and scrambled out from the back seat followed by Fortescue.

'We're late,' she remonstrated in her firm Irish accent, 'If we miss the chance to bid then it's all your fault for insisting on having a cooked breakfast this morning. Why couldn't you just have had muesli like everyone else?' Fortescue shrugged in his typical apathetical manner while they made their way into the sale room and found a place at the back whence to watch proceedings.

*

'Are you sure you're comfortable?' asked Ranald. Elspeth was perched on a bench close to the front with her head buried in the catalogue, intrigued by the variety of possessions which were coming up for sale. She nodded without looking up. Ranald scuttled off and collected Lot 6 before returning to the sale room.

*

Kenny was enjoying himself, fitted out in new brown overalls, resplendent with his curator arm band which was rather a grand title for someone who simply carried the smaller lots to the front of the room to be viewed at close hand.

Now, who was the pretty young lady sitting in the front row in a colourful floral dress with seductive, sparkling eyes and sweeping dark hair? Kenny caught her eye and she returned his look in a kindly way. The rotund man beside her stirred, moving his weight from right to left buttock before speaking,

'I've had a text from Prodius,' he whispered in hushed tones. 'He's agreed to raise the limit to £250,000. Helena raised her eyebrows and then smiled at Kenny when he passed to collect another lot.

*

£38,000 for a Chippendale chair, £42,000 for the Rennie Mackintosh stained-glass coffee table, a Chopard watch made nearly £9,000 and the crowd audibly gasped when Lavery's fine oil painting topped £400,000! Hamish, of course, was in his element. The euphoria of the big day and excellent prices gave a *joie de vivre* to his usually more cantankerous demeanour as he commanded the audience from the rostrum. This was the circus master at his best, raising the spirits with a well-timed quip, engaging with the buyers and squeezing extra bids out of unsuspecting customers, like a cockle picker drawing a whelk. Hamish had flair, Hamish had dash and a twinkle in his eye that Ranald and Kenny had never seen before.

The lots rolled in, the lots rolled out until eventually they reached lot 287 *The Curse of Minerva - a pretty water colour of the*

Parthenon Temple on Loch Leven Island by Giovanni Battista Lusieri 1812.

'Beautiful wee picture,' said Hamish while Kenny held the frame aloft gradually rotating it so everyone could see. Ranald caught Elspeth eye and smiled in excitement. She was on tenterhooks and starting to feel the tension of the big day.

*

'Pay attention,' said Shona briskly, slapping Fortescue firmly on the thigh. Oh, it sent a shiver down his spine as the lovely warm stinging sensation made him quiver just like his old nanny... well, no more needs to be said. 'I'll bid,' Shona continued, barely looking at Fortescue who had come over all meek and mild. He nodded obediently.

*

Helena squeezed her hands together in anticipation while catching Kenny's attention and smiling sweetly. Gladios, yet again, moved uneasily in his seat ready to see if they could at last acquire something of note for the Bureau of Culture, his countrymen, something for Greece.

*

'Now, we've had a lot of interest in this painting,' continued Hamish, 'not just the domestic market but from further afield, mainland Europe and beyond. Of course, Lusieri was the 7th Earl of Elgin's man, responsible for the cataloguing and exporting great artefacts from the Parthenon Temple in Athens – dare I say it... the Elgin Marbles!'

A hush descended on the room and even Hamish was surprised at the effect the mere mention of the Marbles had. Lord Elgin held his head bowed while Fortescue let his left-hand rest on Shona's leg. Helena closed her eyes in prayer.

'As I said, a lot of interest in this picture, we've got book bids at £50,000.' Again quiet as Kenny kept up the steady rotation of the painting from side to side.

'Who's going to start me off then? Can I take £60,000 from anyone... £60,000?

Hamish's beady eyes swiftly scanned the room but not so much as a flinch from the expectant audience who watched in anticipation.

'Okay then, I can take £55,000... who's going to offer me £55,000?

Again, Hamish surveyed the audience like a fisherman waiting for a strike and again the crowd remained transfixed, barely budging while the gnarled old auctioneer eagerly looked on, pulling back his gavel and shrugging his shoulders to invite a bid.

'I'll take the internet bid of £50,000 if no better,' said Hamish and at last the fish struck! Gladios stirred into action and raised his right hand to catch the auctioneer's attention before nodding.

'£55,000 in the front row, £55,000, do I see £60,000 anywhere,' asked Hamish, sweeping his gavel around the room. Shona, realising the Museum's internet bid had been trumped, quickly stood and waved her catalogue in haste.

'I'll take £60,000 at the back,' continued Hamish. Shona nodded signalling her agreement. 'Do I see any more interest at the front?' Gladios came straight back at £65,000 and within a few seconds Shona had raised the stakes, yet again, with another bid. 'In at £70,000 now,' continued Hamish, feeling the mood of the room lift as a wave of excitement began to ripple through the crowd and the palpable tension was being felt by all.

And on the bidding went, in a cat and mouse way, as ever upwards the price climbed: £75,000, £80,000, £85,000, £90,000. Old Hamish's hand became clammy because he could sense something was a foot when the large Greek bid £100,000! The crowd gasped and someone started to clap although they were premature because the race was not yet run. Shona was back with a flick of her hand and Hamish took her bid of £105,000! Silence descended and momentarily the audience was stunned.

Gladios was indignant at being trumped once again; he puffed out his chest, catching Hamish's eye and raised two hands indicating £10,000 more. That will see them off he thought with pride.

Now £115,000 was a jolly good price, more than double the estimate and a little bit more. The bidding should have stopped there; it made no sense to keep spiralling upwards at an ever-greater pace, but up it went: £125,000, £135,000, £145,000 and more. Hearts were in mouths and Hamish was getting hot when Shona hit £185,000! And this was the moment when the big Greek decided to risk all, taking to his feet and offering £200,000! Again the audience gasped.

Hamish looked towards the young Irish girl with the auburn hair and bright emerald eyes. She nodded and the bidding was at £215,000, as quick as a flash. Gladios knew he had to be decisive and kill off the opposition so remaining on his feet at the front of the room he squared up to Hamish for one last roll of the dice.

'£250,000,' he shouted. The auctioneer was flummoxed, not really sure what to do. He had lost track of the increments which had risen so fast. He glanced to the rear where the competition was and saw the catalogue wave and another bid come.

'£275,000,' he said, through his false teeth and… Gladios sank to his seat, beaten and downtrodden by the way events had played out. Helena was incensed at the injustice she felt. With fire in her belly, she stood waving her hand.

'£300,000 at the front, any advance on £300,000?' said Hamish. Gladios pulled her back down and shook his head.

'It's beyond our limit,' he whispered in saddened tones. Helena's face crumpled and the tears began to stream. Kenny was moved and signalling to Ranald, passed him the painting and went to the stricken young lady and helped her out of the room. Gladios followed, a spent force, a broken man.

'Any advance on £300,000,' repeated Hamish while looking at Shona, who appeared to have frozen in the drama, until Fortescue leaned back and playfully grabbed her bottom. It was enough to make her squeal and wave the catalogue.

'£325,000 at the back of the room,' said Hamish, disappointed to see the empty seats in the front row and that the Greek party had left the fray

'Do I hear any advance on £325,000, I'll take £10,000 if that helps.' But the crowd was quiet. Sensing the race for Lusieri's painting had been run, Hamish began to wind up proceedings.

'£325,000 once, £325,000 twice, going at £325,000,' he repeated, raising his gavel. Suddenly, Brenda was waving from her desk below.

'I've got another bid.' Hamish paused to allow Brenda to speak. '£350,000.'

However, Shona had recovered her poise and was now more determined than ever not to be out done. She raised her catalogue to begin a short and frenetic period of bidding while the price grew higher and yet higher. Hamish was coaxing the eager participants as the crowd watched electrified by the renewed activity and mood within the room.

'£475,000,' repeated Hamish before taking a bid from Brenda at £500,000!

'£500,000 any advance on £500,000?' Shona was shocked to have reached their ceiling. Fortescue was sullen, realising they had been pipped.

'Going at £500,000, going once, going twice,' repeated Hamish and barely waiting for anyone to comprehend what was happening, bought his gavel down firmly onto the rostrum.

'Sold for £500,000,' and then looking at Brenda asked, 'to who?'

'The Duchessa,' she replied.

'Ahh the Duchessa,' repeated Hamish in recognition. 'The Duchessa di Canali of Venice,' he announced to the room before reaching for the half bottle of malt whisky under the rostrum.

Chapter 12 – The Aftermath

Gladios eventually found Helena in the café sitting with Kenny drinking a cup of tea and nibbling some fruit cake. Her eyes were red and the mascara smudged. Surprisingly, Kenny had revealed a remarkably compassionate side as he nodded sympathetically while Helena explained the importance of Lusieri's watercolour to the Greek Government. Gladios sat down on the spare seat beside his colleague and shook his head before speaking.

'Unbelievable bidding, we should have secured it comfortably within our budget. I have texted Prodius who is understandably disappointed.' He reached for the remnants of the cake. Helena sighed, her shoulders dropping and her usually upright and well-defined figure slouching into the cheap plastic seat. She caught Kenny's eye and managed a strained smile.

*

'Our final lot,' called Hamish at three thirty that afternoon, looking towards Ranald who held up an old tea set stacked on a tray. Kenny was still nowhere to be seen.

'Wedgewood of course, nothing less for the Late Lady McManus, it was her favourite. I recall being served afternoon tiffin from it; of course, that was before we had something a little stronger,' he prattled on, winking to Lord Elgin who visibly winced. The half-bottle of whisky was having an effect.

£30, £40, £50 and after some spritely competition between a determined old lady from Musselburgh and a dapper Edinburgh antiques dealer, finally, the gavel was brought down at £85. The old lady smiled, pleased with her purchase.

Lord Elgin and his wife stood up which was sufficient to bring the sale to a close. Hamish left the rostrum to greet them.

*

Outside the building in the cobbled courtyard Shona was venting.

'Can't believe it made £500,000 – crazy price.' Fortescue felt his phone vibrate and withdrawing it from his pocket saw Professor Don Donavan's name flash up on the screen. Guessing who it was Shona raised her eyebrow skywards while Fortescue took the call

*

'Now the painting sold well,' blurted Hamish, inadvertently coughing up some phlegm which landed on the lapel of Lord Elgin's immaculately pressed dark blue blazer. Spotting the mishap, he quickly took the silk handkerchief from his top pocket and rubbed the jacket clean.

'There we are now, all spick and span.' Lord Elgin was too shocked to speak. Lady Elgin picked up the mantle.

'And who is the Duchessa di Canali of Venice?'

'Long standing client, known the Duchessa for many years. Old money, of course, just like yourselves. The family have been in Venice since the start. Now when was it? Middle Ages, I think. Splendid Lady!'

*

'Crikey Ranald, what a price the water colour made,' said Elspeth, 'Kenny and you can't have been the only ones to have hallucinations over it.' He nodded as they made their way to the café where they found Kenny and his new Greek friends.

'Take a seat,' said Kenny, jumping up and offering Elspeth his chair. She politely accepted, easing herself downwards while carefully caressing her bump. The twins playfully kicked.

'Oh, mama mia!' exclaimed Gladios, seeing Elspeth condition and suddenly becoming distracted from their earlier woes. 'Wonderful,' he continued, pushing his seat backwards to create more space; 'Is it your first?' Elspeth smiled and nodded. 'Oh, I will never forget our first. My wife, Fatima, blossomed through pregnancy, put on nearly twenty kilos. Twenty kilograms, can you believe it. Developed a craving for Moussaka, couldn't eat enough of it; then spanakopita, souvlaki and just before she gave birth, figs were in season. She ate more figs than our dear old donkey that year!'

Ranald was hovering on his feet, not sure where to sit, when Kenny sidled up and tugged his sleeve.

'I hope you dinnee mind me slipping out of the auction? The young lassie was awful upset at missing the picture. Here, let me introduce you.' Ranald stretched out his hand to greet Helena while Gladios became further engrossed in his conversation with Elspeth.

'I was telling our friends about the outer body experience we had with the Lusieri painting,' continued Kenny, grinning sweetly.

'Quite something,' said Helena, not really believing Kenny's version of events.

'Some evening,' replied Ranald, rather hoping to forget the following morning when he awoke on the floor with the course hearth rugs pattern imprinted into his face.

'You wouldn't believe the images which came out of the painting, a constellation of stars or something like that,' said Kenny, trying, yet again, to persuade Helena as to the truthfulness of his colourful tale.

'Yes amazing,' interjected Ranald, realising his friend was struggling to convince his newfound belle.

*

Hamish scuttled into the café and despite finding Ranald and Kenny fraternising with guests was not particularly concerned.

'Record auction, a delightful day. The Scotsman was covering events and if the wee lassie who interviewed me afterwards is good to her word we will be on the front page tomorrow. How about that!' exclaimed the old rogue, simultaneously slapping Kenny and Ranald on the back. Gladios, who had become distracted by the sudden intrusion, recognised the cheery old auctioneer and stood stretching out his hand to introduce himself.

'Gladios Fatiakos of the Greek Bureau for Culture, Athens. We were disappointed not to have bought the Lusieri painting.'

'Ohhhhh, made a helluva price did that lot. Ten times the guide, way over the top, ridiculous really, but there we are. That's the art world for you.'

'And who was the successful bidder?'

'Lovely lady, Italian… The Duchessa di Canali. We've sold her quite a few paintings over the years.' Gladios nodded.

*

Shona and Fortescue entered the café and instantly recognised Hamish They moved towards him and hovered politely waiting for an audience with the wizened old man. It wasn't long before Hamish's roving eye noticed the attractive Irish girl. He turned to Shona which was her cue to interrupt.

'Hello, we were the under bidders for the Lusieri painting. We're here on behalf of the Museum.'

'Museum?' questioned Hamish.

'Oh, yes, of course... The British Museum,' replied Shona. Gladios instantly stiffened as the hairs on the back of his neck began to tingle. Helena's eyes narrowed.

'Made a helluva price it did,' said Hamish, now captivated by Shona's charm and hypnotic smile. 'These good people lost out as well,' he continued, gently wafting his hand in the direction of Gladios and Helena who instantly stood up. 'They are from the Greek Govern...' trailing off, Hamish realised the significance of his innocent remarks. Shona nodded to her counterpart while Gladios eyed up Fortescue.

'Lovely to meet you,' blurted out Kenny breaking the impasse. Shona smiled although otherwise ignored the gesture and looked back towards Hamish.

'And who was the successful bidder?' she asked. Recovering his composure, Hamish managed a smile before speaking.

'The Duchessa – The Duchessa di Canali of Venice!

Chapter 13 - The Duchessa di Canali of Venice

Luigi Bianachi crossed the Rialto Bridge and then scurried along a side street to the rear entrance of Palazzo Toscano and entered. He pushed the bell to the Penthouse Suite, an enormous apartment which stretched over two floors and had wonderful views down the Grand Canal. The housekeeper opened the door with a smile and young Luigi, the tall, dark haired and handsome delivery boy from Lorenzo's Grocers, stepped inside.

'The Duchessa is waiting for you.' Ignoring her quip, Luigi strode to the double doors leading into the grand saloon where he knocked, pausing momentarily and then coughing loudly walked in with his box of vegetables.

The room was quiet but for some gentle humming emanating from the small bar at the far end. Luigi left the box on the central table and walked to the open French doors and leant over the balcony to take in the view.

'So, what have you brought this week?' asked the Duchessa as she appeared from behind the bar and approached in a dressing gown, loosely tied and with her hair wrapped in a towel. Luigi turned to meet her.

*

Recently widowed, the Duchessa still retained her striking good looks and smiled as she elegantly glided over the fine Persian carpets, not at all showing her forty-two years of age. She was meticulous in how she looked after herself and had retained a lovely, buttery complexion and classic shape which was largely down to her voracious appetite for… any fad which grabbed her attention.

First it had been Pilates – stretching and bending, baths in goats milk lasted almost six months, detox weekends, a month's retreat in a monastery and even regular admittance to rehab was slotted into her busy timetable, despite having no particular issues. Veganism was now her most recent craze: organic muesli for breakfast, vegetable soup for lunch, potato fritters for dinner with whatever else her private chef could rustle up from the well-stocked larder.

*

Luigi moved towards the Duchessa, confidently, not showing his tender twenty-six years of age. Her smile widened, welcomingly, in readiness to speak.

'Anything interesting on offer today?' He nodded, taking her by the hand and leading the Duchessa to the central table where the vegetables sat. She peered into the cardboard container and gently prodded the produce while reciting the contents.

'Carrots, beetroot, celery...' holding up a bulb of fennel, squeezing the bag of spinach and delicately running her right index finger down the full length of the courgette! 'No cabbages,' asked the Duchessa, looking expectantly at Luigi.

'Cabbages?' questioned the errand boy.

'Yes cabbages,' insisted the Duchessa.

'But I haven't bought cabbages for weeks, they're not in season,' replied Luigi slightly mystified as to their relevance.

'Oh Luigi, you surprise me,' continued the Duchessa, teasingly, while moving away from the table to face her young man. 'You see... these are the cabbages I like best of all; well sized, curvaceous and firm.' She reached behind and gently grabbed his buttocks! Luigi smiled. He knew what was expected of him.

*

An hour later the doorbell to Palazzo Toscano rang again. A short, thick set man stood on the side street waiting for the housekeeper to buzz him up. Shunning the lift, he took the three flights of stairs to the Duchessa's Penthouse, striding upwards, step by step, defying his sixty-one years of age. No smile awaited Brialto Corolla from the housekeeper, who could barely bring herself to look at his wrinkled old face with a wide scar running through his eyebrow and down the left cheek. A caustic shiver ran down through her. Offering a seat on the hard wooden bench in the main hallway, she eventually spoke.

'Wait here and I will find out if her ladyship is ready to receive you.' A minute later the housekeeper returned and led Brialto into the Duchessa's boudoir where she lay in the magnificent four poster bed with Luigi casually draped over her. Brialto was not fazed, nodded to his client and then ambled to the wicker chair in the corner where he sat down. Neither was the Duchessa bothered, barely acknowledging his presence while she continued to run her hands through Luigi's dark matted hair.

'Wallpaper sales are up this month,' grunted the old man. 'The new industrial range seems to have gone down well in North America and even the Canadians are showing an interest. Total turnover €687 million for the half year, it's a record.

'Good,' replied the Duchessa while continuing to toy with her supple little plaything.

'Usual arrangements on profits - 50% siphoned off-shore, 30% into your loss- making vineyards and country estates, 10% into your personal account; do you think you can manage to live off €2million this month?' asked Brialto sarcastically. 'Of course, no tax payable.'

'And of course, 10% to the Corolla family. Brialto Corolla to be exact,' piped up the Duchessa, getting out of bed and standing stark naked while she lit a cigarette before slipping her dressing gown on. 'Always 10% for the Corolla family. And what exactly do you do for my generous largesse?' Brialto, at last, showed a little emotion letting a smirk spread over his face as his scar pulled his eyebrow down, partially obscuring his vision.

'We look after you, just like we looked after your late husband, the Duca. The factory workers never strike, the government inspectors pass everything, import and export licences are forthcoming and we make sure you get paid on time. Nothing stands in the way of your business and anything or anyone who does… how shall we phrase it… let's just say problems disappear,' lectured Brialto with a sadistic smile.

The Duchessa recalled the tax inspector – nice young man – who visited last year, only to be involved in a tragic boating accident, late at night, close to the Basilica di San Marco.

'And what of my painting? Has it arrived yet?'

'No, it's still in storage in Edinburgh. We've had an enquiry from the British Museum to loan the picture. No payment but they will cover the insurance.'

'I'm related to Lusieri' replied the Duchessa, ignoring the request. 'Only distant, but nevertheless there is a tenuous connection.

'And what of the Museum,' persisted her trusted advisor.

'Oh, I don't know, what do you think?' Brialto shrugged his shoulders not really caring what happened to her new acquisition. The Duchessa glanced towards Luigi who was now sitting up in bed.

'What do you think Luigi? Should I loan my picture to the… who was it again?' she asked.

'The British Museum,' replied Brialto. Put on the spot Luigi wasn't very sure what to say. He nodded.

'Okay let them have it for a year. I can always visit if I wish.' Brialto stood up and made his way towards the door. The Duchessa returned to the four-poster bed and young Luigi.

'Now where were we?'

Chapter 14 – Taking Stock

It was still hot in Greece; baking hot, day after day, as the unseasonably warm, early summer sun beat down on Athens relentlessly. Gladios arrived at the Sarcophagus Tavern to find Helena and Prodius sitting at their usual table. Nodding, he shuffled into the spare place opposite the fish tank and eyed up the octopus. Almost a decent size he thought, admiring the cephalopod and momentarily wondering what he should eat tonight.

'Terrible shame about the painting,' said Prodius before taking a sip of wine. Gladios nodded, acknowledging his comments and then picked up the menu and scoured the specials.

'Astonishing price,' said Helena who was now coming to terms with their loss. 'The salesclerk, who we met after the auction, claims it harbours secret codes: images of the stars, metopes, classical sculptures and all sorts. Need a few drinks though to unlock it.'

Gladios glanced at Helena and then signalled to the waitress to take their order.

'Mongolian Lamb!'

'Do we know who purchased the painting?' asked Prodius. Picking up the wine bottle, Gladios splashed a liberal helping into his glass and took a swig before replying.

'A Duchessa from Venice. Duchessa di Canali, ever heard of her? No, neither had I. Mrs Fatiakos did a google search and apparently she is recently widowed. Her late husband, the Duca di Canali, was a billionaire according to the papers.' Prodius sighed before speaking.

'I suppose it explains why the picture made such a good price.'

'I've done a little more research,' piped up Helena. 'Not on the painting but on the effects of alcohol on eyesight. Apparently it does have short term vision altering properties. It's all to do with the co-ordination of the brain and the eye muscles.' Prodius and Gladios looked at Helena intently, not really sure where her ramblings were going. 'I mean it's a long shot, in some ways completely absurd … but do you think the salesclerk may have a point?'

'A point,' repeated Prodius, struggling to follow Helena's line of thought. Gladios' eyes narrowed and brow furrowed, inquisitively. He started to speak.

'That the painting holds clues as to where some of our precious Parthenon Temple remains are?' Helena nodded.

'Large parts have never been recovered since they disappeared during the Ottoman Empire.' Gladios was distracted as a large tray of lamb chops arrived on a silver salver.

'Ohhh', said Prodius. 'It's quite an ambitious theory.'

'Well, sections of the frieze have never been found, numerous pediments and metopes too, let alone the statutes. Almost half of what was originally built is still lost,' offered Helena. Prodius sighed before replying in his gentle sympathetic tone.

'Oh, the battering our Temple has taken over the years; blown up in the late seventeenth century, pillaged by all down the ages, both Turks and the British. It pains me to say it, but much will have been destroyed forever.'

'But it's worth a try,' insisted Helena. 'What's a bottle of ouzo and half an hour in front of the picture?' Prodius looked towards Gladios, who was piling up lamb bones on his side plate, but now a little satiated he was more amendable to Helena's suggestion.

'Why not, we've nothing to lose. You'll need to contact the new owners, the Duchessa,' he scoffed mockingly. 'Provided she lets you then give it a go by all means. I remember drinking a bottle of ouzo on my wedding night… Gladios paused as a warm sensation radiated throughout his body. Helena smiled.

'It's agreed then?' Prodius nodded.

Chapter 15 – Shona's Wise Intervention

Fortescue left his flat in Knightsbridge which he shared with his girlfriend, Miranda, who had only recently moved in. He was in a dreary mood though, not his usual bumptious, confident self. There was no particular reason to be glum. Life was always kind to Fortescue, in fact effortless. No worries, no cares just a steady march towards his substantial inheritance while his feckless trustees dished out his generous monthly allowance. He wanted for nothing, or so it seemed on the outside to the innocent onlooker. Deep down though something was bothering Fortescue and deep down he knew exactly what it was.

Miranda! No, it wasn't Miranda; she was perfect in every way, the darling of his mother's eye. Father adored her too. No, it wasn't Miranda who was bothering Fortescue, on what was a bright, sunny morning when he should have been feeling upbeat and full of the joys of life. Yet he wasn't and he knew exactly why... Shona O'Leary, that hot, red headed Irish bint!

Foulmouthed on occasions, cheeky and plucky when the need arose, not at all suitable for someone of his social standing. But there was something about Shona which Fortescue found irresistible, something he tried not to admit, something which aroused him – oh, it made him quiver... the way she treated him with disdain! Damn it, the woman had got under his skin.

Bundling into the meeting room on the fourth floor of the Museum, Fortescue found Professor Don Donavan sitting at the head of the table with Miss Jones, the ever dependable and reliable Miss Jones, on his left, prim and proper as always. He helped himself to a coffee from the sideboard and then turning around… there she was, sitting smugly with a sarcastic grin on her face – Shona!

'You're late.'

'Morning,' replied Fortescue, ignoring the quip and returning Shona's defiant look. Miss Jones coughed politely, which as everyone knew, was the signal that Don was ready to start the meeting.

'I'm pleased to say that the Lusieri painting has arrived and is being safely stored in the vaults. Very kind of the Duchessa di Canali to let us have it on loan.' There was some gentle nodding and a general murmur of approval from the room. 'We've also had a request from the Scottish National Gallery. They want to borrow the picture for their upcoming exhibition: *Early 18th Century Landscapes – the start of the Romantic Movement.* The sale caused quite a stir in Edinburgh.' Fortescue nodded indicating his ambivalence.

'COURTAULD,' screeched Shona. 'Let's get it checked out at the Courtauld, I know the research team there, Oliver Chetwin is the main man and he can work wonders with all sorts of wizardry. You never know what secrets these old paintings harbour: sleepers, cryptic messages or even a pentimento.'

'Pentimento?' repeated Big Don.

'Painting within a painting,' replied Shona, a little too tersely for Miss Jones's liking. Don shrugged indicating his agreement.

'Okay, they can have it for a fortnight prior to the painting being transported back to Edinburgh for the exhibition.'

'Leave it with me,' replied Shona. Big Don shuffled his papers before referring back to the agenda.

'Next item – Hellenistic Urns. Andrew, I think you may know of some coming up for auction?'

Shona smiled, staring at Fortescue, who felt a quiver run down his spine.

*

'What do you think of the colour?' asked Elspeth, picking up the small blankets in the "Mother and Baby" store at 70 Sauchiehall Street, Glasgow. 'Two pink and two blue, hedge our bets depending on if they are twin boys or girls.'

'Or one of each,' replied Ranald, matter-of-factly.

'I think we need four blankets,' insisted Elspeth. Ranald shrugged his shoulders before changing the subject.

'And what do you think of Kenny and this Greek girl, what was her name… Helena? Rather pretty, in fact too good for young Kenny. He seems properly smitten though, barely talks about anything else, even missed a Hibernian match the other day to facebay her.'

'Facebay her? Don't you mean Facetime her?' questioned Elspeth.

'Yes, yes that sort of thing, you know what I mean. Apparently she is keen to visit and Kenny is planning for her to stay at his parent's house in Prestonpans.

'Lucky girl,' replied Elspeth, rather unconvincingly, while putting two pink and two blue blankets into her shopping trolley.

'Yes, quite a change from Athens but that's young love for you!'

Elspeth smiled and the twins kicked.

*

Unusually, Helena knocked on Gladios' door before entering. Prodius was sitting in the uncomfortable, rickety chair opposite the desk with his legs crossed. The overhead fan could be heard clattering above but otherwise was proving hopeless at cooling the room. Athens continued to simmer in the early summer sun. Looking towards Helena, Gladios pushed the spare chair forwards, gesturing for her to sit down.

'Prodius was just explaining that poor Mrs Polopidus' summer cold continues. Fig syrup has failed to ease the coughing. How did you describe it… still braying like a donkey?' Prodius nodded. He had been rather sleep-deprived of late. Helena delicately eased herself into the seat and smiled angelically which, as Gladios knew only too well, usually meant that she wanted something. His colleague was less perceptive.

'I heard that the Duchessa, what was her name?'

'Di Canali,' interjected Gladios with a smirk.

'Yes, di Canali,' replied Prodius, 'Duchessa di Canali of Venice. Very grand and very rich by all accounts, now that the Duca has passed away.' Gladios nodded and Prodius continued. 'Anyway, I understand the Duchessa wasn't amenable to you viewing her painting.' Helena smiled languidly before replying.

'Well, the picture's staying in the UK for the time being. Annoyingly, the British Museum beat us to it. The Duchessa has agreed to loan it to them so they can display it in their wretched museum.' Prodius sighed. 'However, I've just heard this morning that it's going to be exhibited in Edinburgh at the Scottish National Gallery in a fortnight's time. One of the centre pieces for a major exhibition: *Early 18th Century Landscapes – the start of the Romantic Movement.* I was planning to visit and wondered if… we could agree the trip as a work assignment? I would pay for my flights and accommodation but I am desperately short of holidays.'

Gladios looked up from the papers he was browsing and glanced towards Helena, momentarily catching her eye, before letting his gaze settle on Prodius.

'What do you think?'

Uncrossing his legs, Prodius began to fiddle with the pen in his left hand, pushing the cap upwards until it eventually popped off and landed on the floor.

'Oh, why not then?' It's so hot in Athens at the moment you may as well depart for cooler climes and see if you can find the whereabouts of some of our missing treasures.' Helena smiled.

Chapter 16 - The Courtauld

'Samantha, bring the painting over here', shouted Oliver Chetwin while moving from his office into the adjoining laboratory where his assistant, Gus Hertwhistle, was working.

Signing the receipt, Samantha smiled at the pleasant young man from Corinthian Deliveries as she took hold of the picture, neatly wrapped in brown paper and tied with string. Down the corridor, past the small kitchen she ambled, hips swaying provocatively. Arriving at the entrance to the laboratory, she teasingly leaned against the door frame.

'Now who would like an early Christmas present, then?' Not falling for her playful charm Oliver nudged Gus, signalling for him to retrieve the picture so they could examine it together.

'Gently,' cautioned Oliver as Gus ran the paper knife along an edge and cutting the painting free.

'Ohhh quite something,' muttered Samantha peering towards the desk where the picture lay – the Parthenon Temple on a windswept island near the shores of Loch Leven.

'Ridiculous,' said Oliver jovially, shaking his head while holding the painting up to the light to examine it closer.

'Quite a price,' replied Gus, recalling the full-page article on the fourth page of the Daily Mail. '£500,000,' he sucked in through his half open mouth making a gentle whistling sound.

'One helluva artist was Lusieri,' continued Oliver. 'Not very well known in this country as he spent most of his time in Southern Italy and Athens. But just look at the detail and precision of the brush strokes not to mention the depth of colour... remarkable.'

They all stared at the painting in silence until the phone rang in Samantha's office which curtailed the mood and ended their contemplation.

'Well Gus, you know what to do; back off, full ultraviolet and infrared scans, test the paper, the pigments, check the frame out and look for any details of provenance: stickers, galleries, auction houses the usual stuff. It would be nice to have the result by Friday before I go on holiday.' Gus nodded.

*

'Have you had your hair cut, Kenny?' asked Brenda. 'Washed it as well? You're looking bonnie, are you courting?'

The communal room at Forbes and McKillop was silent while everyone looked on in amusement at Brenda's sudden intrusion.

'Lovely young lady - pretty too,' said Ranald mischievously.

'Well, what is she doing with him?' jabbed Brenda, looking towards Kenny who was still reeling from the verbal attack.

'Awwh leave him be,' replied Heather, jumping to Kenny's defence as for once he looked vulnerable, less self-assured than normal. He blushed under his neatly cut crop.

The door swung open and in walked Hamish wearing his best tweed jacket and a mottled old cravat. Cravat ! Crikey what was Hamish doing wearing a cravat, but as he moved into the centre of the room, his guests, who were trailing a yard or so behind, came into view. Ranald instantly recognised the noble features of Lord Elgin who had been at the auction with his elegant wife. They smiled warmly.

'Meet our team,' said Hamish jovially. 'Heather catalogues entries and prepares the auction brochures and Brenda works in accounts.' Lady Elgin stretched out her hand in greeting and as Brenda grasped the immaculately pedicured fingers she panicked and curtsied. It was now Kenny's turn to snigger.

'She's not the Queen.' Hamish spun around and glared at him. But before he had a chance to reprimand the boy, Lady Elgin laughed aloud.

'No, I am not the Queen.' Lord Elgin had now moved alongside his wife, both standing next to Hamish who continued making introductions.

'Ranald has recently joined us and helps with the removals. Paints in his spare time. Not bad, some of his works; he even manages to sell a few pictures from time to time, don't you Ranald?'

'Aye, but they don't make as much as Lusieri's,' interjected Kenny who suddenly seemed to have recovered his confidence. Lord Elgin raised his eyebrows before speaking.

'Unfortunately a lot of his work was lost in a shipwreck… but never in a million years did we expect Auntie's watercolour would make £500,000 – amazing!'

'And how did she come by it?' enquired Kenny, whose curiosity in the picture had grown considerably since his new belle, Helena, had shown an interest.

'Well, that seems a mystery; we're not really sure, but there were many things about Lady McManus we never fully understood. She was quite a character in her day.'

'Splendid Lady,' interjected Hamish.

'You seem particularly interested in the painting,' continued Lord Elgin.

'Aye, well it's strange, the Parthenon Temple on a wee island in Loch Leven?'   Lord Elgin nodded.

'Now come,' insisted Hamish who had become bored with Kenny's ramblings. He ushered his guests out of the staff room and into the courtyard where a driver was waiting to take them for lunch at a local hotel.

*

'Well, what do you make of that?' chortled Brenda, looking towards Ranald who shrugged his shoulders in his usual carefree way.

'Lovely Lady,' said Kenny, who had been quite taken with Lady Elgin's effortless charm.

'Lovely indeed,' repeated Brenda fastidiously. 'Now back to your pretty wee maiden… what's her name then?'

'Helena, like Helen of Troy,' replied Kenny. 'The most beautiful woman in the world - and she's coming to stay with me in Prestonpans!'

'Prestonpans,' repeated Brenda.

'Yes Prestonpans,' said Ranald. 'Fitting for a Greek goddess,'

'Yep, Mum has already changed the sheets on the spare bed,' continued Kenny.

'Has she now!' said Brenda with a wry smile.

Chapter 17 – Bruno Corolla

Bruno raced up the street in his bright red Alfa Romeo as the speedometer nudged 100, 110, 120 kilometres per hour.

'Idiota,' screamed a woman with a pram, shaking her fist as he went straight through a red light at the pedestrian crossing, stirring dust and disturbing the litter on the kerbside. Screeching around a right-hand corner he entered Saint Augustine Street while continuing to push his little red car devilishly fast along the cobbled streets as passers-by looked on in amazement. And then, towards the top of the road, Bruno took his foot off the accelerator and jumped on the brakes! The wheels locked and the tyres squealed with smoke rising from the arches. Eventually the Alfa ground to a halt in front of *El Doreados* – Ristorante Spagnolo.

Pedestrians halted on the pavement and starred in bewilderment. Bruno looked admiringly in the rear-view mirror at the thirty-yard tyre marks he had left on the road and then glanced at his own reflection: chiselled features, bulbous moustache and gold framed Ray-Ban sunglasses. Opening the car door he stepped out, his tall, imposing stature towering over the pretty little vehicle which now had steam wafting out from under the bonnet. Bruno started walking towards the restaurant slowly, controlled and purposefully. Kicking the door open with his suede cowboy boots, he arrived at the main desk where the new receptionist stood, smiling innocently, unaware of how events were likely to unfold.

'Si?' he asked politely.

'Si,' replied Bruno sarcastically.

'And can I help?'

'I've come for lunch.'

'Your name please,' enquired the receptionist, reaching for the big black reservation book and opening it.

'Bruno... Bruno Corolla.'

'Bruno Corolla,' he repeated, unaware of the significance of the name. 'And how would you be spelling Corolla?'

Reaching inside his jacket Bruno pulled out a machete which he raised above his head and then slammed it down onto the desk, narrowly missing the young man's hands and cutting the book clean in two.

'Corolla – C.O.R.O.L.L.A – COROLLA!' screamed Bruno, punching the receptionist with menacing force, splitting his nose open and then slamming his head into the desk. Blood spilled onto the floor. Holding the ashen faced employee by the tie, Bruno dragged him towards the dining area, pushing him through the double doors with such force that the panes shattered as he was bundled into the room and cast to the floor.

'AAAAAAaargh,' wailed a plumb lady on table fifteen, who had seen the wild look in Bruno's eyes and the glint of the machete blade, which he pointed threateningly at the receptionist who was now crawling away from him.

'AAAAAAAAAAAAARGH,' screamed the diners in blind panic while standing up, knocking over glasses and stampeding towards the exit.

'SILENZIO,' shouted Bruno... 'Silenzio,' he repeated gradually lowering his voice. The diners stopped in their tracks with the exception of the Maître d' – Senor Gonzalez - who was scuttling around table twenty-six, partially obscured by some rather tall Americans, and heading towards the rear exit.

Raising his hand Bruno threw the machete towards the back door, the shimmering blade spinning clockwise as it travelled down the central isle and came to a shuddering halt when the blade imbedded itself into the wooden panel with a splintering crack. Gonzalez froze, not even daring to turn around. The room fell silent.

Bruno moved forwards, slowly at first, the gentle thud of the executioner as his cowboy boots clinked against the wooden floorboards. But as he neared the rear of the dining room his pace gradually quickened and quickened, like a whirlwind gathering momentum and energy. Crashing into the Maître d', he violently grabbed him by the scruff of the neck while retrieving his machete and dragging the poor soul across the floor.

'AAAAAARGH,' the diners wailed again when Bruno slammed Gonzalez onto a table and then swept the plates, glasses and cutlery onto the floor with his machete.

'COROLLA wants lunch,' he sneered, pushing his face, nose to nose, into the Maître d's and eyeballing the poor Spaniard with intensity. He slowly bought the machete upwards and gently placed the blade against his neck. 'COROLLA WANTS LUNCH... fillet steak, rare, in fact raw - bleeding.' He nicked Gonzalez's neck and a thin trail of blood began to appear.

KERBOOM! a loud shot echoed around the room when Brialto Corolla fired his semi-automatic Beretta. Bruno froze as the bullet whistled past his head and cracked into the solid stone wall. The diners remained silent, shocked by the sudden turn of events.

Brialto walked slowly down the central isle at a constant pace with his pistol held in front of him. Eventually, he arrived at the scene of destructions where his son still held the Maître d' with the machete to his neck. Placing the barrel against Bruno's head, Brialto cocked the gun with a chilling click.

'Drop the weapon,' he commanded, and the solid metal blade fell to the floor with a noisy clunk. 'Stand up.' Slowly Bruno elevated himself, letting go of Gonzalez who slumped to the ground. Staring into each other's eyes, there was an inaudible tension within the room until Brialto lowered his gun.

'IMBECILLE,' he screamed, slapping his boy firmly in the face with his forehead. 'LUNATICO,' he continued, slapping him again with the back of his hand. Bruno started to cower from his father. 'For the sake of the Virgin Mary, what are you doing? He no pay the rent for one week and you almost kill him.' Gonzalez nodded in agreement. 'Go home you fool,' ordered Brialto, raising his gun again and pointing towards the doorway. Bruno moved quickly and within a jiffy he was back in his Alfa, revving the engine, before squealing tyres indicated he had left.

Gonzalez had stood up and was now smiling at Brialto, grateful for the intervention, only for the hardened Italian to swing the Beretta in his direction and fire another bullet into the wall - KERBOOM.

'We want the money this time next week or... Bruno comes back on his own!' The Maître d' gulped, fully aware of the implications. 'NOW SIT DOWN,' Brialto shouted to the diners, waving his gun in their general direction as they instantly took to their seats. 'You eat your food,' he chided, through gritted teeth, to a table of Japanese tourists who instantly picked up their knives and forks. 'You eat your food, you pay your bill and Señor pays me - Si?' Within seconds Brialto was gone as the distant sound of the Polizia sirens could be heard.

Chapter 18 – Heysham Drive, Prestonpans

Number 9 Heysham Drive was a semi-detached house where Kenny lived with his parents; Malcolm who drove the No 64 bus along the east coast route between North Berwick and Edinburgh and Hazel who helped out at the charity shop in the high street three days a week. It was not an affluent household but it was a happy home where Kenny had lived, since birth, with his elder brother Cameron, who had now left to work on the oil rigs off Aberdeen.

Hazel pulled the divan straight and fluffed the pillows on the double bed within the spare room. Check: clean towel on the rail, fresh flowers in the vase, wardrobe tidy.

'They're here,' shouted Malcolm from the front room, watching Kenny reverse his car into the space on the opposite side of the road. Hazel peered out from behind the bedroom curtains and muttered, 'Lordy be' as Helena clambered out of the passenger's side and collected her bags from the boot of the car. Kenny was remarkably attentive, carrying her rucksack. Up the neatly paved footpath they ambled arriving at the front door.

'Hello,' said Malcolm, greeting Helena with a firm handshake before leading her towards the living room while Hazel prepared afternoon tea in the kitchen. Check: best china tea set, four cups, four saucers, four plates, four knives, tongs for the sugar cubes – where are the tongs? Frantically going through the cutlery draw – phew! One set of tongs. Paper doilies on the cake stand, salmon and cucumber sandwiches on the lower tier, fruit cakes and shortbread on the middle, macaroons on top. Oh… who can resist a macaroon? Overcoming the temptation Hazel placed the china tea pot on the trolley and wheeled it towards the living room in her slippers. Slippers! 'Lordy be,' she muttered for a second time while scrambling up the stairs to change her footwear.

'I'll just see where tea has got to,' said Malcolm, only to meet Hazel entering the room with the trolley which she wheeled in. Looking up she caught Helena's eye, her gentle smile and warm glow… the frisson of meeting her son's new girlfriend! The womanhood was felt in nanoseconds. She liked Helena before she had even muttered a word. Smiling, Hazel embraced her and said, 'Welcome to Scotland.'

*

The New Acquisition Committee were gathered around the table in the main board room on the top floor of the British Museum. Andrew Johnstone was waxing lyrical about the vases he had bought for the Museum at a recent auction while Professor Don Donavan nodded ambivalently with the ever-attentive Miss Jones sitting by his side

Fortescue arrived late, not that there was anything unusual about that. He seemed to have been distracted recently, not quite his usual confident self, he looked slightly dishevelled. Shuffling, he made his way to the end of the table to recover from the blazing row he had earlier with Miranda. Shona was constantly on his mind and playing with his raw emotions. Looking around the room… where was she?

*

'Right, I didn't realise Oliver was going on holiday for a fortnight, is there no one else who can run the tests?'

Shona hung up and re-entered the board room. Glancing towards Fortescue she held his gaze, neither smiling nor frowning, she betrayed no emotion to dear old Fortescue who seemed to be tormented by her presence.

'Well?' asked Don, looking at the Irish beauty with the sunlight streaming through her auburn hair. Sitting down, Shona re-ordered her papers in readiness to speak.

'I have the initial report from the Courtauld. They have taken the picture out of the frame and done the usual visuals. No labels on the backs, although the carbon dating indicates it's from the correct period. The ultraviolet and infrared tests have been completed but no results yet. Rather annoyingly, Oliver Chetwin has gone on holiday and no one seems to have any idea where he left them. One thing though, they found some faint writing on the rear of the backer. It's in Italian, but we have had it translated: *'Yet still the Gods are just, and crimes are crossed: See here what Elgin won and Elgin lost.'* There was quiet in the room. Don twiddled with his pen. 'Any ideas anyone?' asked Shona, looking around at the blank faces. 'Clearly Elgin is associated with the Parthenon although I am not sure…'

'The Curse of Minerva,' interrupted Fortescue breaking the silence. 'A Byron poem about the looting of the Parthenon Temple. He was quite politically motivated in the day and strongly disapproved of Elgin's work.' Everyone was rather surprised. Dear old Fortescue – it all seemed a bit cerebral for him.

'Thanks,' said Shona softly, fluttering her eyelashes and teasingly holding his gaze.

'My pleasure,' Fortescue replied, regaining some smugness and putting his smart phone back in his pocket with the google search results still displayed on the screen!

'It's a riddle,' interrupted Andrew Johnstone, suddenly excited by the discovery.

'A riddle?' questioned Don.

'Yes, a riddle,' continued Johnstone. 'Think about it... much of the Parthenon has never been recovered: metopes, friezes, pediments and all sorts. Then, out of the blue, we have a painting by Lusieri of the Parthenon Temple situated on a small island in deepest Scotland near to where Elgin lived. It's got to be more than coincidental.' There was silence in the room. Don moved uneasily in his chair before commenting.

'So, what are you suggesting? There are parts of the Parthenon buried on the island in Loch... what do they call it?

'Leven, Loch Leven,' said Shona, suddenly animated by the wild suggestion. 'It is strange,' she continued, 'I mean Andrew is right – the image of the Temple on Loch Leven, what an oddity? It must indicate something more. I mean Lusieri was a serious painter, detailed landscapes on big canvases, he wasn't known for frippery.'

The room was quiet until Fortescue stood to get another cup of coffee. Don caught his eye and Fortescue instantly recognised the vacant look of a clueless mind. For once he was benevolent and decided to help out.

'And what is being suggested? A full-scale dig?' Shona's eye lit up at the prospect.

'Not necessarily a full-scale dig. I think Oliver at the Courtauld will know how to scan the area, in the first instance.'

'When he's back from holiday,' said Fortescue with a grin.

'When he's back from holiday,' repeated Shona with a touch of sarcasm.

'So, what do you think?' persisted Johnstone, looking towards Don, rather pleased with himself for coming up with the idea.

Don rocked in his chair, moving the weight from right buttock to left and then left to right. The committee looked on expectantly as Miss Jones straightened her poise, her shrew like eyes darting back and forth while taking in the facial expressions and subtle messages they conveyed. Turning, she caught Don's attention as he swivelled to face her. There was a nod and Don now knew what to do.

'Well let's organise a dig then!'

Murmurings of approval rippled around the room.

Chapter 19 - The Scottish National Gallery

Kenny led Helena into the Udny Arms, Rose Street in the heart of the New Town, Edinburgh. The heavy double doors swung behind them as they moved into the brightly lit reception area and strode towards the bar, taking a seat on the high stools. The locals looked on bemused, even though they were used to tourists invading their space and cluttering their pub.

'And what will you be having,' asked Kenny, retrieving a wad of notes from his back pocket and slapping the cash onto the counter.

'Double whisky Mac,' said an old man, rather cheekily, while perching on his seat close by. Kenny nodded un-flinchingly and the bar man retrieved his glass and filled it from the optic fastened to the wall. The old man smiled, acknowledging the gesture.

'What would you like?'

'I don't know, what do you recommend at this time in the morning?' replied Helena, glancing at her watch – eleven o'clock!

'Oh, something strong,' insisted Kenny. 'Ranald and I were completely blootered when we saw that wee painting reveal its hidden secrets; eight pints of lager, maybe ten, can't say I can properly remember we were that drunk. Then a couple of shots of – Kawatachi whisky – and crikey the wee painting sprang into life, images of all sorts leaping out at us.'

'I'll have whatever you are drinking,' replied Helena. Catching the bar man's attention Kenny nodded, signalling that he was ready to order.

'Two double whiskies with a shot of Baileys in each and a pint and a half of your house lager.

'Tennent's do?'

'Aye, Tennent's will be just fine.' The old man slid his glass down the bar. 'And whatever you put in that,' said Kenny rather generously.

*

Ranald was with Elspeth at the gallery in the Merchant City, Glasgow. So was Iona McKinty, her younger cousin, who was now settling in and becoming an integral member of the team. New paintings had to be catalogued and put away, takings had to be reconciled and accounted for and boy, hadn't cashflow improved recently since Iona had found her feet and taken over the shop floor duties. In the admirers flocked, one after the other, usually hovering aimlessly until eventually they would pluck up courage and ask Iona out on a date. And on the whole Iona nearly always accepted, certainly at the outset she did, gradually working her way through Glasgow's better eateries at her customer's expense. Second dates, of course, came at a price – the odd purchase from time to time. She had sold the whole of the Mora McBegg collection, only two Karl Pearson's remained and to particularly persistent admirers Iona had even managed to shift a couple of Ranald's Glasgow skylines. Elspeth was delighted and if Elspeth was delighted, Ranald was happy too.

The doorbell rang and in walked a tall, smartly dressed gentleman.

'He looks married,' whispered Elspeth as he approached the desk and enquired.

'Do you mind if I look around?'

'Oh, by all means,' replied Iona warmly. 'Come, I will show you our new collection by Ranald Milngavie, he's very talented you know.' Iona led the unsuspecting customer into the adjoining room.

'Never a truer word said,' muttered Ranald while stretching back in the comfortable leather chair and admiring his wife's bump.

*

'Buurrrp,' belched Kenny as he staggered out of the Udny Arm into the brightness of daylight. His eyes squinted when looking back for Helena who bounced off the door frame when she stepped into the street.

'Cooo, what a morning,' she said, momentarily leaning on the metal railings with her head hung low, appearing as if she might be sick. But Helena's constitution was like that of the wild goats of the Kolonos Hills in her native Greece - steadfast. She smiled to herself, stood upright and with a warm glow slipped her arm through Kenny's and started to lead him down the cobbled road in the direction of the Scottish National Gallery.

Tootttttttttttttttt, blared the horn of a passing motorcar as they staggered over Princes Street.

'Watchey where you're going,' remonstrated an irate taxi driver when they reached the other side. Kenny clipped the kerb with his smart brown brogues and stumbled, desperately trying to regain his balance, before eventually crashing into the waste bin on the pavement side. Helena sniggered while watching him stand up.

Now hand in hand they traipsed up the Mound and arrived at the front entrance of the National Gallery looking for - *The Romantic Movement Exhibition.*

'Through the double doors and join the queue on the left,' said the doorman, looking rather suspiciously at the inebriated couple who were swaying towards the kiosk.

'Tttttwo adults please,' slurred Kenny when he reached the head of the queue, breathing toxic fumes over the attendant as she took the money and began printing the tickets. She pressed the red button with her knee summoning the security guards.

*

Sitting in the second last cubicle on the left in the Gentlemen's WC, Kevin, of Northern Protection felt his pager vibrate. It began to flash.

'Blast, Blast, Blast, Blast!' he exclaimed excitedly while pulling up his trousers and flushing the loo.

*

'Shouldddd be around the corner,' said Kenny who had become increasingly impatient waiting for the kiosk lady to pass him the tickets. Eventually, he strode off with Helena in tow.

'Slim guy with an attractive girl, they went that way,' directed the attendant. Kevin the security guard looked flustered.

'Heading towards the exhibition,' he spat into his walkie-talkie.

'Okay, I'll meet you there,' replied Ray, getting up from the staff room table and putting on his Northern Protection jacket.

*

There was a throng of tourists surrounding the curator in the middle of the room where Lusieri's painting was on display. The publicity from the auction had raised the profile of the *Romantic Exhibition* and in particular the obscure water colour of the Parthenon Temple situated on Loch Leven Island. It was drawing in the crowds

All sorts were there, a jamboree of a gathering from academics in tweeds, connoisseurs wearing blazers to jostling students who were vying for a space on the small bench with the central view. American,

European and Far Eastern tourists wafted in and wafted out, snapping the scene with their smart phones before eventually moving on.

Kenny and Helena staggered to the front, barging between all, until they stood behind the bench with a clear view of the picture.

'Here, have a quick swig,' said Kenny, unscrewing the top of his half bottle of whisky and passing it to Helena who took a gulp much to the disapproval of the nearby visitors.

'This is not a pub,' someone said, irately. But ignoring the comment Kenny raised the bottle upwards and poured the amber liquid down his already well lubricated throat. He then settled down to look at the picture and see what it would reveal. And abracadabra... there were two images of the Temple slightly off-set from one another. Kenny was seeing double but not the fireworks or extravaganza of images he first saw when he viewed the painting in Grantown-on-Spey. Suddenly, a double man wearing a blazer and tie came onto the scene, walking towards them and obscuring the view.

'No drinking or eating in here, Sir,' said the curator firmly. He advanced on the drunken couple and tried to take hold of Kenny's bottle. Momentarily, the old hands clasped the Whyte and Mackay label only for Kenny to wrench it free and take another swig. Helena stumbled and half landed on a Chinese student sitting on the bench in front as a small fracas broke out in the room. Kevin and Ray arrived.

'Backup required in the Main Exhibition Room,' muttered the burly guards into their walkie-talkies. They started running towards the melee.

The curator, despite his advancing years, had now wrestled the bottle out of Kenny's grasp and stood triumphantly with it held aloft while holding onto Kenny with his right hand. Helena had recovered her poise and with her notebook and pen to hand stared at the painting waiting for it to unveil its secrets.

Kevin and Ray pounced on the curator and soon battered him to the ground and removed the half whisky bottle from his hold.

'Not me you numbskulls!' he remonstrated while pinned to the floor. Kenny was now stood beside Helena also staring at the painting and waiting for it to erupt into life. But there was not so much as a whiff of the little watercolour revealing her bounty.

'There they are,' shouted the kiosk lady, pointing toward our embattled heroes as they continued to gaze at the painting, almost oblivious to the furore they had caused. Another burly Northern Protection guard stepped forward reaching to apprehend Helena. She looked up, gulped and then vomited over the unfortunate soul. And again, as the whisky began to take its toll. By now Kenny was having a semblance of common sense while realising their quest was proving pointless with all the mayhem going on around. The security guard was flabbergasted by the quantum of seemingly warm diced carrots dripping from his uniform. Kenny pulled Helena in the direction of the lobby, looking to escape. The kiosk lady shouted.

'Stop them!' However, a wave of visitors was already moving towards the exit and Kenny and Helena were swept up in the mass of bodies looking for the door. The remaining guards were too busy dealing with the surge of guests to notice them slip out of the main entrance and back onto the street where the sudden illumination of daylight took them by surprise. They squinted to avoid the full glare. Kenny draped Helena over his left shoulder and they staggered down the road back towards Princess Street in search of a taxi.

Chapter 20 – To Dig or Not to Dig

Kenny was sitting in the staff room at Forbes and McKillop idly stirring his coffee.

'You're not your usual self,' said Brenda in her typical rumbustious way. 'Now how is that wee Greek girl treating you? Is she enjoying her stay in Prestonpans?'

Crikey, Kenny was hung over from the previous day's excursion to the Scottish National Gallery. He was also fed up that Lusieri's painting had not revealed any clues. Stiff lipped and positively frigid when compared to the last time he had seen the little beauty in Grantown-on-Spey after their session at the Taj Mahal, Helena was despondent and had even questioned at breakfast if it was worth staying any longer. Hazel had persuaded her otherwise.

'Now you haven't seen Edinburgh Castle, been up to Arthur's seat or even had a day trip to the countryside. There are some wonderful wee fishing villages around the Fife coastline.' Hot toast and Dundee marmalade had persuaded Helena to stay a little longer. She was due to meet Kenny, who was on a half day, for lunch.

Ranald looked on slightly bemused, feeling rather sorry for his newfound friend. However, but the chit-chat was soon disturbed when Hamish burst into the room coughing and spluttering.

'Now, I don't pay good money for you all to sit around gassing and passing the time-of-day drinking coffee. We've auctions coming up, catalogues to prepare, antiques to be collected, deliveries to be made, invoices to be issued; all the usual stuff to keep the wheels of Forbes and McKillop turning.' No one budged. Kenny kept stirring his coffee while Brenda continued reading the Daily Record. Ranald looked away to avoid Hamish's gaze.

'MOVE,' shouted the fiery old man, slamming his fist onto the table, spilling Kenny's drink and glowering with rage. His leathery old face contorted in pique.

'We've only just sat down,' said Brenda, not cowed by Hamish's fury.

'Well, you had only better just stand up,' replied the old auctioneer. Brenda remained put, burying her face into her newspaper. She was used to these sudden outbursts. But Kenny shifted to avoid the warm coffee dripping onto his trousers and Ranald eventually stood, realising discretion, on occasions, was the better part of valour.

'Right, on you go,' said Hamish in more gentle tones, pleased his authority had not been completely undermined and then he swivelled, leaving the room and returned to his office and the bottle of whisky he kept in the bottom drawer. Kenny collected his jacket from the stand and left for his lunch date with Helena.

'See you in the morning.'

*

The Monday afternoon meeting at Historic Scotland was usually a tedious affair. A plate of plain digestive biscuits lay in the middle of the table and there was instant coffee and tea bags on the sideboard beside the hot water urn. Regional Managers were huddled close by and as the time neared quarter past two, everyone took their places around the circular table.

'Updates from the regions,' barked Lara Patterson, who was in charge of the group's activities. New toilet block at a visitor attraction in Argyllshire, pathways in the Cairngorms, sponsored events, repairs and maintenance and … a request from the British Museum to undertake a dig at Loch Leven Castle!

'Did I hear you correctly?' questioned Lara.

'Yes,' replied Judith Caldwell, the area manager, thrusting the letter across the table. 'They are a bit elusive as to exactly what they think they may find but otherwise a very thorough application: method statement, environmental policy, mitigation works and a risk assessment. Two hundred pages long,' she continued, allowing the pages to flick between her forefinger and thumb before lobbing the bundle onto the table. Lara picked up the document and momentarily stared at it in silence.

'What do you think?'

'Well, it's quite exciting; I'm all for it,' replied Judith decisively.

'And the SSSI designation,' rebuffed one of the other managers.

'All taken care of. It's covered in some report or other they had commissioned.'

'And what are they expecting to find,' pressed Lara.

'Well, as I said they have been a bit elusive on that point, so I phoned the lady at the Museum, Shona O'Leary, a nice Irish girl by the sounds of her, but feisty. You know the sort, used to getting her way. But that aside, I did manage to winkle out of her the real reason for the dig and it's all to do with that painting which sold recently. You know the one; it was splashed on the front page of the Scotsman, made a phenomenal price – £500,000 from memory.'

'Really?' queried Lara, raising her eyebrows, her interest now whetted.

'Anyway, I was slightly off with the girl, despite her Irish charm, and let it be known that we wouldn't be granting permission unless they were a little more open on their real intent – she sang like a canary! Could hardly get her off the phone. And that was when our charming Irish friend let us know what they actually think … Elgin Marbles, they reckon! There was stunned silence within the room; nobody was sure what to say until Judith picked up the conversation again. 'The Museum has had some tests completed on the picture.

Apparently, it's come up with a clue that there may be some lost artefacts from the Parthenon Temple buried on our wee Island. Imagine that!' Again quiet. 'Well, what do we think,' continued Judith. 'Is it dig or not to dig?'

Lara pulled herself together and again flicked through the pages of the Museum's weighty bundle. She sighed!

'Someone will have to go through the application in detail, make sure it stacks up, in particular that any damage to our site is mitigated and repaired. Judith, can I leave that to you?' She nodded. 'We will have to notify our public relations department to make sure they are on side. Council will have to be informed and there will need to be some signage informing our visitors what is going on. We seem to have made a decision ... any questions?' Silence returned until Judith coughed politely.

'And what if they find something? I mean what happens if they do discover some relics from the Temple?' Again, there was quiet contemplation.

'Good point, I hadn't really thought about that. Presumably it will belong to us. Let's get group legal to check it out and advise.' Looking around the table Lara raised her eyebrows and smiled.

'Dig it is then!'

Chapter 21 – Breaking News

Ranald weaved his way through the rush hour traffic before parking the Forbes and McKillop van on the private drive outside 19 Huntly Gardens in Glasgow's West End. Up the stairs he bounded, keys jangling, and after fumbling with the lock he opened the front door of the marital home and stepped inside.

'Hi darling.' Not a word from Elspeth. Placing the milk carton in the fridge, Ranald was drawn to the sound of the television coming from the living room. 'Hi,' he said, reaching down to peck his wife on the cheek, who was sitting on the sofa staring at the TV.

'Ssssshhhh,' rebuffed Elspeth, pointing to the BBC news reporter coming live from outside the Scottish National Gallery.

'Breaking news on the theft of a priceless Lusieri water colour,' spouted the self-assured arts editor while looking at the camera. She turned to interview the Chief Superintendent of Edinburgh's Police Force.

'Crikey,' exclaimed Ranald, gasping in astonishment. Elspeth nodded still barely acknowledging her husband's presence.

*

Shona left the Museum early. Fed up with working late she was due to meet a friend for a drink at the Utopian Wine Bar sandwiched in a back street between theatre land and Fitzrovia. She bumped into Fortescue in reception, who rarely worked beyond his allotted hours. He had mellowed towards her though and was no longer the self-centred toff who she had first met when she joined the Museum. Now quite meek, Fortescue was almost subservient in his demeanour.

'You coming for a drink?' asked Shona. He smiled and nodded.

*

At a small table in the corner of the bar, cradling a glass of chardonnay, was Shona's friend. She smiled when Shona entered, her expression turning to a smirk on spotting Fortescue lolloping along behind. Eyebrows were raised. Introductions were made and as Fortescue turned towards the bar, she nudged Shona and gave her the thumbs up. But Fortescue, who was fiddling with his smart phone, never reached the bar. He stopped abruptly in his tracks while staring at the little screen.

'Bloody hell!'

Shona, who had been watching her colleague out of the corner of her eye, saw him returning in haste. Within a flash Fortescue was back at their table.

'Look at this,' he exclaimed, thrusting his smart phone forward. The BBC news bulletin was clearly on display – Theft at the Scottish National Gallery! Grabbing hold of the phone Shona began to read the article.

'Feck, it's our painting – Lusieri's water colour. Did we have it insured?' Fortescue shrugged his shoulders.

'I think it's time we had a drink.'

*

It was eight o'clock in Venice. The Duchessa was sitting on the terrace of Ristorante Riviera in the heart of San Marco with the ever-attentive Luigi at her side. Oh, how the Venetians gossiped: *'She's only been widowed six months… would you believe it - a grocer boy! What would the Duca have made of it? Lovely man was the Duca.'*

Luigi stretched his arms upwards and yawned, tired from the constant deliveries of organic vegetables to his lover, nearly every day, twice sometimes; only for them to be liquidised by the housekeeper, made into soup and left in the freezer.

'Gabinetto,' said Luigi standing up, flexing his back and stretching his legs and then disappearing to the gentlemen's loo.

The music system gently hummed in the background, the soothing voice of a soprano carried on the early summer air as the

Duchessa let her head fall backwards and closed her eyes. But the moment was soon disturbed when her smart phone vibrated and a tweet came in. Looking at the screen the Duchessa quickly scrolled to her twitter account to see a message from the Scottish National Gallery: *'#Romantic Exhibition #missing painting # Lusieri.'* Stunned silence. Then switching to the BBC Scotland web site to see if it would corroborate the message, her worst fears were confirmed. The Duchessa's painting had been stolen!

Luigi returned and began to massage his lover's shoulders, but she was unreceptive and tense, not soft and supple like she usually was. Moving out of reach, to escape his roaming hands, the Duchessa put the phone to her ear and waited while the handset rang out.

'Ciao Duchessa.'

'Ciao Brialto. We have a problem …'

Chapter 22 – Inspector Donald Mackenzie

At precisely six thirty in the morning Donald Mackenzie stepped onto the Meadows in central Edinburgh for his early morning fitness regime. Tight shorts, tight vest, bulging muscles and white socks neatly pulled halfway up his calves. Dainty white plimsolls too. Fit as a fiddle was Donald, bow chested with muscular thighs. And not surprising because every morning on weekdays this fine figure of a fifty-eight-year-old bachelor, who still lived with his parents, would run around the perimeter stopping regularly to complete his circuit training. Sit-ups, squats, burpees, star jumps and press-ups – phew, what a man!

But nearly every morning, without fail, calamity would strike at some point. Almost run over crossing the road, ripping his shorts, straining a muscle or dirtying his immaculate white exercise wear. And this morning was no different. Hot and sweaty, Donald slowed to a walk at the end of his session only to shuffle a couple of yards before stepping into a filthy, great dog turd!

'Christ,' he cursed, feeling his plimsolls slip underfoot as the intolerable stench arose from the ground. 'Blast,' he swore again dragging his foot through the grass to remove the offending … he could hardly bring himself to mutter the word while looking down in dismay at his stained white footwear.

Of course Donald was no stranger to mishap. He had been an accident-prone kid, ill co-ordinated and perpetually blundering into catastrophe from the day he was born. But despite his calamitous tendencies his parents had loved young Donald as only a mother and father can. Private schools and a university education followed before he graduated with a disappointing third in Criminal Behaviour. Eventually, Donald had enrolled in the Edinburgh Police Force where the rules and regulations of the Constabulary had suited him. But despite his enthusiasm, Donald's career had never blossomed in the way his parents had hoped it would. Well, that was until his big break arrived when he was invited to join the Serious Crime Squad as an Assistant Detective.

Small scale felony to start: petty pilfering, shoplifting and others of the sort before he was assigned as the second in command to the infamous - *Mission Marijuana* – a global drug busting case. No longer could Donald talk about his work, instead, he had to stay stumm while mopping up his gravy with Yorkshire puddings at Sunday lunch.

The Mission gained pace though: house raids, covert operations, arrests galore and the grand finale of seizing a shipping container, full of high-grade marijuana heads, at Leith Docks. The reward for two years painstaking planning, £10,000,000 of taxpayer's money, and almost the whole resource of the serious crime squad. Such a shame, such a crying shame that Donald who had lived, breathed and worked tirelessly on *Mission Marijuana* – should have impounded container 122.

'Look there, it's on the slip,' he protested, pointing to the handwritten note scribbled by his superior.

'172… IT SAYS 172!' boomed the Chief Detective, his face glowering with rage, his cheeks reddening in pique.

Donald gulped but resisted any back chat. Realising the error, he sprinted to the security gate only to discover that container 172 was last seen on the back of a Scania truck registration AK62 CDE heading for Halifax. A national alert was put out but AK62 CDE was a bogus number belonging to a Vauxhall Astra registered in Dunfermline.

Then the recriminations started. It was convenient for all the senior officers on the case to point the finger at Donald. Within six months he was transferred to the Criminal Art Department where he was deputy to an elderly officer who retired shortly afterwards, leaving Donald in charge with a paltry budget of only £100,000 per annum. Barely enough to keep the lights on.

But, as Donald tried again to wipe the dog turd from his plimsolls, he did so with a spring in his step for he knew that today would be different. The Criminal Art Department had a mystery to solve - the stolen painting from the National Gallery!

*

Ranald was clearing the breakfast table and loading the dishwasher when Elspeth arrived in the kitchen still in her dressing gown.

'What time will you be back tonight?'

'Usual darling, about 7 o'clock,' replied Ranald as he leant forward and pecked his wife on the cheek before reaching for his jacket and heading towards the door.

It was fresh outside, early morning weather with the sun only just starting to warm the mellow stone buildings of Huntly Gardens. Unlocking the rear door of the van Ranald placed his rucksack in the back and moved the sheet lying on the floor... He was aghast at what he saw! 'HOLY MOSES,' he said out aloud, in a partial state of shock, because there before him was Lusieri's painting! Ranald shut the door and relocked the van. His head was a spin of speculation – how on earth did it end up in his truck? But it was a quandary which pointed him in one direction only... Kenny was surely implicated! Must be. He was obsessed with the Greek girl and she equally infatuated with the picture. They had been to see it at the National Gallery on a couple of occasions, but really, was Kenny so stupid as to actually steal it? Preposterous as it seemed Ranald couldn't think of any other explanation.

Of course, a sensible husband would have gone straight back home and discussed it with his wife. Elspeth would have known what to do and Ranald knew very well what she would say – hand it in! Made sense. Drive to the Police Station in the heart of the West End and deliver the great work of art to much acclaim. Television interviews would follow, coverage in the press, he quite liked the idea of a moment of fame. But there would be questions. Ranald felt his heart thud. Yes, there would be questions and recriminations.

'And do you know how it came to be in the back of your van Mr Milngavie?' was ringing through his ears while he imagined himself sitting at a sterile desk being interviewed by plain clothes police officers with a tape recorder whirring in the background. He suddenly felt overwhelmed by a sinking feeling as an air of despondency crept into his normally up-beat persona. Ranald knew full well where the questioning would lead - straight back to Kenny and his new Greek girl!

He climbed into the driver's seat and started the engine.

Chapter 23 – A Reported Sighting

Donald Mackenzie entered the Police Station in Kincardine Street and took the lift to the third floor where his small office was next to the gentlemen's loo. On opening the door he was greeted by a mop of long blonde hair, bright white teeth and sparkling blue eyes.

'Hannah, what are you doing here?'

'I've been seconded. The guvnor thought it would be useful for you to have an extra set of hands.'

'The painting?' questioned Donald. Hannah nodded.

'It's high profile, the media are all over it, so he wants a smooth and orderly outcome. It's not one to get wrong.' She instantly regretted her comments. Donald winced at the haunting memory of *Mission Marijuana*. Nearly ten years ago now but still he occasionally heard sniggers and whispers when he entered a room, the spectre never leaving him. The phone on his desk started ringing.

'Inspector Donald McKenzie. Yes, no, yes … I see' – within ten seconds Donald had put the receiver down and was reaching for his coat.

'Come on, let's go. The painting has been spotted in Glasgow!'

*

Bruno was standing in the cramped WC within the first-class section of the British Airways flight from Venice to Edinburgh.

'Bollockio,' he spat when the turbulence caused him to stagger and crash into the toilet, dropping his spliff. Pupils fully dilated he regathered himself and managed to find the joint rolling on the floor. 'Phewwww,' he sighed, leaning against the wall, inhaling the smoke and closing his eyes while allowing his head to roll backwards. Euphoria engulfed him while he let himself be absorbed in the moment, the ambience, the occasion, the… BBBBBBBBringgggg, the smoke alarm went off!

'Everything okay in there?' asked a stewardess who had rushed to the cubicle. She heard groans of contentment through the thin door. Within two minutes Bruno was back in his seat beside Brialto.

'Where have you been?' snapped his father, looking into his son's eyes and instantly recognising the vacant look.'

'Idiota,' he barked, slapping Bruno forcibly on the cheek. He ignored it, rolling away to one side.

*

Elspeth arrived at the Gallery, in the heart of Glasgow's Merchant City, at quarter to ten that morning. Iona had already opened the shop and the coffee was percolating in the kitchen. The smell of Colombian beans radiated throughout. Good mornings were exchanged and Elspeth busied herself sorting out paperwork before checking the window display through the net curtain.

'OH MY!' she shrieked at the top of her voice. Iona came running, shocked by the sudden exclamation. 'What's that doing here?' said Elspeth, staring at the central stand where Lusieri's painting was mounted. Iona looked perplexed, her brow furrowing in confusion. She shrugged her shoulders.

'It was in the safe when I checked this morning. It looks good in the window. Where did you get it from?' Bamboozled by Iona's response Elspeth stared at her in disbelief.

'It's the stolen painting from the Scottish National Gallery. Do you not recognise it?' Iona ignored the quip as the faint sound of a police siren could just be heard in the distance. Elspeth was now in a state of panic. Yes, it had been stolen but how on earth did it end up here? The sirens were gradually getting louder. 'Oh god, it must have been Ranald,' she muttered, jumping to conclusions. Why? How? When? What? - all racing through her thoughts with the sirens getting ever louder. Her mothering instincts took hold. Whatever that half-witted duffer had done, he was her husband, her lover, her soul mate and soon to be the father of their twins. A set of blue flashing lights pulled up outside the gallery.

Car doors were flung open, armed policemen clambered out and within seconds they had entered the shop to be met by Iona's disarming smile. They lowered their guns and the burly sergeant stepped forward.

'We've had a tip off that there's a stolen painting is being displayed in the shop window.' Suspiciously, he eyed the empty stand through the net curtain.

'Oh, replied Iona, thinking on her feet. 'Is it any of these?' she asked waving her hand in the general direction of the gallery wall where many pictures hung. Stepping forward the sergeant began to scan the paintings before walking to the net curtain to examine the empty easel.

'It was reported as being in the front window,' he said, turning to look at Iona questioningly. She raised her eyebrows.

'And what does it look like?' The sergeant appeared confused.

'It was on the telly last night – ten o'clock news, err... Jones, what does it look like?'

'Dunno Sarge,' the constable replied, looking equally perplexed.

'Well look it up then,' said the sergeant with the faint trace of annoyance creeping into his voice. He turned towards Iona. 'And where has that painting gone?' he asked, pointing at the empty easel.

'It will be in the safe,' interjected Elspeth who appeared from the storeroom wheeling a pram laden with baby accessories.

'And who are you?' asked the sergeant.

'The owner,' riposted Elspeth firmly. 'Now, what exactly are you looking for?'

The sergeant shrugged while glancing at the constable who was still fiddling with his smart phone trying to find an image.

'We had a report of a stolen painting being displayed in the shop window.'

'Well, from who?' questioned Elspeth. The sergeant shrugged his shoulders again, looking at his constable and hoping for some support. But he was otherwise too engrossed. 'Are you sure it wasn't some drunken time waster? We get all sorts of wino's, alcoholics and dropouts hanging around here in the mornings. The pavement's usually splattered with vomit, kebab papers scattered everywhere; it could have been a mistaken identity.' The sergeant nodded, feeling slightly intimidated by Elspeth's cool and confident manner. 'Anyway, Iona will show you inside the safe and any other painting you care to see. I've a mid-wife's appointment in half an hour.' Elspeth ran a hand over her bump to emphasize the point. She collected her jacket.

'Please come this way,' said Iona leading the policeman towards the storeroom while Elspeth left with the pram!

*

Inspector Donald McKenzie and Hannah arrived at 38 Strathallan Avenue on the south side of Glasgow. Joanna Gloag answered the door and was surprised to see the plain clothes policeman and his pretty assistant. After a short explanation, she led them into the living room then went to the hall and yelled upstairs.

'JOHN – the police are here to see you.' Hannah smiled at Donald, amused by Mrs Gloag's manner and within a couple of minutes a dishevelled John Gloag arrived in the room wrapped in a dressing gown. Mrs Gloag bought in a pot of tea and doughnuts, lots of doughnuts: plain doughnuts, pink doughnuts, jam doughnuts, doughnuts with holes in and doughnuts without. 'Go on help yourself,' she said while pouring from the pot. Recovering from the night shift, John helped himself to a sugar-coated treat and a cup of tea before he sat down.

'We're here to get a statement about the stolen painting you saw in the gallery window,' said Hannah with her laptop on her knees ready to type.

'Is this the picture you saw?' asked Donald, holding his smart phone out with an image on the screen. John took a bite causing the jam to squelch from the side.

'Aye, it is. I saw it on the news and there it was in the shop window. You would have thought they would have waited a bit before trying to flog it.' Donald sighed. The witness seemed a trustworthy chap but when Strathclyde Police had checked the premises the painting had not been found. He helped himself to a doughnut, leaving Hannah to continue with the statement.

*

Ranald had arrived at the Forbes and McKillop Auction House but there was not a sign of Kenny anywhere. Sick according to Brenda. Nor was he returning any calls. Ranald's phone vibrated and he saw Elspeth's name flash up on his screen. He took the call.

'Hi.' There was momentarily silence until Elspeth exploded into life.

'HI, HI, you say HI as if it's an ordinary humdrum day', she was suddenly lost for words and unable to continue.

'Elspeth calm down, what's up?' With the rage burning within, Elspeth rediscovered her voice which had now taken on Olympian proportions.

'THAT BLOODY PAINTING IS WHAT'S UP!'

'Oh,' said Ranald. 'I can explain.'

'We've had the police at the gallery this morning,' continued Elspeth. 'What on earth was it doing there?'

'But I left it in the safe.'

'Yes, and Iona found it this morning and decided it would look good mounted in the front window.'

'Crikey, she's ditzy that girl,' replied Ranald innocently.

'DITZY?' screamed Elspeth. 'DITZY? She's ditzy is she? Well, who put that blasted painting there in the first place? Crikey, mother alive, how on earth did you end up with it?'

'So where is it now?' asked Ranald meekly after his caustic rebuff.

'Safe!' snapped Elspeth. The twins kicked, sensing the mood, and suddenly the flood gates opened and the tears began to flow. 'What are you mixed up in Ranald?'

'I'm coming straight home,' and with that he hung up.

*

Kenny looked down at his smart phone and saw numerous missed calls and messages from Ranald. He guessed the painting had been discovered in the back of the van and he knew he should phone and let him know what had happened, but he was still in a state of shock as to how events had played out when they had revisited the Scottish National Gallery.

Yes, he had been drinking with Helena again, in the hope that the painting would at last release her secrets but, in truth, it hadn't worked. It was the heart attack which had caused the mayhem. Not theirs, but an elderly gentleman who had been in the main viewing room taking in the exhibition until he rasped and clutching his chest fell into the wall, knocking a Landseer to the ground. The curator panicked, hit the alarm and the whole building was put on alert with flashing lights and a wailing siren. Lock down! Security guards burst into action, scurrying to the room but on realising the nature of the emergency they relaxed and called for a first aider.

That's when Helena struck, quickly snatching the Lusieri painting from the wall and concealing it under her jacket. The alarms were still ringing so no one noticed, well, not until they had left the building, anyway. Oh, they had laughed while walking towards Princess Street amused by their luck and the audacity of the theft – right under their noses! But by the time they made the interchange the place was crawling with police cars, flashing blue lights and noisy sirens, making their way to the National Gallery. That's when the panic set in and they both started to realise the gravity of their misdemeanour. With little idea of what else to do Kenny had popped back to Forbes and McKillop and slipped the painting into the back of the works van which Ranald used. The news headlines that night did little to allay their fears. They went to ground, contemplating what to do next.

*

The Boeing 747 touched down at Edinburgh Airport. Brialto and Bruno left the plane and made their way through customs and on to hail a taxi from outside the main entrance. Thirty minutes and sixty pounds later they were dropped off outside the Charleston Hotel in the centre of the city where they booked into their luxurious suite: marble bath, gold shower head and as much complimentary champagne as one could feasibly drink. Bruno sat on the balcony and smoked another joint.

*

Ranald arrived at Huntly Gardens and parked the van on the private drive. Bracing himself, ready to meet Elspeth, he felt his phone vibrate and saw Kenny's name flash up on the screen.

'Hello,' he answered with a monotone note.

'I can explain Ranald. It wasn't planned. Helena and I went to revisit the Gallery and this old geezer had a heart attack …' Unconvinced by Kenny's revelations, Ranald's keys rattled when he unlocked the front door and entered to find Elspeth, stony faced, standing in the hallway with her hands on her hips.

'I can explain,' said Ranald, putting his phone back into his pocket. But Elspeth said nothing, holding her steely gaze and allowing her intense brown eyes to bore into her husband. Ranald looked at Elspeth, ready to face the music.

'I can…'

'Sssshh,' said Elspeth, cocking her head, listening to the faint noise in the background.   'Can you hear it?

'What?' replied Ranald, perplexed by the response.

'There, it's getting louder.' Ranald still looked confused but within thirty seconds all started to become clear when a police car, with flashing blue lights, pulled into Huntly Gardens.

*

Ranald opened the door to meet Donald Mackenzie with his I.D. card held out in front of him.

'Criminal Arts Department, Edinburgh Police. We have a warrant to search your flat!'

Chapter 24 – The British Museum in a Panic

It was early evening. Shona and Fortescue were in the lobby of the Charleston Hotel, sitting at a table with a half-empty bottle of chardonnay resting in an ice bucket. Occasionally sipping from their wine glasses, they waited tentatively to meet Brialto and Bruno Corolla.

Guests came and guests went, uniformed porters scuttled back and forth, collecting suitcases and escorting visitors to the lift. But the background hum of comings and goings was disturbed when the steady clip of purposeful strides could be heard on the marble floor. They instinctively picked up on the regularity of the step and swivelled in their chairs.

'Ciao,' said Brialto, removing his darkened sunglasses so he could see more clearly. Shona felt Bruno's gaze bore into her with real intensity while her eyes were drawn from his suede cowboy boots to the crumpled denim shirt and then the wild eyes under his tousled brown hair. She felt a pleasant shiver run down her spine.

'Good evening,' said Fortescue, stretching out his hand to welcome the Duchessa's people. Brialto ignored the gesture and, instead, sat down at their table. Without being asked Bruno poured two glasses of wine, emptying the bottle.

'Thank you for agreeing to meet us,' continued Fortescue as Shona for once appeared lost for words. 'We just wanted to reassure you that the Edinburgh Police Force is in control of the investigations. It's early stages although they are confident of a speedy resolution.' Silence. Brialto was looking at them curiously while swilling the wine around in the bottom of the glass but, otherwise, said nothing.

'The picture is well insured,' said Fortescue in a final act of reassurance. Brialto nodded, finally acknowledging his presence. Bruno drained his glass, and his father beckoned them to huddle in with a flex of his index finger.

'You see, the painting, it's very valuable.' Shona and Fortescue nodded. 'But it's not the money which concerns the Duchessa. No, she has a lot of money, more money than she knows what to do with especially since the Duca died. Lovely man was the Duca di Canali. Our families have been, well, how should I put it... entwined, yes, entwined for many years. We helped the Duca and the Duca helped us. Well, paid us, if you know what I mean?' The menacing look on Brialto's scarred face was sufficient for Fortescue to glean the message. Shona remained transfixed on Bruno's chiselled features.

'Let me explain more clearly,' said Brialto, withdrawing the Beretta pistol from his inside pocket and harmlessly placing it on the table beside the ice bucket. 'The money is not important. It's nice, but of no significance to the Duchessa. But the picture painted by her great, great, great, maybe another great, her uncle anyway – Lusieri - now that is priceless.' Brialto picked up his pistol and innocently returned it to his inside pocket before continuing.

'You see we lent the painting to the British Museum and what we want is our picture returned, not a big pay out from your insurers. Do you understand?' Shona had started to take a keen interest in where the conversation was going. She nodded unquestioningly. Again, there was quiet while Brialto sipped his wine before placing the glass back on the table. 'Let me explain how things work in Italy.' Bruno smirked aware of what was coming. 'We want something, you deliver it... you get what I am saying?' Fortescue was struggling with the concept.

'As I have said, the Edinburgh Police are investigating matters.'

'No, no, no,' said Brialto, almost laughing at the prospect. 'We don't care about your police force. We lent the picture to you and we expect you to return it or we get... VERY ANGRY,' he shouted. The lobby was silenced. The receptionist looked up from her desk as a porter walked over to investigate.

'Everything okay, Mr Corolla?' he asked politely.

'Yes, yes,' said Brialto, waving his hand to dismiss him. Lowering his voice he crouched forward. 'The Duchessa wants her painting back. You find it and return it... Okay?' Fortescue and Shona were dumbfounded. 'Or... I ask Bruno to help out.' The tall Italian smiled while standing up and subtly opening his jacket to reveal a glinting machete blade strapped to his side. Fortescue and Shona gulped. 'NOW GO,' shouted Brialto. The pair left without finishing their wine.

*

'So, you own the gallery?' asked Donald while Hannah tapped away on her laptop.

'Yes,' repeated Elspeth for a second time.

'And you are sure that the missing painting has never been on your premises?' continued Donald.

'Yes,' said Elspeth with the faint trace of exasperation creeping into her voice.

'Yes, it has never been on your premises or yes it has?' asked Donald, simply confusing matters.

'No, no,' said Elspeth defiantly.

'Well, is it yes or no?' continued Donald, tying himself up in knots. Elspeth sighed in exhaustion. They had searched the flat but found nothing and since then they had been round and round the block on the same line of questioning for the last forty minutes. She hated lying. It was against all her principles, not the way she had been bought up, not the Brownie code of honour, which she had sworn at the tender age of seven years old, not the way to bring up children. Elspeth was guilt-ridden in her denial of the paintings whereabouts.

'Look, the police visited the gallery this morning. It wasn't there and neither is it here. Are you sure the sighting was kosher?' Donald sighed, even he was getting tired.

'We interviewed the witness earlier today. Married man in his late fifties, he seems reliable enough.' Hannah's smart phone bleeped when a message came in. Instinctively she stopped typing and picked up her handset.

'Boss can I have a quick word?'

'Do you mind?' asked Donald standing to join Hannah in the hallway. Elspeth stared stony faced at Ranald while they gossiped outside. Returning to the living room Donald Mackenzie appeared to have a spring in his step and glint in his eye. Without even sitting down he turned to Ranald.

'Now, I understand you work at Forbes and McKillop!'

BBBBrrrrring the bell rang. With Ranald now coming under scrutiny Elspeth went to the door and opened it.

'Hi, I work with Ranald. Is he in?'

'You're Kenny?' hissed Elspeth, her voice lowered. 'What the hell are you doing here?' He was flummoxed by the greeting. Helena stood behind him smiling sweetly.

'Everything okay out there?' shouted Hannah.

'Yes,' replied Elspeth, stepping outside the flat and quietly pulling the door shut so they could speak without being overheard. And speak they did while Kenny explained how events had played out over the last twenty-four hours. Elspeth sighed, her shoulders dropping.

'Look, here's the key, now go.'

*

'And how long have you been at Forbes and McKillop?' asked Donald. Hannah yawned, she was becoming increasingly weary at the monotonous tone and predictable questions. Elspeth re-entered the room.

'Anyone for tea?' Donald shook his head as he turned to face Elspeth.

'It doesn't look good, does it? The picture was seen at your gallery and your husband works for the auction house who sold it. Coincidental? We have just received another warrant to re-search your premises.'

Hannah held up the smart phone in Elspeth's direction.

*

Kenny and Helena arrived back at Heysham Drive in Prestonpans around nine thirty that evening.

'You're late tonight,' shouted his mother, on hearing the door close and them enter the hallway. 'There's some supper in the bottom oven if you are hungry,' Hazel continued while getting out of her armchair and making her way towards the kitchen. Helena was putting the kettle on when she arrived although there was no sign of Kenny who had scampered upstairs and seemed preoccupied in his bedroom.

'That picture is still missing,' mentioned Hazel. 'It was on the news again tonight. Apparently, the police have been searching some place in Glasgow.' Helena winced. Kenny entered the kitchen.

'What's for supper?' he asked, quickly changing the subject.

*

It was just after eleven o'clock when Elspeth locked up Hutchinson's Gallery and the police left empty handed. Meticulous and organised in their search; all pictures carefully laid out on white sheeting and catalogued, cupboards cleared, ceiling spaces checked, even the bins had been emptied and searched. But not a clue where the painting could be.

'I told you it wasn't here,' said Elspeth triumphantly. Donald and Hannah nodded reluctantly before calling it a day.

'Where is it?' asked Ranald once the police had departed.

*

Kenny and Helena were sitting on the edge of the bed staring at the painting propped up on the chest of drawers while sipping whisky. The amber liquid, mixed with a smidge of diet coke, slipped down rather pleasingly and began to work its magic as their sight became blurred, then hazy, before finally they began to see double. Two Parthenon Temples lying lazily across one another, two islands, two foregrounds and two sets of clouds in the distance. But while two gave them promise that at last the secretive little water colour would reveal her secrets, she teased rather than pleased, never quite letting her robe fall to the ground and reveal her wares. Oh, it was frustrating for Kenny who had glimpsed the dark secrets which lay within, only last month when they were in Grantown-on-Spey. But whatever had coaxed the little beauty then, half a bottle of Whyte and Mackay just didn't seem to cut it this time around. Within half an hour Helena had slumped on the bed and was gently snoring. Kenny laid a duvet over her and then stumbled to the spare room where he slipped between the sheets and closed his eyes. Within minutes he was sound sleep.

Chapter 25 – Let the Dig Begin

Lara Paterson opened the car door when she saw the lorry arrive.

'Come on Judith, let's see what this is all about.' There was toing and froing on the mainland as workers with hard hats and high visibility vests loaded equipment into the small boat which would ferry them to the island. Within a couple of minutes they had crossed the water.

'Hi,' shouted Shona when she saw them arrive at the pontoon. After collecting coffee from the mobile servery she led them inside a portacabin and to a Formica table, with cheap plastic seats, where Oliver Chetwin was sitting with his assistant, Gus. They had an array of plans spread out in front of them. Fortescue appeared.

'Good to meet you,' said Oliver, in his usual matter-of-fact tone, not really wanting to be disturbed from his discussions on how to operate the *Ecografia Scanner*.

'*Ecografia* what?' asked Lara.

'*Scanner*,' replied Oliver firmly. 'Wonderful piece of equipment, latest technology from Italy and the first one to be imported into the country.' Unusually, he hesitated… 'the instructions are in Italian. Do you speak any Italian?' he enquired with a little hope in his voice. They both shook their heads decisively. 'Shame. The Italians who delivered it didn't speak much English either so it will be a matter of suck it and see.' Gus smiled nervously.

'Oh, and that reminds me,' said Oliver. 'The tests we did on the painting are back.' He reached down and retrieved a small file from his briefcase. 'We've now got the results from the ultraviolet and infrared scans. Interesting,' he continued while spreading some papers across the table. 'All fairly typical although the deep pigment screen came back with some faint images.' Oliver drew their attention to the relevant sheet. 'Classic water colour patterns in the main,' he said, pointing to the outline of the island, the Parthenon Temple, foreground and sky. 'But here, can you see a light smudge,' pointing to the bottom left corner. 'And here, and here…'

'A pentimento,' asked Shona with glee, her hopes inflating.

'A pentimento?' queried Lara and Julia in unison.

'A painting within a painting,' replied Fortescue, suddenly taking a keen interest. Oliver turned to the next sheet.

'Much clearer on this one where we have lessened the tone of the other images. There's a sequence of shapes in a loose circular pattern.' He pointed to the outline with his index finger.

'Yes, I can see it,' said Shona, now visibly excited. Fortescue stood up and was peering ever closer at the intriguing discovery before speaking.

'We'll have to let the Duchessa know.'

'But what does it signify?' persisted Shona.

'Haven't a clue,' replied Oliver with a big grin on his face. 'That's your job to find out.'

*

Ranald arrived at Forbes and McKillop where he found a police van parked in the courtyard. He sighed, guessing what they had come about, and then made his way into the main building in search of Kenny. He found him in the common room.

'Ah, there you are,' said Hamish, who suddenly appeared in the doorway. 'The Edinburgh Police are here and they want to search our premises.' Ranald was ashen faced, not really enjoying the constant attention of the men in blue, while Kenny began to fidget nervously realising they were hot on the trail. Sitting in silence, neither of them said a word.

Hannah strode in amidst the hubbub of uniformed policemen scuttling backwards and forwards to begin their work although before she had noticed Ranald, Hamish had whisked her away to find Inspector Mackenzie who he had left in his office.

'Where's the wretched picture?' asked Ranald in heated breath, once the coast was clear.

'Safe,' replied Kenny firmly but not giving anything away.

'They will be round to search your house soon. It won't take them long to make the connection and once they do there will be a fleet of blue flashing lights outside of your home with armed policemen knocking on the front door.' Kenny sighed. He knew Ranald was right.

'The ruddy thing just won't give up her secrets. Tight lipped and frigid compared to when we saw her in Grantown-on-Spey. Can't work it out. Drunk pints of whisky staring at that painting and just when I think it's going to happen it all seems to fizzle out with not so much as a sniff of what we previously saw. It's got secrets Ranald, I'm sure of that and all we need to do is work out how best to get her to release them.'

Ranald was hesitant, taken aback by Kenny's commitment in what he thought would be a doomed quest. He sighed, letting a deep breath of air escape his lips and his chest deflate. The boy was in love, caught up with his exotic Greek belle, distracted from reason and no longer caring about his reckless actions.

'Have you tried the whisky?' asked Ranald.

'Yes, yes, yes,' repeated Kenny, 'drunk more whisky than I care to think about staring at the little beauty.'

'No, I mean THE whisky,' replied Ranald with a glint in his eye.

'THE whisky?' repeated Kenny.

'Yes, THE whisky… the Kawatachi whisky. We brought it back, remember? It was placed in miscellaneous property along with all the other odds and sods we pick up from house clearances. Mysteriously, it's appeared in the Guvnor's bottom draw.'

'GENIUS!' exclaimed Kenny, standing up and smiling. Within seconds he had left the room. Brenda looked up from her paper.

*

Kerplunk – a couple of minutes later Hamish thrust the door open and strode into the common room with Donald and Hannah in tow.

'Where's Kenny?' Brenda looked over the newspaper and shrugged her shoulders.

'He was here a second ago,' before looking towards Ranald for help.

'Gone to the loo,' he suggested while exchanging glances with the police officers. Surprisingly, they ignored him.

'Brenda, can you let these people know where he lives. The address ought to be on our files somewhere.'

'Data protection?' she queried.

'Obstructing our enquiries,' quipped Donald. Brenda began to stir and lead the entourage to her office.

*

'Ciao,' said the Duchessa answering her phone while wafting between the main salon and boudoir within her apartment at Palazzo Toscano.

'Ciao Duchessa,' replied Brialto formally, not forgetting his position.

'Any news?' The doorbell rang and Luigi entered the building taking the lift to the top floor with his box of vegetables.

'Si, si, si,' replied Brialto, 'we've told the Museo. Bruno has given them a warning. You know a Corolla warning … that normally does the trick. He's a good boy is Bruno,' who was sitting in front of him with his cowboy boots resting on the table. Brialto leant forward and slapped him on the cheek and shook his head. He let his boots fall to the floor.

'As I was saying, we have told the Museo that you want the picture back. I think they got the message. We'll follow it up with a Corolla visit in a couple of days' time.'

The Duchessa was feeling her way around the vegetable box: broccoli, always had broccoli, potatoes, carrots too, always had potatoes and carrots. Under the brown paper her delicate well-manicured hands scuttled, stopping to press the tomatoes while smiling at Luigi.

'Anyway,' continued Brialto. 'We've also made contact with some distant family friends in Edinburgh. We Corollas, we have friends everywhere. Distant friends, but friends are friends as far as we are concerned. We help them and they help us. It works well, si. Onaldo Mackenzie. That right, Bruno?' he questioned, looking at his son. Bruno nodded and Brialto continued. 'Anyway, Onaldo he's the police officer in charge. We can keep tabs on him.'

The Duchessa now had her hands wrapped around a couple of firm avocados as her pink fingernails slowly scratched over the wrinkled skin and gently stroked them! Luigi exhaled a long sigh and the Duchessa reached behind his midriff, placing a hand on his bottom and slowly dragged him towards her.

'Buono Brialto, buono. You keep tabs on Onaldo and make sure you find my picture.' With that she dropped the phone and dragged Luigi towards the boudoir!

Chapter 26 – Heysham Drive

'Coffee?' asked Hannah, removing the flask from her shoulder bag and unscrewing the top. Donald nodded.

'May as well.'

It was almost eight o'clock in the evening and they were sitting in an unmarked police car in Heysham Drive near Kenny's home. The light was fading and the temperature was beginning to fall. Hannah was well-wrapped in a padded body warmer although Donald just had a

Harris tweed jacket and was starting to feel the chill. They could see some headlights approaching in the rear-view mirror and a wee car sped past and ground to a halt outside of number 9. Kenny jumped out and briskly made his way to the front door.

'It's our man,' said Donald excitedly, placing his hand on the handle ready to leap out. Hannah grabbed his arm.

'Steady, let him go inside first.' As Kenny disappeared into the house Donald bounded out of the car.

'Come on, let's do it.'

'Not so fast,' said Hannah, breaking into a jog to keep up with her colleague who was striding purposefully towards number 9 Heysham Drive. Up the neat, paved path he galloped, brushing past the well-trimmed hedge and arriving at the newly varnished front door. A side light illuminated the outside and Donald turned, waiting for Hannah to catch up. Within a split second she was there. No need to talk, no need to delay. Donald pushed the doorbell. They both waited in suspense as the ringer buzzed inside.

*

'Malcolm, Malcolm, can you get that,' called Hazel from the kitchen while balancing pots and pans on the draining board and clearing up after supper.

'Hello,' said Malcom, standing in the doorway dressed in his cardigan and slippers not sure why they had visitors at this time of night.

'Edinburgh Police, Criminal Art Department,' said Donald, holding up his I.D. Barging past, he entered the hallway. Hannah followed him in. 'We want to speak with Kenny. We know he's here.'

*

Bruno nodded and opened the door of the black Mercedes Benz.

'No killing, now,' said Brialto as Bruno left the car, firmly shutting the door behind him. Slowly he walked, the heel of his cowboy boots clipping the pavement with a chilling regularity. No need to rush, no one was going anywhere. On he strode in his controlled gait, sucking in the fresh evening air, filling his lungs with oxygen. Bruno was in control, Bruno knew what needed to be done and Bruno was slipping into the zone - a psychotic state where all was blanked out; no emotion, no cares, just... explosive fury!

*

Hazel arrived on the scene to investigate the commotion in the hallway.

'It's the Police, they want to speak with Kenny,' said Malcolm, slightly alarmed.

'Kenny?' questioned Hazel, equally confused.

'Yes Kenny. It's all to do with that picture which went missing, you know the one? it was on the ten o'clock news last night. The auction house sold it.'

'Kenny, Kenny... come downstairs,' shouted Hazel, looking up towards the landing. Buzzzzzzzzzzzzzz, the bell rang again. 'Malcom, get the door,' barked Hazel now flustered by the sequence of events. Still no sign of Kenny from upstairs.

*

'Sei, cinque, quattro, tre,' counted Bruno until he heard the rattle of the key being placed in the lock. Before Malcolm could open the door, he heard a terrifying scream and then the splinter of wood when Bruno bought his machete downwards smashing through the door panel!

'AAAAAaargh,' screamed Hazel as Kenny appeared on the stairs. Donald looked stunned although instantly stepped forward shielding Hannah from the impending storm. CRASH - the machete splintered through the wood again and again until a firm kick from Bruno's cowboy boots bust the lock out of its fastening. The door swung open, hanging limply off its hinges.

The big Italian stepped inside. Donald moved forward but with the back of his hand Bruno slapped him so hard he was stopped in his tracks, dazed by the blow. Opening his eyes, Donald found the wild

Italian and his bulbous moustache leering into his face as he felt the cold metal blade pressed against his neck.

'THE PITTURA,' Bruno screamed, 'I WANT THE PITTURA.' Throwing Donald to one side he walked down the hallway with the machete held out in front of him.

'Okay, okay,' said Kenny, sensibly intervening before he disappeared back upstairs. Hannah squeezed the button on her panic alarm

*

'Category one emergency,' shouted the duty officer within the control room of the Edinburgh Police Station in Kincardine Street.

'We've got a fix on the location in Prestonpans, need a chopper in the sky and armed police to the scene, as soon as'.

'Whose alarm?' asked the Sergeant, rushing into the room.

'Hannah Wright's. Logged here as a covert surveillance operation,' said the duty officer, pointing to the screen. The Sergeant leant forward to read the details.

'MACKENZIE!' he exclaimed. 'What is she doing with Mackenzie?' All thoughts returned to *Mission Marijuana*.

'Secondment, sir. The Guvnor thought she would be a safe pair of hands to help with the art theft. You know the painting it was all over the press. Made the ten o'clock news. Biggest case since the Yarwinder went missing.'

*

Kenny sprinted up the stairs and entered his bedroom.

'Helena,' he shouted, staring at the cupboard with its door wide open and the window curtain fluttering in the breeze. Thrusting his head outside he screamed... 'HELENA.'

Bruno was standing in the hallway as all cowered on the floor before him with their hands behind their heads. He drew steadily on a

115

cigarette and eyed Kenny carefully when he came back down the stairs. Shrugging his shoulders he spoke.

'No painting.'

*

A convoy of police cars were streaming down the A1, blue lights flashing and sirens screaming as the helicopter flew overhead.

'Eight minutes to target,' barked the lead officer into his handset, keeping HQ abreast of progress.

*

Bruno had Kenny pinned up against the wall and, holding him by the throat, calmly bought the machete up to his neck.

'You no understand. We want the pittura returned or... he perforated the skin with the sharp blade as blood began to seep onto Kenny's collar.

'Nooooo,' screamed Hazel, getting to her feet and charging at Bruno. She started punching him in the back. Effortlessly, he cast her to the floor as Malcolm moved to restrain his wife.

'Leave him,' said Brialto, walking into the hallway and sauntering down the corridor with his Beretta in hand. Cool and calculated he raised the pistol, waving the barrel and pointing it towards the stricken group. 'We want the painting. We want it undamaged, unscathed and we want it soon. You understand? Soon, pronto, quickly.' Cocking his gun Brialto swung it towards Donald. 'You in charge? You Onaldo?' Raising his chest upwards to bulk out his frame and shield Hannah he nodded. 'I thought so, I can smell it, I can smell the fear in your sweat. Your little heart pounding while you contemplate if tomorrow will ever arrive.' He stepped forward and waved the barrel of his gun in front of his nose threateningly.

Donald wondered if his time was nigh when he felt cold steel being pressed against his forehead. He peered into the dark, soulless eyes of his tormentor, taking in the deep scar of his disfigured face.

'You find the picture,' said Brialto calmly and then you give it to me. Comprendo?' Donald nodded. Bruno let Kenny slip to the floor, superficially damaged but otherwise unharmed. Calmly, he followed Brialto out of the doorway and back to their car.

*

Bruno indicated right and pulled on to the A1, turning towards Edinburgh as the convoy of blue lights could be seen coming in their direction. He shrugged his shoulders and smiled at Brialto when they sped past.

*

Helena was running across a corn field, the long stems brushing her legs with the ears of grain sticking to her skirt. She was warm with small beads of sweat appearing on her forehead. Towards the lights of Wallyford she went with the watercolour safely tucked under her arm.

Chapter 27 – The Dig Continues

Shona and Fortescue arrived at the Kinross House landing pontoon and boarded the launch. It was a blustery day which was causing the water to lap against the boat as they cast off from the shore. Windswept spray dampened their clothes although their spirits were undiminished thanks to the excited voicemail Oliver Chetwin had left, the previous evening, extolling the results from the *Ecografia Scanner* !

*

'... *get yourselves down here as soon as possible in the morning.'*
Shona had returned the call although it went straight through to the
answerphone.

'Frustrating,' she exclaimed while sitting with Fortescue at the
hotel bar, pondering the recent events and their meeting with the
Duchessa's people. 'Should we let Don know?' Fortescue had shrugged
while looking down at his smart phone. There had been two missed
calls from Miranda and a number of texts. He was guilt ridden, not
returning her messages, and dreading what would be a difficult
conversation. Shona grabbed his thigh to catch his attention. Looking
up he longingly gazed into her bright emerald eyes. The Irish temptress
had cast her Celtic spell and he seemed unable to resist her wicked
charms.

*

'Morning,' shouted Oliver from the pontoon, waiting for the launch to
come alongside. Up the path they scuttled as drops of rain began to fall
and within a couple of minutes they were in the portacabin and Oliver's
makeshift laboratory. Gus was sitting at the table logging the readings
on to his laptop and mapping the site.

'Come and look at these,' said Oliver, leaning over and
pointing at the screen. 'There, see the pattern?' Gus flicked onto a
different tab and everyone stooped, straining their eyes. Confusion
reigned at the sight of the images which sat before them - two mottled
grey screens with indecipherable dark smudges on both. Shona plucked
up courage.

'We're struggling.'

'Colour the infrared data,' commanded Oliver. Gus moved the
mouse and clicked on the icon. Darker shades appeared on both screens.
'Can you see it now?' continued Oliver taking a biro out of his top
pocket and pointing to a section. 'Add more colour, Gus, to accentuate
the difference.' Still silence from the onlookers. 'Crikey, have you lot

been drinking? Look at the pattern here, which comes from the infrared images we found in the painting and these from the *Ecographia Scanner*... there's a match... almost!' Oliver moved his pen across both images, illustrating the shapes. 'I mean there's minor differences but generally a close correlation.' Shona nodded, although looked unconvinced.

*

'Let's just run through it once more Mackenzie,' insisted the Chief Superintendent of Edinburgh Police Force who was a large boorish man with a pot belly and a grizzly demeanour. He had beady, pig-like eyes and was staring oafishly at Donald and Hannah. 'You say a tall dark man with a foreign accent attacked you with a machete?' Donald looked at Hannah for support then nodded.

'Yes, the other witnesses have corroborated the story.'

'So, tell me about the man who arrived with a pistol.' Donald sighed. He had already made a statement as clear as could be. Breathing in, he summoned up the energy to try again.

'Medium height, older man, say late fifties, maybe sixtyish, stout though and solid; the sort of guy who could look after himself in a fight, if you know what I mean. Oh, and yes, his most distinguishing feature, a deep scar which ran down the left-hand side of his face. The Superintendent nodded. He had read Donald's statement which had been comprehensive in fact meticulous in its precision and detail. Hannah looked at her watch wondering how much longer this would last.

*

It was early evening when Kenny arrived at the reception of the Holiday Inn, Wallyford. The polite receptionist smiled welcomingly and then directed him towards the bar where he found Helena perched on a stool and enjoying a long gin from a highball glass with a cocktail stick poking out of the top. Her legs were elegantly crossed as she sat tall, confidently poised as if nothing had happened over the last twenty-four hours. Kenny hesitated. The attack last night had shaken him to the bone. His mother had been in tears, almost hysterical at times, whereas his father had hyper-ventilated and required a sedative to calm him down. He had never seen his parents in such a state. Normally dependable, boring in their routine and the humdrum of everyday life they had been rocked to the core, never slept a wink last night and had even called off work this morning.

Helena turned instinctively, sensing Kenny's presence and cast her intoxicating smile in his direction. Without speaking she casually patted her hand on the adjoining bar stool, inviting him to sit down.

'Drink?' Kenny shook his head and climbed onto the stool. For the first time his unrelenting devotion to Helena was being questioned. She sensed it and put a reassuring hand on his knee. Kenny flinched and the fragile glass cocoon of their impregnable love seemed shattered, splintering like breaking shards falling to the ground. Slowly, Helena swivelled back towards the bar and took a long sip of gin before speaking.

'You don't understand what the Marbles mean to us Greeks. They are not just inert lumps of stone… they're our heritage, our being, the conduit which connects us to our classical roots and the ancient Gods and Goddesses of distant times.' Emotion and feeling was shown with her every syllable. Kenny shifted uneasily in his seat, slightly unnerved by Helena's unrepentant demeanour. Silence returned and Helena took another sip of her drink.

'Have you got the picture?' asked Kenny. Helena nodded.

'It's upstairs in my room. Have you got the whisky?' Kenny opened the holdall he had brought and there, loosely wrapped up in an old football shirt, nestled the treasured bottle of ten-year-old Kawatachi malt whisky – cask 264. Helena downed the rest of her gin and standing up jangled her room keys.

*

Gladios entered the Sarcophagus Tavern to find Prodius sitting at their usual table and nurturing a glass of rosé. Noisily dragging a chair across the tiled floor and banging into the radiator he sat down with his usual bluster. His attention was distracted while he looked for the octopus in the fish tank. Eventually, grunting to acknowledge his colleague, he picked up the menu and quickly glanced down the Chef's Specialities saddened to see the Mongolian Lamb was no longer there.

'We still haven't heard from Helena. It's been almost a week since the painting was stolen and not a peep from her aside from a couple of brief texts,' said Prodius. Gladios helped himself to a glass of rosé before signalling to the waiter that he was ready to order.

'Yes, it's not like her,' he agreed. The waiter arrived and took his order, scribbling frantically before repeating it back to him.

'Tzatziki to start, Moussaka main with a side plate of fries?'

'Large fries,' corrected Gladios, 'and another bottle of ...' he picked up the empty rosé and waived it in the waiter's direction.

'I received a phone call from Helena's mother yesterday morning,' continued Prodius, 'she hasn't heard from her for nearly a week. Do you think she is okay?'
Gladios sipped his wine letting his gaze be drawn back towards the fish tank and the octopus. He sucked in the foggy restaurant air with the faint whiff of tobacco teasing his nostrils while he mulled over the circumstances of Helena's travels.

'Would you like me to visit Scotland?' he asked.

'I had been thinking the same,' confessed Prodius with glee. The Tzatziki arrived on the table. Gladios helped himself with a fork, devouring a mouthful before speaking.

'Presumably expenses paid, decent hotel, generous daily allowance?' Prodius smiled, knowing it would be futile asking Gladios to economise despite the era of austerity.

'Agreed,' he muttered before helping himself to some more wine.

*

Hamish lay on the double divan within the main bedroom of Agnes's flat above the Black Dog while clutching a tumbler of whisky and drawing on his fag. Agnes was showering in the ensuite and within a couple of minutes she appeared in her dressing gown and pair of woollen slippers. Letting her robe fall to the ground she slipped between the sheets and cuddled up to the bony old auctioneer.

'Oh, that's lovely, Agnes,' said Hamish, feeling her warmth through his winceyette pyjamas. She slipped a hand between his buttons and rubbed his chest.

'No, no, no, not tonight, darling,' said Hamish, restraining her hand while he stubbed out his cigarette in the ashtray which sat on the bedside table. 'The flesh is not what is used to be, my dear, and to be honest something is troubling me.' Agnes sat up in bed, disappointed with the evening's outcome.

'So what's up; tell me what's concerning you?'

'It's that picture, you know the one which we sold at the auction; made a helluva price and then mysteriously was stolen from the National Gallery. They still haven't found it.'

'Ummm,' said Agnes coyly, seeking to winkle out of the old man what was really bothering him. 'Come on tell me more.'

'Oh, it's probably nothing, nothing at all really… it's just that Kenny and his Greek girl had shown a real interest in the painting, been to view it a couple of times at the exhibition even on the day it went missing, according to Brenda.' Hamish paused not sure where his ramblings were leading.

'Go on, get it off your chest,' nudged Agnes as she firmly gripped his knobbly knee.

'It was the description in the Scotsman which got me thinking: *slim built male in his twenties with a tall female accomplice, noticeable by her foreign accent.* That's Kenny and the Greek!'

'Are you sure?' questioned Agnes, finding the connections quite tenuous.

'Well, I've seen Kenny with her before, on the day of the auction. It's just how I would describe them.' Agnes sighed, not really understanding old Hamish, and wondering if the years of whisky were finally taking their toll.

'You may be wrong, of course.' Hamish nodded, accepting that was a highly plausible answer but deep down something was niggling him. In truth he quite liked young Kenny. Of course he didn't pay him much but on the whole, he had worked hard since joining the firm and with Ranald's guidance had proved to be a useful addition. That was it... obvious really, not sure why he hadn't thought of it sooner... ask Ranald! He would surely know if Kevin was mixed up in something or not. Hamish put his arm around Agnes, cuddling into his loving landlady and sleeping partner.

*

Helena and Kenny sat on the single bed in the Holiday Inn with the picture perched on the sideboard and resting against the wall. The central pendant brightly illuminated the room and most importantly the beautiful little water colour which was standing in front of them. Kenny eyed her warily. Far too many times, of late, he had sought to look into the soul of the painting, beyond the thin veneer of water colours and into her bowels in search of the deep secret which he was sure she possessed. And far too many times she had shown a little leg, the hem of her skirt; teasing young Kenny, taunting him with her wares but keeping him from her inner sanctum and the secret he so desperately wanted to uncover.

'Enough?' asked Helena who was pouring the Kawatachi ten-year-old malt, cask 264, into a couple of teacups which were beside the electric kettle. Kenny nodded. 'Mixer?' He shook his head. Breathing in he readied himself as he took the cup from his Greek belle who moved closer so their shoulders touched. The tension, the intimacy, sparking a fission and the flicker of a lost love which appeared that it may revitalise and burst back into life. But on this occasion, within the Holiday Inn, love was to be denied because young Kenny knew what lay ahead. He had ridden the Kawatachi rollercoaster before and he was fully aware they were in for a frenzied trip.

'PHWOARRRR,' he shouted, sipping the amber liquid as its fulsome flavour tickled his tonsils and burned the back of his throat.

'WHOARR,' replied Helena, losing her Kawatachi virginity and sipping again. Kenny followed, downing the contents of his cup before getting up to pour some more. Three inches of the bottle were sunk between them while they sat on the bed looking at the picture with double vision, waiting in expectation as they had waited before. But something felt different this time; they were elated and in a euphoric state, surfing on a wave of expectation and they were not to be disappointed. The picture had taken on a whole new persona, no longer the pretty wee girl who sat on the side lines waiting for a dance. This was a behemoth of a woman who was dancing provocatively before their eyes, a wanton wench working the floor and drawing in the unsuspecting observer. The Parthenon Temple sparkled, its classical columns leaping out of the frame as ancient Greek Hoplites ushered them inside, through the entrance and into the cavernous innards of the iconic temple. And there before them the constellations shined, reflecting their formation onto the tiled floor.

'Ccccopy it,' stammered Helena, scribbling with pen on paper, noting the pattern which they saw. But the Kawatachi rollercoaster had only just begun; throwing them around corners, up and down, like never before. The floor of the temple began to crumble and splinter with lava bubbling up from within, erupting and spewing and then… there was no more!

Chapter 28 – Treasures Uncovered!

The mini digger moved into position. Oliver jumped up to the cab and spoke with the driver.

'We don't know precisely how deep to dig so once you get to six feet can you let us know? We will then check with a probe.'

'Aye,' said the driver, moving the joystick so that the long arm extended before flexing downwards, ripping up the turf and moving it to one side.

'Exciting isn't it,' said Lara Paterson, looking around at her colleague, Judith, who had a beaming smile. She nodded in agreement while watching the digger toil away.

Oliver had now moved back from the works area and was standing beside Shona who had Fortescue to her side. No one spoke, instead, they were transfixed watching the yellow machine grunt and groan as it piled up the earth in the back of a trailer. All would be sifted by the volunteer archaeologists who were waiting in anticipation for the first load to arrive.

Fortescue glanced at Shona, catching her eye, and she held his gaze with a gentle smile. For once, she came over all meek which wrong-footed Fortescue who was more used to her high-handed manner. His composure was ruffled and in panic he spoke.

'Miranda and I have split up,' he blurted in surprise, not sure why he felt compelled to share his hurt. But it was wasted on Shona who barely blinked. In reality she knew it was on the cards, she knew Fortescue liked her and she knew just how much. Shona had teased and tortured him with her indomitable spirit and now when he appeared most in need of her, she had acted with... reproach, ignoring his plea. Fortescue stuttered, surprised by the lack of a response. He changed tact and went back to all that seemed to interest her... the Curse of Minerva by Giovanni Battista Lusieri and where it may ultimately lead them.

'The Byron verse mystifies me.' Shona's ears pricked up and she momentarily swivelled to glean some more. 'I studied Byron,' continued Fortescue. 'It seems odd that a verse from the Curse of Minerva should have been scribbled onto the back of the picture. He was an avid critic of Lord Elgin, there were spats in the press and all sorts between them.'

'May have been added later,' replied Shona, looking at her colleague and staring into his eyes. Oh, what lovely gentle eyes, deep blue with an irresistible spark. Fortescue smiled while returning her gaze. What a lovely smile, thought Shona, admiring his pursed lips and the curl of his mouth. She wanted to touch his face, run her fingers through his floppy hair and... no it was too soon. Not just yet, plenty of time to pull dear old Fortescue in.

BANG! everyone heard the digger's bucket make contact with something rather solid.

'STOP,' screamed Oliver, running towards the hole and waving frantically.

*

A dark Mercedes Benz pulled up at Kinross House. The occupants got out and slowly walked over the forecourt, heading in the direction of the garden and the landing pontoon beyond. The steady crunch of gravel under a pair of suede cowboy boots!

*

Kenny stirred and rolled over in bed. Crikey, a splitting pain ran through his head as he felt the onset of a whopping hangover. Gently shaking himself he sat up and glanced towards the alarm clock on the bed side table – eleven am! Where had time gone? Stretching to his right he felt the dozing shape of Helena, curled up under the duvet but otherwise still fully clothed. He leaned over. She was breathing. Well, in the circumstances, that was at least something. Off to the bathroom he tottered to splash some cold water around his ruddy face and to clean his teeth. Helena was sitting up in bed when he arrived back in the room.

'Here look at these,' she said, passing Kenny the sheets of paper they had scribbled on the previous night. Remarkably, their sketches were very similar: a circular shape of smudges. Otherwise, the watercolour sat on the sideboard resting against the wall, no longer the wanton temptress, now demure and small.

'I've been thinking,' said Kenny, hesitantly.

'Thinking?' questioned Helena, her head starting to clear. 'Thinking? Never a good idea to think too much. So tell me Kenny, what have you been thinking about?'

'You know what's troubling me,' he said, pointing to the painting while hanging his head despondently. Helena sighed. Things had gotten a little out of hand, that she could not deny. Firstly, taking the picture which had caused a hullaballoo. Hullaballoo! - more than a hullabaloo, good heavens it had made the Greek national news, precipitated a ferocious attack only the night before last and… What had happened to her? Sensible Helena with a staid job at the Bureau in Athens, always dependable, always reliable, pastiche in her outlook and now being chased hither and thither around the suburbs of Edinburgh by a machete wielding lunatic.

'Okay, what do you suggest?'

*

Bruno and Brialto arrived on the island after borrowing a small rowing boat they had found. The Duchessa had tipped them off following a telephone conversation with the British Museum, who felt obliged to keep her up to date with developments. Yet, despite their reassurances, there was still no sign of the missing painting.

*

Oliver was in the hole with a shovel with numerous faces peering over the side including Nancy O'Donnell from the Courier and her erstwhile competitor at the Fife Times, big Brendan McCluskey. Both had managed to blag their way onto the island, following a tip-off they had received. And now they were both jostling for position and vying for the attention of any of the so-called experts to interview. None cared to indulge them. Oliver put up his hand, steadying the driver who carefully raised the bucket so he could clear the soil and fully reveal the hard object he was standing on.

'What do you think it is?' shouted Shona, impatiently. Oliver shrugged his shoulders and kept shovelling.

*

Bruno and Brialto appeared on the scene.

'What are they looking for?' asked Bruno, approaching Nancy who was momentarily at a loose end. She was a little taken aback by the tall Italian and his bulbous moustache. Within a few seconds Brialto had joined them and after raising his eyebrows questioningly, Nancy got the message.

'Oh yes. What are they looking for – treasures of some sort…I believe.'

'Treasures?' repeated Bruno.

'Yes, Greek treasures, apparently. Artefacts from the Parthenon Temple.'

'Parthenon?' said Bruno, ignorantly.

'Yes, the Parthenon Temple, the Acropolis, ancient Greece… '

'Imbecilic!' interrupted Brialto, cuffing his son around the head. 'No educated,' he continued while shrugging his shoulders and looking at Nancy who was now regretting ever speaking to the foreign oafs. She smiled patronisingly which was lost on the Italians who missed the subtly of her icy stare.

'So why?' pressed Brialto, 'why do they dig for Greek treasures in Scotland?'

'They bothering you luv?' interrupted the site foreman, a brusque chap with a shaved head who had taken a shine to young Nancy.

'No, no,' she replied waving him away, not sure how having another oaf on the scene was likely to help. In whispered tones she spoke. 'It's something to do with that painting which was stolen'

*

Oliver had uncovered a portion of the large solid object the digger driver had partly dug up.

'A sarcophagus?' suggested Gus.

'Not sure. There's a door, but it's not like an ancient tomb.' There was now quite a crowd surrounding the hole, waiting in glee to discover what had been unearthed. 'Gus, get down here,' barked Oliver. His eager assistant scrambled downwards with earth tumbling beside him and landing on their precious find. 'Steady.'

Brendan McCluskey had stolen a march on young Nancy and moved in close onto the edge of the dig, with the best view. He tottered daintily on his feet, leaning over the safety tape so he could see what was going on. And, typically of Brendan he leaned a bit too far, slipped on some mud and lost his balance…

'Bloody hell,' cursed Oliver when spherical Brendan landed in the hole and clattered into Gus, knocking him over and causing a scrum.

'Idiot,' he bellowed on realising what had happened. Brendan apologised profusely and then tried to scramble out, although the stocky little reporter wasn't used to such athletic feats and nor were his slick leather-soled shoes best suited to the task.

'Whooa,' shouted Brendan as he slipped and came tumbling back down again.

'Get a rope,' said Oliver, glaring at the mud-stained journalist. Nancy, who had kept a safe distance, was now enjoying the debacle unfolding in front of her. Brialto's scarred face managed to muster a smile. Even Bruno grinned before drawing on his cigarette and casually tossing the butt end into the hole. As for Lara and Judith... they both had to walk away, with tears streaming down their faces, as muffled sniggers grew into howls of uncontrollable laughter.

Gus tied the rope firmly around Brendan's extensive girth and gave the thumbs up to the workmen who took the strain and started to haul. Oliver was shaking his head and muttering under his breath...

'Ruddy ape!'

*

Two hours later the digger's telescopic arm elevated upwards, raising the enormous rectangular box which swung in a hessian net. Cameras flashed, Nancy and Brendan recorded events and even Lara and Judith watched eagerly, in anticipation, having recovered their composure. The tension was building all the time.

'Gently,' urged Oliver as the great artefact landed on the waterproof mat and the net fell down around it. The rope was unhooked and the now burgeoning crowd of scientists, archaeologists - ists in this – ists in that - hangers on, waifs and strays and our dear beloved Italian psychopaths, started to move in.

'Look here Gus, ancient writing, can you read it?

Peering at the rusty figures, they were difficult to decipher so he took the soft brush from his inside pocket and delicately wiped away the dirt before placing tracing paper on top and scribbling with his soft leaded pencil.

'Anything yet?' asked Oliver with growing impatience.

'Z. First symbol Z.'

'Z?'

'Next... A'

'A? A?' .

'N and U, S, S, I.'

'WHAT!' bellowed Oliver. 'Let me have a look,' snatching the tracing paper from Gus.

'Z.A.N.U.S.S.I!'

'Zanussi,' they repeated in chorus. Oliver grabbed the lid and in a pique of indignation wrenched in open.

'Fluck, it's a fridge!'

Chapter 29 – The Charleston Hotel

'Name please?' asked the receptionist at the Charleston Hotel while sitting in front of the computer screen and completing her supermarket order.

'Fatiakos, Gladios Fatiakos.' The receptionist moved her mouse and right clicked purchasing a three-pack of ready ripe avocados.

'And how would you be spelling, fatty... what was it?' But before Gladios could answer there was a commotion in the foyer as the

Duchessa arrived with her entourage of assistants and helpers. The concierge scurried in all directions, collecting cases and bags from the small fleet of chauffeured cars which had ferried them from the airport.

'Duchessa di Canali,' announced the po-faced PA, arriving at the reception desk and speaking over Gladios, whom she totally ignored. The receptionist right clicked accidentally ordering an extra bottle of olive oil. Another assistant arrived and demanded,

'Which room? Which room, please? We've had a long journey and the Duchessa wants some down time.' The receptionist moved her mouse left, then right, clicking here, clicking there, shutting down shopping sites and social media chats until she arrived at the hotel homepage and went to reservations.

'We booked the suite of rooms two days ago,' insisted the PA adding, 'the account was paid in advance.' By now the receptionist was starting to panic, realising this was no ordinary guest, but before she could make any headway the crowds of minions shuffled and gasped, parting like the Red Sea for the Duchessa who strode towards the reception desk with young Luigi in tow.

'Keys,' she demanded holding her hand out flat. On the screen the icon was whirling round and round, but otherwise was proving futile in directing the receptionist to the correct area of the booking system.

'Va bene Duchessa?' asked Brialto who had just returned to the hotel with Bruno. She smiled acknowledging his presence and then looked back at the receptionist expectantly. Still the icon circled. Bruno, with eyes on stalks, stepped forward and grabbed the receptionist by the hair, dragging her head backwards and thrusting his bulbous moustache and snarling grin into her face. This proved too much for Gladios who had been standing patiently while the riff raff pushed in.

'That's no way to treat a lady.' Onlookers gasped in shock. A porter went to her aid, although was quickly shrugged off by the powerful Italian who sent him crashing to the floor. But Gladios was made of stronger stuff and a good deal sturdier. With his sleeves rolled up, revealing the Hellenic Navy tattoo, he thumped Bruno in the back of his ribcage and at last the big man flinched and released his grip. Turning to face his assailant he stood tall, towering over Gladios while they eyeballed one another. Bruno clenched his club like fists with the veins in his forearms bulging.

THWACK! Brialto brought the solid metal handle of his Beretta down onto his wayward son's skull.

'Idiota, imbecille,' he raged, cuffing his boy around the ears with real force. Bruno recoiled backwards. Fires burned within, just once too often Brialto had sought to humiliate him in public. He lashed out, grabbing his father by the throat and clenching his fist strengthened his grip on Brialto's windpipe. But despite the intense pressure being exerted, he smiled sarcastically at his son and then spun the Beretta taking hold of the handle and easing the barrel into Bruno's hard packed and well-toned stomach. He said nothing, he didn't need to. Instead, he slipped the safety catch off and cocked the pistol with a firm – click! His smiled widened when he felt the pressure on his windpipe begin to ease as Bruno released his hold.

Brialto gave a gentle cough as oxygen surged back into his lungs, revitalising his being. He smiled sarcastically and then spat into his son's face.

'Balmoral suite, top floor,' said the receptionist, recovering her composure and reaching into the draw of her desk to retrieve the swipe cards.

'Thank you,' said the PA, taking the bundle and turning towards the Duchessa.

*

Hamish entered the staffroom at Forbes and McKillop where everyone remained seated, gossiping idly amongst themselves and drinking coffee. No sign of Kenny who had rung in sick. Ranald was back at work, sitting in his usual place at the table close to the kettle.

'Can I have a word?' asked Hamish softly, looking at Ranald and gently coaxing him out of his seat and down the corridor to his office where they could have some privacy.

'Drink?' Ranald shook his head. 'No, I thought not,' continued Hamish taking the whisky bottle from the bottom right drawer of his desk and pouring himself a measure which he diluted with a dash of Crabbies. 'I had a lovely bottle of Japanese whisky, left over from Lady McManus' sale. Err, what was it called, Kawachi... something or other, can't say I can fully remember. As I said, a lovely bottle, pretty label; but Christ it was hooching, proper fire water, hadn't drunk anything like that since I tried my hand at home distilling back in the 1960's. Wonderful times the 1960's; I don't suppose you remember them?' Ranald shook his head. 'No, I suppose not, before your time. Anyway, I haven't dragged you to my office to chat about whisky and what not, no... I am concerned about Kenny.' Ranald felt his stomach tighten while he momentarily flushed and his hands became clammy.

'Kenny?' he repeated.

'Yes Kenny,' replied Hamish. 'There's been something odd in his behaviour of late. He's been off work a lot recently and Brenda tells me he has a new Greek girlfriend, the one we met at the auction. She was very interested in the Lusieri painting. You remember the girl, attractive, far too good for young Kenny, but there you are, no accounting for taste.' Ranald sat in silence, still not sure where the conversation was going. Hamish continued. 'They were both fixated on the picture, visited the exhibition on a number of occasions and then, as you know, it went missing.' Ranald nodded feeling his face redden. 'It was the description in the Scotsman which got me thinking,' said Hamish. 'Local man, mid-twenties with an attractive foreign lady. You don't think they are involved in any way?'

Ranald was now beginning to feel queasy. He knew full well Kenny was most certainly involved, right up to the gunnels, in the soup as plain as could be, and it alarmed him that even old Hamish had become suspicious. Crumbs, he felt a suffocating feeling as if the walls were closing in around him while he began to wonder how long it would be before Kenny's folly would be discovered. He would surely be found out.

'Anyway, I just thought, I would mention it,' prattled the old auctioneer, oblivious to the strain Ranald was feeling. Brenda knocked and opened the door.

'The Duchessa is on the phone and wants to speak with you.'

*

It was almost four o'clock in the afternoon when Kenny and Helena got off the bus in Prestonpans and began the short walk to number 9 Heysham Drive, ambling gently, not sure what to expect when they arrived at the new front door. Opening it they walked in. Malcolm and Hazel were sitting in the front living room sipping tea and aimlessly watching daytime TV. Neither had gone to work today.

'We're back,' said Kenny, trying to sound upbeat while poking his head around the doorway to see his parents. Hazel, always polite, stood to welcome them, although her demeanour remained solemn. She was no longer the joyful mother looking forward to spending time with her son's girlfriend. Bzzzzzzz, the doorbell rang. Everyone jumped, startled to be disturbed again.

'Hello,' said Inspector Donald Mackenzie when Malcolm opened the door. 'Is Helena Tattius here? We would like a word with her.'

Chapter 30 – A Pleasant Surprise

'Meet Brialto Corolla and his son Bruno,' said the Duchessa, leading Hamish into the main dining room at the Charleston Hotel. The old auctioneer shook hands and smiled as they all sat down while the waitress took an order of drinks and placed menus on the table.

'Fish of the day is turbot, cooked in a lemon sauce,' she announced before leaving them to choose. Luigi arrived late. After kissing the Duchessa on the cheek, he took the seat to her right and placed a hand on her leg.

'Nice to meet you,' said Hamish, breaking into conversation. 'You must be the Duca's son. Lovely man was your father a gentleman through and through. I remember the time I sold him a Canaletto. Who would have thought, hey, a Scotsman selling a Canaletto to a Venetian, of all people.' Hamish took a generous swig of wine which had just been poured and continued before anyone had chance to interrupt. 'It was 1978, I remember the picture clearly. It turned up at a house sale, well, when I say house I mean castle, really. Recognised it straight away and let the Duca know.' He took another large swig of wine.

'Can I take your orders?' asked the waitress.

'Turbot,' said the Duchessa before anyone could reply. Brialto put his menu down in surprise and raised his eyebrows.

'Pescatarian,' she replied, dismissively.

'Flexitarian,' piped up Luigi, 'sometimes vegan, sometimes fish.'

'Duchessa,' said Bruno through a haze of fug, his brain intoxicated from the spliff he had smoked earlier on the balcony of his hotel room.

'The British Museum,' he continued, 'they're digging for treasures. Treasures which your picture has revealed, priceless pieces of great importance... You should have them.' For once Brialto agreed with his son and nodded. Anything which belonged to the Duchessa also belonged to them. Ten percent was their usual cut; ten percent of any treasures which the picture uncovered would only be fair recompense for their time in Scotland.

'It's finders-keepers in Scotland,' sparked Hamish, striking a match to light a cigarette.

'No smoking,' barked the waitress, snatching the fag from his hand before he had time to inhale.

'So, who gets the treasure if they find something? asked Brialto. 'The British Museum?' Hamish shrugged before replying.

'Possibly.'

'NO,' snapped Bruno slamming his fist onto the table, rattling the cutlery and spilling some wine. 'It's not right. Not the British Museum. The picture belongs to the Duchessa and so does the treasure.' Brialto agreed.

'Seems fair to me.' Hamish was catching up with the conversation, slightly puzzled that there was such talk of riches.

'Just so I am clear, are you saying the painting I sold the Duchessa harbours lost secrets?' She nodded.

'The British Museum arranged for the picture to be scanned at the Courtauld and found a verse from a Byron poem and what they think is a pentimento.

'Byron poem,' repeated Hamish, quite taken with the romance of the idea. The Duchessa continued.

'The Curse of Minerva, the title of the painting. It's also a poem Byron wrote about the looting of the Parthenon Temple. What was the verse? ... *Yet still the Gods are just, and crimes are crossed: See here what Elgin won and Elgin lost.* Yes, that was it. Fascinating, isn't it?'

'And where are they digging,' enquired Hamish keen to find out more.

'Loch Leven Island,' spilled the Duchessa, without any thought.

'Oh,' said the old auctioneer. He had a swig of wine while he took in the news.

*

'Forty-two minutes passed eight - interview formally terminated,' said Hannah, clicking the off button on the recording machine. Donald pushed back in his chair and holding his hands behind his head he stretched out his legs and began to sprawl.

'Could I have a few words with my clients?' said the duty solicitor as he stood, pleased to move after the two-hour ordeal. Helena was exhausted, the nervous tension having sapped her energy while Kenny, who had accompanied her, was showing some signs of strain.

Number 9 Heysham Drive had been searched, much to Malcolm and Brenda's distress, although after a couple of hours of ransacking their well-kept suburban home there was still no clue as to where the painting might be.

*

Bruno was now standing at the reception desk while the fearful receptionist scrolled through the computer system looking for the booking. It was against all rules, broke the data protection act and could lead to her being sacked, if management found out. But after her previous encounter with the mad Italian she was only concerned for her own well-being. In the interest of safety, the young girl began to blather.

'Gladios Fatiakos from the Greek Bureau of Culture, room twenty-eight on the second floor.'

'Greek Bureau of Culture?' repeated Bruno inquisitively. The girl nodded while keeping her eyes on the screen.

'That what's down on the booking form.' Bruno smiled sadistically.

'Good, now you keep an eye on him and let me know what he is up to. The times he comes, the times he goes. Comprendo?' The receptionist nodded.

*

'Lost property, put it in lost property,' shouted the Station Master of Edinburgh Bus Depot.

'But it's got an address,' replied the bus driver, walking through the doorway and placing the parcel, wrapped in brown paper and tied with string, on the desk: CHIEF SUPERINTENDENT, EDINBURGH POLICE STATION – HANDLE WITH CARE.

'Edinburgh Police Station?' repeated the Station Master, picking up the package and looking more closely at the handwritten label. Typical, no postage… stick it in lost property.'

'Is that a good idea?' pressed the driver. 'I mean, you said that about the cat we found in a basket… remember?' A shudder ran through the Station Master. Tabitha, that was its name, dear old Tabitha left in a wicker basket on the bus by a senile old lady, with a fading memory, on her way home from the vets. Tabitha, the name was etched on his memory. How could he forget dear Tabitha and the RSPCA inquiry which followed, the jibes at his Golf Club and the sketch which the drivers performed at the Christmas party, too much hilarity. And then there had been the headlines in the local press: *Tabitha's Torment – Left in Lost Property...* Frankly he had done well to keep his name out of the papers.

'Okay, okay, make sure it is delivered as soon as.'

*

'Donald, Hannah, a word please?' demanded the Chief Superintendent, standing in the doorway watching Kenny and Helena collect their belongings and leave with the duty solicitor. Donald felt a dark cloud gathering while looking at the formidable stature of the overweight, pot-bellied Chief and his stern grimace. 'My office,' he barked, leading them down the corridor and into his plush abode with a Cappuccino maker in the corner. It hissed, spewing out steam and gurgled while he filled a cup and promptly sat down, creaking into his leather seat. Donald and Hannah were left standing in trepidation. They knew what was coming. The storm clouds were gathering, billowing in ever greater spirals and darkening with menace.

'The picture,' said the Chief, glaring at them. Donald stepped forward to shield Hannah from the impending rage. 'It's been a week, a whole week and still no leads.' There was silence. Donald nodded, acknowledging the fact. It was futile to speak. Let the storm pass and then try. 'The press are starting to ask difficult questions...' His face was reddening, his lips were pursed and there was a wild look in his eyes. 'WHAT ON EARTH HAVE YOU BEEN DOING?' he screamed, like a crack of lightening as the winds started to blow.

'Excuse me sir,' said the receptionist, bursting in. 'This parcel has just arrived and I was asked to bring it straight to you.'

'AAAARGGHHHH,' shouted the Chief Superintendent, furious that his tirade had been interrupted.

'Let me help with this,' said Donald, seizing the initiative and unwrapping the parcel. He left the contents sitting on the table.

'I can report the picture has been recovered, Sir.'

'AAAARGGHHHH,' screamed the Superintendent, again.

Chapter 31 – Back to the Dig

'How many cubic metres?' asked Oliver.

'One hundred and forty-six thousand, according to the *Ecografia Scanner,*' replied Gus while standing beside the operator's screen and scrolling through the menu. 'Almost two acres covered to a depth of a metre, fifty-three hours of operational time and oh, what does it say here… service required?'

'Service, service required!' riposted Oliver. 'Wretched pile of Italian junk. How much did we pay for it? Never mind, I don't think I want to know.'

'They're here,' interrupted Gus when he saw the representatives from Historic Scotland and the British Museum making their way to the temporary office within the portacabin.

The local press had lost interest after the debacle with the Zanussi fridge. What was it the Courier had said? *Cold shoulder for the British Museum.* At least they hadn't mentioned the Courtauld, reflected Oliver. Everyone was flat and no longer brimming with expectation as to what may be discovered. Their anticipation had been quelled by nearly five days of digging with little reward. The *Ecografia Scanner* had ground on, spewing out readings, graphs and maps with varied shadings. But what was thought to be a match to the pentimento proved to be a false dawn and a great disappointment. The buried circular sheep flank had been nothing of great note and the excitement of the large rectangular object in the centre... well, a cheap 1960's Italian fridge hadn't done much to whet the archaeologist's appetite. They too were beginning to wonder why they were mindlessly sifting through soil to find little more than broken pieces of glass and the occasional coke can. The weather had turned with intermittent downpours and their spirits had been sapped.

Oliver still had bustle and his usual impetuous manner but even his ever-optimistic disposition was beginning to flag. The only one who seemed up-beat was dear old Fortescue who, after almost a week in Shona's company, was surprisingly chipper.

*

'We've now covered the whole site,' said Gus, sitting at the top of the table beside Oliver. 'It's not what we had hoped for, in fact it's a little disappointing, in truth.' Oliver nodded in agreement before speaking.

'We would have expected to find something of substance by now.

'And the pentimento?' interrupted Fortescue, 'the circular shape, similar to the sheep... flank? Is that what you call it?' Gus nodded. 'Could it symbolise anything else?' Oliver breathed in with a heavy sigh before speaking.

'There was a similarity with the reading from the *Scanner,* but we all know the outcome of that.' He paused before continuing. 'Realistically, we've been at the site for almost a week and nothing to show other than...' his voice tailed off.

'What do you suggest?' asked Shona, cutting to the chase. Gus looked downtrodden. Oliver sighed again.

'It seems pointless to keep aimlessly digging when there is little indication that we will find anything of note.'

'And the verse from the poem?' asked Fortescue in a more positive tone. *'Yet still the Gods are just, and crimes are crossed: See here what Elgin won and Elgin lost.'* Oliver remained unmoved and

Gus looked equally blank. Shona shook her head. She was confused, unable to decipher the clue and bamboozled by its relevance.

'It must mean something though,' she muttered her face terse and contorted in thought. Oliver shrugged.

'Nothing instantly springs to mind.'

Lara and Judith from Historic Scotland had been watching the conversation ebb and flow and the theories develop, although they were concerned that their ancient monument was now looking like a building site with piles of earth and tape everywhere.

'Does that mean you're going to call a halt?' asked Laura, wishing to get to the bottom of the mornings meeting. There was instant quiet. No one spoke. Instead, there were quizzical glances across the table until eventually all eyes settled on Oliver, the elder statesman. He paused, drawing in breath and readying himself to deliver the news that no one really wanted to hear.

'I think it's time we called it a day.'

*

The Duchessa met the Principal of the Scottish National Gallery, as agreed, at precisely four o'clock that afternoon. He was a small erudite man dressed in a neatly ironed corduroy suit with a bow tie and well-polished shoes. Luigi had been sent to amuse himself in the city, leaving Brialto and Bruno to accompany the Duchessa to seek re-assurances about the painting's security and to see if they could find out any more about the secrets it held.

'Please do sit down,' said the Principal, waving his hand magnanimously at the row of seats in front of his mahogany desk. There was a knock on the door.

'Sorry we're late,' apologised Shona, entering the room with Fortescue lolloping along behind. They saw Brialto and Bruno sitting either side of the Duchessa and were instantly apprehensive, recalling the gruesome threats when they last met.

'Don't worry about them,' said the Duchessa, sensing their trepidation. 'They are not as harmful as they look.' Bruno sneered at Shona. They took their seats in front of the Principal who began to speak.

'I thought I would just confirm the additional measures we have taken to protect the painting now that the police have found and returned it.'

'No, no, no, no,' interrupted Brialto, shaking his head. Bruno stood up towering above the desk and looked threateningly at the little man who came over all queasy. 'The Duchessa decides on the security measures, it is her painting. We see the room where you show the picture and we want four, no eight guards; four on the entrance and four on the exit, or… the Duchessa takes the painting home.'

'Ah, but' said the erudite little man, 'we have a contract with the British Museum which was agreed by you.' Bruno slammed his clenched fist onto the table with real force, knocking the small espresso cup over and causing coffee to spill onto some papers.

'We don't care about your contract,' he spat. 'The painting belongs to the Duchessa and she take it, if she wants.'

'I think he's right,' said Brialto, enjoying the stricken look which appeared on the Principal's face.

'Well, let's not get too technical,' said the Duchessa, asserting her authority. Shona plucked up courage and started to speak.

'The contract was agreed by all.' Fortescue winced, knowing her comments wouldn't go down well with the Italians. Bruno swivelled and shot her a sinister stare. Oh, there was something about Bruno which unnerved and excited Shona in equal measures. The Duchessa was starting to become fed up with the bickering.

'I want reassurances that the painting will be safe.' The Principal nodded while beginning to speak.

'We have increased security immeasurably, doubled the staffing at the exhibition and there is a rotation of guards who watch over the painting when we're open to the public, otherwise, it's stored in the vaults when not on display.' The Duchessa seemed placated.

'And the pentimento,' enquired Brialto, staring at Shona. 'We hear rumours that the painting harbours clues to lost treasures?' The Principal appeared confused. Shona sighed, if only, she mused. She looked towards the Duchessa and began to speak.

'The painting is a bit of a mystery, I mean the Parthenon Temple on Loch Leven, the connection to Byron, the pentimento and that Lord Elgin's ancestral home is close by. The dig was worth a punt.' There was silence while Shona paused. She breathed in before continuing. 'Initial surveys were promising but we found little more than an ancient sheep pen with an old fridge buried in the middle.' She sighed, deflating as her shoulders sagged and the body language betrayed how she actually felt – hacked off that they hadn't found anything on the dig.

'And do you still think it can lead to treasures?' pressed the Duchessa, interested to find out as much as possible about the picture's murky past.

'Maybe,' replied Shona, realising the conversation was now presenting more questions than answers. But the Duchessa was enjoying herself, soaking up the mystery which lay behind Lusieri's lovely water colour.

'Now, I want you to keep us informed of any developments. The picture can remain in the exhibition but you must let Brialto and Bruno know of any new clues or inclining's as to potential treasures it may reveal. Agreed?'

'Okay,' said Shona.

Chapter 32 – Hutchinson's Gallery

BRRRIINNGGGGG - the doorbell rang.

'Iona, can you get that?' shouted Elspeth from the kitchen as a large man and slender young woman stepped into the shop.

'Good morning,' said Iona, greeting the visitors in her usual courteous manner. The gentleman smiled in a friendly way. He had soft eyes and a gentle look.

'Is the owner in?' Elspeth appeared from the kitchen with a slightly perplexed expression on her face. She recognised her visitors, although she just couldn't place them. Foreign, definitely foreign with dark sun-drenched looks.

'Hello, Gladios Fatiakos from the Greek Bureau of Culture and my colleague Helena. The auction, we met at the auction,' continued Gladios. Elspeth's face lit up in recognition, recalling the kind spherical man who had offered her a chair.

'Hello,' was all she managed, surprised by their sudden appearance as she recalled the day when the sale of the picture had set the auction room alight. Helena smiled sweetly and stretched out her hand in welcome.

'We should have warned you,' said Gladios, realising their arrival had taken Elspeth by surprise.

'And do you want to look around the gallery?' asked Iona, mystified by the foreign visitors.

'Yes, yes of course, we would love to look around your fine gallery,' replied Gladios, casually glancing at the walls, feigning interest which was clearly not there. Elspeth could see straight through it.

'And that's it, just a quick look around the gallery?' she asked.

BRRRIIINNG - the doorbell rang again as another visitor entered the shop. Elspeth was gobsmacked to see Donald Mackenzie and Hannah arrive.

'I hope we're not disturbing you,' said Donald, walking towards the reception desk, oblivious to the others.

'I'm with customers,' Elspeth replied tartly. Gladios, forever affable and completely unaware of the significance of the new arrivals, stretched out his hand in welcome.

'Gladios, I'm from Greece.' Helena, who had been shielded from view by her bulky colleague, stepped out from his shadows and the sight of her left Donald and Hannah momentarily lost for words.

'What are you doing here?' they eventually chortled in unison.

'A question I might well ask you,' replied Helena coolly. Gladios said nothing while he tried to piece together the various relationships. Iona looked at Elspeth, not sure of what her next move should be. Hannah eventually broke the impasse.

'We've come to chat about the painting.' Helena moved uneasily. She knew all about the painting, where it had been over the last couple of days and how it had mysteriously turned up on an Edinburgh bound bus. She knew how it felt, its touch, its feel and most importantly the secrets it held.

'The picture's been returned. It was all over the news,' piped up Elspeth, not sure why they should be continuing with their enquiries.

'That's correct, although a crime was committed which we are still investigating,' replied Hannah. 'Where were you the night before last?' It was a clichéd question to ask. Elspeth broke out into a smile.

'What are you suggesting? I travelled to the far side of Edinburgh and left the painting on a bus? Would have been easier to put it on an Edinburgh bound train from Queen Street Station, that is of course, if I even had the picture, which I didn't.' Donald sighed. It did seem a waste of resources to pursue inquiries, but the Chief Superintendent was adamant they should do so.

NO STONE UNTURNED were the words he had screamed at them following the debrief about the mysterious re-appearance of the stolen painting.

There had been sniggers in Police HQ when Donald passed in the corridor and some light-hearted leg-pulling in the common room about the discovery of the highly valuable and controversial piece of art which was found on the back seat of a bus by the driver when he finished his shift. Even Hannah had received comments regarding the so-called *dead hand* of poor, old Donald. She hadn't been amused though, most certainly not. Hannah had enjoyed working with her new colleague; his gentlemanly ways and polite manner and most importantly how he had protected her when they were attacked by the machete wielding, mad man in suburban Prestonpans.

'Okay, that was a bit crass,' admitted Hannah, much to Elspeth's surprise. 'But we are still working on the case and you are one of our lines of inquiry.' Donald glanced towards Helena.

'And so are you.'

Gladios was now thoroughly confused and completely perplexed as to who the official looking gentleman was and why Helena seemed to be implicated; the quiet young girl who had worked in his department for the last five years without trouble.

'I'm from the Greek Bureau of Culture,' he blurted, not sure what else to say or why he should think it particularly relevant. Hannah's brow furrowed.

'Aren't you also from the Bureau?' Helena reluctantly nodded.

'We work together,' said Gladios.

'Can we all just sit down for a moment,' insisted Donald, realising it would take a concerted effort to work out all the interwoven connections between the various parties. It was a disarming move and seemed to put everyone at ease. They shuffled towards the central table to take a seat while Iona went to put the kettle on.

*

Ranald was sitting in the common room at Forbes and McKillops reading yesterday's Scotsman which Hamish had left behind. Woke articles from well-educated individuals dreaming up ruses on how to bring down the Scottish Government and ditch the likely Indyref. He nodded, tutted and shook his head in equal measure while reading through the headlines. Kenny burst in having arrived late.

'Ranald, I've found something!' Brenda's ears started twitching. Lowering the Daily Record, she took a sip of coffee.

'Look,' he exclaimed, holding out his smart phone to allow Ranald to view the screen. 'The Curse of Minerva! I did a google search last night and found Byron's poem about the looting of the Parthenon Temple.' Taking hold of the handset Ranald started scrolling through the text; verse after verse of eloquent prose, it was a mighty composition of quite some length, written with feeling, written with passion and unmistakable in Byron's disapproval.

'What's up,' asked Brenda who had been watching the pair. Her comments were ignored. Ranald looked at Kenny and shrugged his shoulders.

'Interesting, but I'm not sure how it helps?' Kenny shook his head.

'Neither am I, although it must signify something. I mean the title of the painting makes little sense without Byron's connection.'

'Back to work,' said Brenda as she stood up and looked at her watch. She was disgruntled that they hadn't shared their secret.

*

Fortescue and Shona were sitting inside a coffee house in Edinburgh New Town. Bohemian pictures hung on the walls, leaflets on reiki, pottery classes and talks on various well-being matters were scattered on the side table and the smell of freshly ground coffee radiated all around.

'Oliver and Gus should be here shortly,' said Shona, glancing at her watch while Fortescue stirred his cappuccino with a longing look in his eyes like a lovesick puppy begging for attention.

'The Duchessa coming too?'

'Yes,' replied Shona, 'and that means her Italian lackeys will be joining us as well. The younger one is mad and as for his father... well, he gives me the creeps, his scarred face, obscuring the left eye whenever he smiles.'

'Grimace, I think you mean.'

'Grimace, smile it's all the same for him. Revolting man!'

'Morning,' cried Gus, leading Oliver into the depths of the coffee house and within a couple of minutes the Duchessa arrived with her entourage and was soon sitting at the head of the table with Luigi almost on her lap.

'Duo, expresso duo,' barked Bruno. Brialto took a seat on the wooden bench with his back to the wall. Shona glanced at the tall Italian and Bruno fixed her look with a cold stare. A shiver ran through her.

'Shall we begin, Oliver?' asked Fortescue. He nodded.

'We're here to update you. As you know the infrared scans of the painting revealed a pentimento – a painting within a painting.' He removed a copy of the printout and slid it across the table towards the Duchessa. 'The originals were faint although we enhanced the shading so you can clearly see the sequential marks in a circular shape, twenty-seven in total and an off-lying one here,' continued Oliver, pointing with his finger. The Duchessa picked up the paper and viewed it in silence before passing it to Brialto.

'And do you know what they signify?'

'No,' said Shona abruptly. 'We are doing tests at the Museum including measurements and so forth to see if we can find any patterns or correlations which help us identify the relevance of the image. It's not straightforward though.'

'And then there's the poem,' interjected Fortescue reciting the verse: *'Yet still the Gods are just, and crimes are crossed: See here what Elgin won and Elgin lost.'* The Duchessa looked distracted, reaching beneath the table to stroke Luigi's inner thigh.

'It's a clue, no?' asked Bruno, before finishing his expresso and placing the dainty wee cup on the saucer.

'We think so,' replied Fortescue. 'We have, in short, two pieces of information which hint at something else; the pentimento and the poem although we don't really know what connects them and where they are directing us.'

'Or what will be at the end of the rainbow!' said the Duchessa with a firm grip on Luigi's leg. She was now stroking him vigorously!

'You're quite right,' continued Shona. 'We thought perhaps lost artefacts from the Parthenon... I mean taking into account the subject of the painting. Possibly: metopes, friezes, pediments much of which remain missing to this day.'

'But you didn't find anything on the dig?' sneered Bruno with a half-smile. Shona nodded, hanging her head in disappointment.

'And what may these metopes, friezes and what not be worth?' asked Brialto who was always keen to get down to business.

'Priceless,' said Oliver. 'Many tens, possibly even hundreds of millions.' Brialto's beady little eyes lit up and started darting back and forwards while he did some rudimentary calculations. Ten percent was an awful lot of money.

'And who gets the proceeds?' asked the Duchessa as Luigi began to sweat while she continued massaging his inner thigh. There was silence. No one wanted to discuss the thorny issue of where the treasures may end up, if any were ever found.

'It's the Duchessa's picture which has provided the clues,' said Brialto, positioning her as the natural beneficiary.

'Shall we see if we find something first,' said Oliver, being the pragmatist. 'No doubt the law will be complicated on such matters, and, in any event, I think it would be better to have something to argue over rather than argue for arguments sake.' Even Bruno was silenced by Oliver's common-sense approach.

'Okay,' said the Duchessa. 'But I want Brialto and Bruno to accompany you on any further digs or excursions you embark on.' There were polite murmurings from Shona and Fortescue, indicating their agreement.

*

'Okay, okay,' repeated Donald, sitting at the head of the table with his notebook to hand. 'We have Gladios and Helena from the Greek Bureau of Culture; Elspeth, the gallery owner, where the painting was spotted.'

'Allegedly,' she interrupted.

'Allegedly,' repeated Donald. 'And there's a connection with the auctioneers, Forbes and McKillop, via your husband and the house in Prestonpans where Helena is staying. It can't all be coincidental?' There was quiet, nobody spoke, instead they eyed one another across the table until Gladios cleared his throat.

'But the painting has been found.' Donald sighed while Hannah continued to lazily type notes, appearing to all to be losing interest. 'Is there much to be gained from pursuing your enquiries?' Donald knew that Gladios was right. He had warmed to the spherical Greek and his kindly disposition, his soft voice and gentle nature. A sensible man unlike the hot headed tyrannical Chief Superintendent of the Edinburgh Police Force.

'More tea?' asked Iona lifting the pot. Donald shook his head and Hannah stopped tapping on the keyboard and shut her laptop. She smiled, looking around at the friendly unthreatening faces. They had all answered their questions, tirelessly, in between providing rich tea biscuits and plenty of warm drinks while the congenial Greek had orchestrated the answers in his jovial, rambling Mediterranean way. Helena seemed less combative than when they had last interviewed her and likewise Elspeth appeared to have mellowed. Standing up Donald smiled before he and Hannah left the premises and walked towards their car.

Chapter 33 – Back to the National Gallery

'Are you sure this is a good idea?' questioned Elspeth, sitting in the Rose Street bar with Ranald and Kenny who were already quaffing beer. The twins kicked as she moved uncomfortably on the bar stool and sipped her orange and lemonade. It was only three weeks to the due date and Elspeth was now feeling very large and in truth looking forward to the time when she would no longer be carrying her heavy load. Helena returned from the ladies and was suddenly waving frantically at Gladios, who had just entered the pub and looked rather lost.

Ten thirty in the morning had been the agreed time they would all meet at the Udny Arms for a sharpener before visiting the National Gallery. Kenny and Helena wouldn't go; no, that would be foolhardy after their earlier escapades - they would easily be recognised. Ranald and Elspeth would visit with the remnants of the Kawatachi ten-year-old malt whisky - cask 264, which they would smuggle in and drink discreetly before going to see Lusieri's fine water colour, in the hope that the brazen hussy of a painting would once again drop her robe and reveal all. Gladios was to be the chaperone. The spherical Greek gentleman wished no harm to come to Elspeth who was really not in a condition for such capers. Prodius had asked to be kept abreast of developments although Gladios had been economical with the truth and only sent the odd text, from time to time, confirming all was well.

Gathered at a small table the motley crew made an unlikely alliance: young, old, Scots, Greeks, male and female but in a strange way they had bonded over the enchanting water colour which had brought them all together. More beer was drunk and by midday, with a skin full of booze, Ranald was ready for his foray to the National Gallery.

*

'Three adults, please,' asked Elspeth, removing the purse from her jacket pocket and offering her credit card. The small machine whirred, printing the tickets and then suddenly without warning the security guards stepped forward.

'Please, this way madam,' directing them to a small plain table just beyond the kiosk. 'Routine search. Can I have your bag?' Elspeth hesitated, not sure what she should do as buried in the deep folds of her handbag lay the Kawatachi malt whisky! 'It won't take long,' encouraged the guard. Elspeth reluctantly handed over her smart Longchamp bag which was hastily unzipped. Scarf, lipstick, mirror, hairbrush, sweets… and a water bottle half filled with amber liquid?

'What's this?' Elspeth was dumfounded, the sequence of events and speed of happenings had taken her by surprise. No one had considered a search of their possessions and now that it had happened, she was unsure what to say.

'It's my sample,' said Gladios.

'Sample?' repeated the Guard confused by the answer.

'I'm diabetic,' continued Gladios, thinking swiftly on his feet.

'Oh,' said the guard, as the penny dropped, and he hastily placed the plastic bottle back into the bag and instinctively wiped the palm of his hands against the back of his trousers. Maximum security was the order of the day but a bottle of urine... he shuddered at the thought. 'On you go.' And on Ranald and Elspeth galloped almost fleeing the little table and scurrying into the heart of the building with Gladios trundling along behind.

*

The kiosk lady looked at the thick-set gentleman who was standing in front of the booth and let her eyes roam over his gnarled old features, wrinkled from years of sun, and was drawn to the deep scar over the left-hand side of his face and drooping eyelid. His tall, athletic friend looked equally menacing, stood there in suede cowboy boots with a wild distant look in his eyes.

'Two tickets,'

'That will be £10.60 please,' replied the attendant. Brialto stuffed a handful of notes through the barrier, not remotely concerned if he overpaid. Without waiting for the change, they strode off towards the main exhibition.

*

Ranald was in the gentlemen's loo with Gladios, squashed into a single cubicle. The large Greek was sitting on the pan with the lid down while Ranald stood to unscrew the bottle top. He sniffed. The instant wave of raw undiluted whisky took him by storm, enveloping him in its powerful vapour as the mere recollection made his eyes begin to water and his stomach churn. He tentatively took a small sip and then a larger gulp, then another and another, before screwing the top back on the bottle and handing it to Gladios.

'PHWOARR,' he shouted, much to the distress of an elderly pensioner in the adjoining cubicle. Leaving, Ranald was faced with the mirrors above the wash basins. Peering into the reflection he saw twinkling stars in the background and the apparition of a large god-like figure in a white robe appearing behind him. He was already hallucinating and, realising the effect might wear off soon, or more likely he would simply degenerate into a jabbering wreck, he moved quickly towards the corridor and into the main exhibition room where the painting was on display. Elspeth, who had been waiting outside, joined him as Gladios stumbled along behind.

There were hordes of people surrounding the picture, the recent publicity having swelled the attendance and raised the profile of the Romantic Exhibition which had constantly been in the media and featured in the news. In they barrelled, into the heart of the throng, pushing past tourists, families and all sorts until Ranald was near the front of the crowd with a clear view of the picture.

'Here, draw what you can see,' ordered Elspeth, thrusting a notebook and pencil into his hand.

'Another drink,' demanded Ranald. Gladios at last caught up with them and passed the bottle forward. After further sip of the intoxicating brew Ranald focussed his attention on the picture and let his eyes bore into its soul, its being, its hidden depths. And boy, the pretty little water colour did not disappoint. The Parthenon Temple appeared to leap out of the frame and was there before him, no more than a few yards away, in all its splendour, the warm stone drenched in the soft hues of late evening sunlight. Gladiators and soldiers circled the outside and wrestled one another as the gigantic colonnades seemed

156

to part and once again, he was drawn into the inner depths of the magnificent building where he looked down at the ornately tiled floor.

Ranald hiccupped, breathing whisky fumes over some Japanese tourists who quickly moved away. And then he began to scribble on the note book his hands working frantically, smearing the pencil's graphite over the paper, forming dark shapes in a concentric ring. He staggered, belched again and then his knees buckled. Ranald fell forwards crashing through some bodies and landed on top of the bench in the front row where some school children were sitting. Downwards he tumbled, knocking the infants to the floor. Their teachers began to circle. Security Guards moved swiftly to the scene of mayhem while Ranald grappled on the ground before violently throwing up over a child's rucksack. Elspeth had wisely snatched the notebook from him and was now kneeling over Ranald and tending to his needs. The burly security guards formed a cordon around him and, not wishing to take any risks, began to evacuate the room.

Bruno, who had been watching events unfold, had sidled up to Elspeth and noticed her bag was open and the notebook was protruding out of the top. Instinctively, he stretched his hand forward, letting his delicate fingers rummage through the contents. He had the book in a jiffy and what was this? Pulling out the water bottle with the amber liquid he recalled Ranald sipping from it earlier. Then, removing the top he sniffed the contents and was knocked back by the wave of powerful fumes, filling his nostrils.

Gladios now had Ranald draped over his shoulder while the security guards escorted them towards the exit as the distant sound of police sirens could be heard getting ever louder.

'PWHOARR,' shouted Bruno, taking another gulp, 'PHWHOARR, PWHOARR, PWHOARR,' he screamed at the top of his voice. Ripping his denim shirt open he started to beat his chest like Tarzan!

The pictures in the room were leaping from the walls and dancing in front of him while the ceiling opened up and he was then looking towards a brightly lit star-filled sky. But his gaze was instantly drawn to Lusieri's beautiful painting. The colonnades parted and he was pulled into the Temple's inner sanctum where a celestial pattern suddenly appeared on the pretty tiled floor. Surely a message from the Gods of ancient Greece – stars leading them to untold riches. Then suddenly a meteorite was hurtling towards him as a security guard dived in and rugby tackled Bruno so he fell to the floor. He was no pushover though, even in his highly intoxicated state. Kneeing the assailant in the groin he then head-butted him in the face, breaking his nose. Blood began to spew from his nostrils.

'More assistance,' cried another guard into his walkie-talkie, calling for back up. But Tarzan was now on his feet, a snarling and angry sight with adrenaline coursing through his veins. He reached into his jacket looking for his trusted machete, but no machete was found. Brialto had insisted he leave it at the Hotel. His eyes stood out on stalks, and he began to spit and froth at the mouth while the anger swelled within.

'ON GUARD,' shouted Bruno with his fists raised. He circled on the spot eyeing up the security guards who had now abandoned Ranald and where closing in. Throwing a haymaker of a punch Bruno missed his target and spinning, fell to the floor. Grappling with his demons he was a tormented soul.

The distraction was a blessing for Gladios and all, who were leaving the building when the police car pulled up and out jumped Donald and Hannah.

'What are you doing here?' remonstrated Donald, taken aback by the surprise encounter but before anyone had a chance to answer he was waved into the Gallery to deal with Bruno who'd had a second wind and was ready to take on all comers. Hannah pulled out a Taser gun and with a mighty crack Tarzan screamed, 'AAAAAAAAraghhh,' before falling to the ground.

Brialto watched in amusement from the crowded hall and then looked down at the notebook which he had taken from Bruno amidst the furore. He smiled.

Chapter 34 – Iona Shows an Interest

The Duchessa was sitting on her own at breakfast within the large dining room of the Charleston Hotel. Brialto walked in and without waiting to be asked pulled up a chair and sat down beside her. She smiled politely although otherwise looked distracted. Her usual bright, sparky disposition appeared to have deserted her as she half-heartedly buttered some toast. Brialto sensed that all was not well. He ordered an expresso and cooked breakfast from the polite waitress who was circling.

'Is it the boy, Luigi? Is he starting to lose his sheen?' The Duchessa nodded before speaking.

'I miss the Duca. He wasn't perfect, far from it. In fact, he was downright cantankerous and obstinate on occasions, but for all his faults he had a gentle side to his sometimes-fiery disposition. Luigi is fun, great fun, but he's young, oh mama mia he's young, young enough to be my …' The Duchessa paused not really sure where her ramblings were going and why she had felt it necessary to burden Brialto with her innermost feelings first thing in the morning.

'Coffee?' offered the waitress with the cafeteria poised and ready to pour. The Duchessa shook her head dismissively.

'And what would you like me to do with Luigi?' enquired Brialto, trying to be helpful. 'Do you want rid of him?'

'No! No, no, not in that way,' stressed the Duchessa, slightly alarmed; recalling the gruesome demise of the unfortunate tax inspector who met his end near the Rialto Bridge. 'The vegan diet is beginning to bore me. It's okay for a while, kept me trim, but there is only so many nut cutlets and humus one can eat in a lifetime and I think I may have reached my quota.'

'Here we are,' said the waitress, placing a plate of fried eggs, bacon, sausage and haggis on the table. The smell wafted and the Duchessa looked longingly at the wonderful fayre.

'Another,' barked Brialto, indicating with his knife which he pointed towards the plate. The Duchessa smiled.

*

It was around midday when Gladios and Helena arrived at Hutchinson's Gallery. Ranald and Kenny were already there having been on a job in Glasgow. Helena had now moved out of Prestonpans and into the Charleston Hotel, courtesy of the Greek Bureau of Culture. Prodius had relented when he heard of the machete attack at her previous abode. And while Kenny and Helena were on good terms, realistically their infatuation with each other was on the wane. Breaking up was not proving easy after their whirlwind romance, but the winds had blown too hard, too fast and too early and were now blown out. Both knew they had reached the end of the line, but the final acknowledgment and severing of ties was proving difficult.

'Coffee anyone?' asked Iona, thrusting her head out of the kitchen. There were grunts of approval. Elspeth placed the - *Closed for Lunch* - sign in the shop window and locked the front door. Everyone gathered around the central table as Iona placed a packet of garibaldi biscuits and the cafetière in the centre and then disappeared to find some mugs.

'The notebook has gone missing,' said Elspeth, opening up the discussion. 'Not sure what happened, must have fallen from my bag amidst the scuffle. However, I saw what Ranald drew and it was almost identical to the images which Kenny and Helena produced when they also viewed the painting under the influence of... what was it called again?'

'Kawatachi, ten-year-old malt,' said Kenny proudly. 'And boy it has a kick, never had anything like it before... fire water!' Ranald's sallow facial features contorted, managing the briefest of smiles before the splitting pain in his head returned, reminding him of the previous day, little of which he could actually remember.

'Anyway,' continued Elspeth, 'whatever the whisky was called it's delivered these scrawls,' pushing Kenny's and Helena's sketches into the middle of the table. 'Anyone have any suggestions as to what they mean?' Gladios, the elder statesman, sighed.

'Constellations perhaps?' he offered to a silent audience. 'I mean us Greeks have always been interested in the stars dating back to mythological times. Our Gods liked to reward their heroes and heroines with a place amongst the heavens.'

'And the Byron poem!' continued Elspeth, ignoring Gladios' ramblings. 'Any ideas what that could mean?' she posed as the self-appointed chairperson, sitting at the head of the table. Her question was met with a series of blank expressions.

'Leave it with me,' mumbled Ranald, whose interest in the poem and its connections to the picture and the Elgin Marbles had grown as the mystery developed.

'And the drawings?' re-asserted Elspeth, pulling everyone back to the images Helena and Kenny had produced. Iona had now been drawn into the group while drifting aimlessly around the table with her smart phone to hand. She instinctively reached forward and picked up the papers.

'Ohhhh circular shapes, reference points at set spaces. Ummm, that's not unusual in archaeology.' Everyone was quiet, surprised at the sudden intervention

'You think it's an archaeological image?' asked Elspeth.

'Maybe… Circular shapes often indicates a henge. I could do some research. The number of reference points may provide a clue.'

'Henge?' queried Helena who had been subdued to date.

'Yes henge, like Stonehenge, ancient Neolithic earthworks usually in a circle with stones or pillars on top. Fascinating period; the final chapter of the Stone Age around 5,000 years BC.' Iona was illuminated with rosy cheeks and sparkling eyes lighting up her face.

'Let me get a photo of the drawing,' she continued, reaching over the table and using her smart phone to take a snap.

'Give me a couple of days and I'll see what I can unearth - no pun intended!' Gladios smiled contently. He was happy working with this impromptu young team of Scots and Greeks who had by chance come together.

'You let us know on WhatsApp?' he suggested, looking at Iona. They seemed to have the beginnings of a plan and Gladios was pleased he would have something more positive to report to Prodius when he phoned in towards the end of the week. His tummy rumbled. It was almost time for lunch.

*

The Charleston Hotel had a faded grandeur in keeping with its aristocratic origins. Originally the Edinburgh town house of the sixth Duke of Carnoustie, ennobled for his services in the early 16th century to James VI King of Scotland. Refit, renovation and makeover had followed refit, makeover and renovation of the fine Georgian building which stood in the heart of the New Town. Cutting edge design, bespoke furniture, gaudy wallpaper and mood lighting typified the current décor throughout the Hotel; apart from the private dining room where the intricate wood panelling had been listed, protecting it from cheapskate latte-drinking designers in skinny jeans and pumps. There were French doors which opened onto a small courtyard and the dining table was fully laid with well-polished silver cutlery, elegant crystal wine glasses and neatly folded napkins.

Bruno was already lounging outside, letting the summer sun gently warm his face while he rolled a joint and began to smoke.

'Good afternoon ma'am,' said the portly waiter when the Duchessa entered with her young lover, Luigi, who hadn't been sent home, just yet.

'Hurry up,' snapped Shona as Fortescue followed her through reception. They scuttled along the corridor towards the private dining room. Brialto had just arrived and was helping himself to a sherry from the decanter which was on the fine mahogany sideboard. His skittish eyes darted backwards and forwards taking in the room and the place settings - eight in total. Eight he mused, slightly confused because he had been expecting just the six of them. The door opened and in walked Oliver Chetwin with Gus in tow. Brialto nodded to welcome them. Otherwise, the atmosphere was stilted until Shona and Fortescue bundled into the room.

'Sorry we're late,' blurted the Irish beauty, looking slightly flustered for a change. Brialto poured her a sherry. Bruno came in from the courtyard and stood towering over Shona in his usual indomitable way. A quiver ran down her spine like a sharp bolt of electricity. She found herself blushing, unsettled by his presence.

Oliver and Gus were laying out papers on the table while waiters circulated with drinks and canapes and soon everyone was seated with a sherry to hand, sipping daintily from the crystal cut glasses. Luigi moved his hand onto the Duchessa knee beneath the table, young fingers roaming across the pleats of her skirt, pressing and squeezing ever harder. The Duchessa crossed her legs, deflecting his attentions while reaching beneath the table and slapping his wrist. Luigi looked crestfallen that his lover's affections seemed to be drifting elsewhere. Bruno, who had noticed the interactions, smiled sarcastically. His wild eyes were dilated and on stalks.

'Gus, would you like to take everyone through what we have so far,' said Oliver, kicking off proceedings.

'These are the images of the pentimento which we previously uncovered,' said Gus, shoving copies of the results into the centre of the table. The Duchessa, who hadn't seen them before, picked up a sheet and began to examine the results in more detail, cocking her head to the left then right, enabling her eyes to focus.

'It's a circle,' she eventually announced, breaking the silence. Bruno fidgeted nervously in his chair his eyes darting in all directions until eventually settling on Shona. She felt his piercing stare.

'Yes, spherical in shape,' continued Gus, looking at the Duchessa who was deep in thought. 'Made up of twenty-seven marks, intermittently spread on the perimeter. Anyone have any ideas?'

'Stars?' said Fortescue who had at last sprung into life and was beginning to pay attention.

'Maybe,' replied Oliver. We've looked at the usual constellations, you know: Orion, Taurus, Gemini and what not, although not found a match.'

'They're stars,' insisted Bruno bluntly. Everyone was surprised by his rare intervention. 'I saw stars when I visited the Museo.' It was a story which Bruno had recounted before; how the painting had opened up and revealed what appeared to be a heavenly constellation.

'Show them the picture,' he said, looking at Brialto who for once appeared less sure than normal. He fidgeted in his seat before reluctantly reaching for the notebook he had in his briefcase.

'These are the images our friends produced in the National Gallery.' Brialto tossed the scribblings onto the table. Gus instantly picked them up and comparing them with the pentimento nodded.

'Almost an exact match.' He passed them to Oliver.

'As I said, stars,' repeated Bruno feeling vindicated. Without being distracted by Luigi the Duchessa was maintaining her attention and suddenly became enthralled by the idea that the images may signify a secret message or clue connected to ancient beliefs and the solar system.

'We must investigate,' she announced. 'We must do some research into the stars and see if there is a connection.'

'What do you think, Oliver?' asked Shona who had also gained some enthusiasm. She put a reassuring hand on Fortescue's knee. Oliver sighed, not wholly convinced the images were connected to celestial objects, but he was struggling to come up with an alternative suggestion.

'Okay, let's see what we can find out. Professor Zinbottle is probably the best bet. Cambridge man who works at the Harwell Space Cluster close to Oxford. There isn't much out there which Zinbottle doesn't know about.' The Duchessa smiled and Shona nodded which was sufficient for Oliver to conclude that Professor Zinbottle was to be instructed.

Chapter 35 – The Jigsaw Takes Shape

'Enter,' bellowed the Chief Superintendent of Edinburgh Police Force who stood up and leaned over his desk like an ape. Taking the weight on his knuckles his gut sagged beneath and he grimaced, appearing as if he was in pain. And he was, his lumbago playing up again. Donald and Hannah shuffled in and took a seat in front of their surly boss, waiting for the chastisement to begin.

'Any leads?' the Superintendent barked mercilessly with a splitting pain running down his lower spine and into his buttocks. He visibly winced. Hannah shook her head, not daring to speak while Donald sat in silence eyeing up the behemoth of a man before them. 'Ummmm,' murmured the Superintendent straightening up and putting his hands on the side of his corset.

Metaphorically, mothers called for their children to come indoors, close the shutters and secure all, in anticipation of the impending storm. The cyclone whirled quietly at first, gently whistling, although soon gathered some momentum and exploded in fury.

'WHERE ARE THE SUSPECTS?' screamed the Chief Superintendent, the storm now beginning to swell. 'WHERE ARE THE ARRESTS? WHERE IS THE JUSTICE? WHERE? WHERE? WHERE?' he shouted, whipping himself up into a frenzied rage.

'The painting has been found,' reminded Donald, but this did little more than stoke the fires. Slamming his fists onto the table the Chief Superintendent glared at them and then lowered his voice.

'A crime has been committed and I want the perpetrators… get it? I want covert surveillance twenty-four hours a day. I want you to eat, breathe and live the case until you come up with some arrests. Do I make myself clear?' Donald and Hannah nodded. The Chief Superintendent dismissed them. 'GET OUT.'

*

Elspeth was in the gallery sorting through a new collection of paintings from a lesser-known artist she had decided to support. Urban images of earthy Glasgow scenes: pedestrians at a zebra crossing, children loitering on street corners, queues for a burger van. Everyday life, portraying the City's raw underside. The doorbell rang and Iona entered, full of energy and zest. She could hardly contain herself.

'Did the cat get the cream last night?' asked Elspeth who was a little over a fortnight from her due date and feeling the strains of the latter stages of pregnancy. Swollen ankles, bloated abdomen and a sore back from carrying her precious cargo. Momentarily, Iona looked confused, not really understanding the comment but she just could not contain herself any longer. Fizzing with excitement, her rosy cheeks blushed from the exertions of rushing to the gallery.

'I think, I've got it,' she blurted.

'Got what, exactly?

'The clue, the image and what it signifies.' Elspeth felt some movement in her abdomen as the twins shifted in the womb, appearing to vie for position.

'The sketches, you mean?'

'Yes, the sketches; here, look at this,' continued Iona opening her satchel and taking out a textbook – *The Standing Stones of Callanish and Ancient Scottish Henges.* Flicking to page sixty-three she retrieved her smart phone and scrolled to the photograph. 'What do you think? Elspeth took the handset for a closer look, positioning it between the book and the photograph of ... ?

'What is it?' she mumbled, running her index finger down the page to the footer – *Figure 1 – The Ring of Brodgar!*

'Ring of Brodgar?' questioned Elspeth.

'Yes, Ring of Brodgar,' repeated Iona. 'It's one of the oldest henges in Scotland. Look, twenty-seven stones just like the sketches that Kenny and Helena made... and in exactly the same position around the circle!' Iona was just brimming with energy and visibly shaking with joy at her amazing discovery.

'Well, what do you think it means?' asked Elspeth who was unsure of the implications.

'Haven't a clue, but isn't it exciting,' bubbled Iona while starting to bounce up and down on the spot, barely able to contain her enthusiasm. 'What shall we do?' The twins seemed to have picked up on the mood. Elspeth felt a couple of sharp prods from within.

'I don't know … WhatsApp, put it on the WhatsApp group.' Ten second later Iona pressed the send button.

*

'What do you think?' asked Gus. Professor Zinbottle stroked his beard then stood up and walked towards the window of his third-floor office at the Harwell Space Cluster and peered out across the rolling Oxfordshire farmland. Fields of yellow corn wafted lazily in the breeze. Mid-summer was almost upon them. Gus continued to sit quietly, not really sure what to expect. The Professor walked back to his desk and sat down.

'I would need to do some research. There are eighty-eight constellations in our solar system and I am a bit rusty on some. Although my first impression… it's not instantly recognisable as one of the better-known groupings.' Gus remained seated and quietly nodded. 'Even if it does represent one of the minor constellations, I'm not sure how that will help your search for relics from the Parthenon Temple. Somehow, I doubt they will be in space!' A wry smile broke out across the Professor's congenial old face.

'And the Zodiac?' asked Gus, ignoring the jibe.

'Ummmm, the Zodiac,' mused Zinbottle, nodding his head in that learned way that Professors are inclined to do. 'There are no obvious correlations. I can do some research but nothing instantly springs to mind.'

Gus sighed. He was tired after catching the sleeper to London and then the early morning service from Paddington Station. He yawned in disappointment. Completely unrealistically, he had hoped that Professor Zinbottle might have cast some light on their mystery with some insightful thoughts. However, the reality was much more mundane; a wild goose chase on a whimsical notion that somehow the stars would guide them to ancient treasures. It was starting to feel like a false dawn.

'Is the Duchessa du Canali paying my fees?' enquired the Professor, leaning backwards with his arms stretched out behind.

'I think so,' replied Gus. Zinbottle smiled and it was not the first time he had smiled during their meeting. A confident grin spread across his face. Confident that these twenty-seven smudges, set out in a circular configuration, were unlikely to have any correlation, whatsoever, with the zodiac, the stars or anything even remotely heavenly.

'Give me a few days and I will see what I can come up with.'

*

'You both want the rest of this week off?' asked Hamish.

'YES,' Ranald and Kenny replied in unison while standing in the staffroom next to the coffee machine.

'Ohhhhhh,' said Hamish, sucking in through his teeth with his lips tensed as he considered the request. 'Both of you?' They nodded.

'There are no auctions coming up,' said Kenny.

'We seem to be on top of things,' chipped in Ranald. Hamish was quiet while scrutinising his storemen, both new to the role, both now settled in and both proving their worth, helping with the grunt and graft of the auction days. But Kenny's movements had intrigued him of late. New Greek girlfriend who he had met on that fateful sale day when Lusieri's water colour had made a record-breaking price. And then there were the afternoons when he and his girl went to see the picture at the National Gallery before it went missing.

'And this has nothing to do with the… Lusieri painting?' asked Hamish. Ranald and Kenny looked uncomfortable, in fact shifty, both avoiding the old man's gaze.

'And what makes you say that?' questioned Ranald just a little too quick, ever so slightly defensively which was sufficient for Hamish to guess that his suspicions were likely to be true.

'It was the description in the Edinburgh Evening News - *medium height, slim built man in his mid-twenties with an elegant foreign lady…* Was it you?' asked Hamish, looking pointedly at Kenny who blushed but said nothing.

'He was with me,' snapped Ranald, rather too quickly, rather too forcibly. He was not at all convincing. There was quiet while they all looked each other up and down. Hamish's beady eyes were darting back and forth between his storemen. In truth, he had become intrigued by the painting and the secrets it may hold. The dig on Loch Leven Island hadn't produced anything although he was sure Ranald and Kenny were onto something with their exotic Greek friends and he craved to know what.

'You know about the Byron verse?' spilled the old man, realising he may have to indulge his boys to get something in return.

'The Byron poem, you mean?' replied Ranald, not sure why Hamish had broached the subject.

'Not just the poem,' said Hamish. 'There's a verse inscribed on the back of the painting, oh what was it? - *Yet still the Gods are just, and crimes are crossed: See here what Elgin won and Elgin lost.'*

Kenny and Ranald were dumfounded and not sure what to say. The poem remained a mystery to them and although the news of the verse didn't instantly shine a light on the conundrum, perhaps it would help them later once they had had a chance to think it through.

'Thanks,' said Ranald, breaking the impasse.

'And the holiday?' persisted Kenny.

Hamish smiled, realising they were not going to share anything with him, just yet. Maybe they needed a little longer, he mused.

'Okay, you can both have the time off. But no funny business and look after yourselves.'

Brenda waved from the office window as Ranald and Kenny left the premises together and walked towards the Forbes and McKillop van and jumped in. Turning left into Corphistine Road they motored towards the main interchange and onto the ring road. A solitary car pulled out behind them and began to follow.

*

Bruno was towering over the attentive receptionist while standing by her desk and rubbing his moustache.

'When they leaving?' he barked mercilessly, unappreciative of the great risk the girl was taking in divulging the guest's information. Without making eye contact she folded a piece of paper and handed it to the threatening Italian.

'Here's their travel itinerary.' Without saying thank you Bruno smiled and walked off.

Chapter 36 – To Orkney to Orkney

'You can't come.'

'Why not?' remonstrated Elspeth, not used to having her decisions questioned.

'You're only two weeks away from your due date. It would be crazy.'

'Well, in that case you can't go.' Ranald's shoulders slumped as he exhaled with a long sigh. Elspeth was right of course, she always was. Two weeks to go and the babies could come at any time, two of them, a double helping of trouble. Ranald knew he couldn't leave Elspeth… she would have to come!

*

'Can I see your tickets, please?' muttered the guard who was standing in the carriage as the train began to pull out of Waverley Station, heading for Inverness. Helena smiled politely, all innocent and meek, not the wild impetuous young lady who only a week or so earlier had jumped out of a first storey window with the painting tucked under her arm to make a dash for safety and the Holiday Inn on the outskirts of Wallyford. Gladios passed the tickets to the Guard who stamped them and continued on his way.

'Tickets please, tickets please,' repeated Gladios mockingly while looking at Helena who didn't really pick up on the nuance of his joke. He was in a good mood this morning and excited by their trip to Orkney in search of long-lost treasures from the Parthenon Temple.

On the guard trudged, entering the first-class carriage where he saw a pair of suede cowboy boots resting on a seat.

'Feet off please,' he said in a polite, courteous manner, not at all confrontational in the way he asked. The boots didn't move and nor did the paper – *Il Figaro* – behind which… 'Tickets please?' asked the guard, simply doing his job, but the paper and the cowboy boots

172

remained steadfast. He was clearly being ignored. 'Excuse me sir,' said the guard, trying a different tack, and then reaching forward pulled the paper away to reveal a finely chiselled faced with a bushy moustache and dark sunglasses. 'Can you take your feet off the chair?'

'Are you sure you want me to do that?' asked the boots. The guard nodded. The cowboy boots came off the seat and the perpetrator stood up, towering over the poor little man who instinctively cowered. Removing his sunglasses Bruno stared at the snivelling wretch, striking fear into guardsman' heart. Reaching forward he grabbed the tie and slowly but firmly began to tighten the knot, his knuckles clenched white as the veins in his hands started to bulge. The guard began to turn pale. He tried to speak.

'Uurghh,' was all that he managed with his face reddening and his mouth beginning to dribble. Whoosh, the door slid open and in walked Brialto, carrying a coffee with a copy of the Scotsman tucked under his arm.

'STUPIDO,' he shouted at his errant son, throwing the hot coffee over him and then attacking with the paper, slapping him here, slapping him there. 'Stupido, stupido,' he repeated, his slaps becoming more intensive and his paper beginning to fray. The guard was now choking with the last gasps of breath appearing to slip from his body. CRACK, Brialto hit Bruno on the head with the butt of his pistol and at last the big man released his grip, letting the guard slump to the floor. He stirred and coughed as Brialto helped him to his feet and stuffed a bundle of cash into his hand to send him on his way. Bruno sat down and picked up the *Il Figaro* and continued to read.

*

Hamish left the Black Dog around mid-morning. He had stayed the night after drinking the best part of a bottle of fine malt whisky, as he always did, during the Forbes and McKillop quarterly partnership meeting. It had followed the usual format; starting just after closing time once the drunken waifs and strays of Corphistine Road had been thrown out to make their way home and Agnes had finished the washing up. Of course, she could have done much better in her heyday. Quite the beauty of this end of town was young Agnes; she had suitors from all over the city, young, old, slim, fat, tall, short, greying and bald. But after two unsuccessful marriages and a broken heart she had been left with little more than her grandfather's share in the auction house. And while the pub paid the day-to-day bills, Forbes and McKillop gave her a half-decent profit share which Hamish provided. And that was the rub; dear old Hamish with his greasy hair, nicotine-stained teeth and putrid breath. Not to mention his octopus hands which were inclined to roam if he had half a chance. However, Agnes was a lady of a certain age and a lady of a certain age has certain needs and as much as she knew it was wrong to be cavorting around with a married man who had seven children and attended church nearly every Sunday; it was quite simply the best she could do.

'Another dram?' Agnes would ask when sitting at the bar with Hamish who would run through the figures while she listened, perched on the stool with her legs crossed; allowing her skirt to ride indecently high and revealing a generous calf. And what ageing gentleman, also of a certain age, doesn't enjoy a well-sculptured calf. On the meeting would grind until Agnes would lean forward, letting her well-filled blouse heave up and down, distracting Hamish from the P&L. Eventually, she would reach over, taking hold of his gnarly old hand and lead the wizened old auctioneer upstairs.

And now Agnes stood in the pub doorway, resplendent in her pink dressing gown and sheep's wool slippers. She drew on a fag and waved him goodbye. And off Hamish motored in his clapped-out old Jag, heading towards the centre of Edinburgh and the Charleston Hotel for his lunch appointment with the Duchessa.

*

Kenny was waiting at the service station when Ranald and Elspeth pulled up.

'Jump in,' mouthed Ranald from the driver's seat of the Forbes and McKillop van. Elspeth waved to catch his attention. However, Kenny remained steadfast, standing beside his luggage.

'Come on,' shouted Ranald with the window now down, looking towards his work colleague and then at the scruffy camouflage rucksack placed on the ground. There was also a holdall. A bright floral pink holdall! His gaze remained transfixed unable to understand why there should be a second bag on the floor. Elspeth had now eased out of the passenger's seat and stood, beckoning him over. But Kenny stayed put not bothering to move until, without warning, the familiar figure of Iona burst onto the scene. Elspeth was agog as they walked towards the van, threw in their bags and jumped into the rear seats.

'Too exciting to miss,' said Iona, putting her seat belt on.

'But what about the gallery? We are supposed to be open today.
'

'My sister Megan's got it covered.'

'Well, you might have asked,' riposted Elspeth firmly, wrong-footed by Iona's sudden appearance. Ranald slipped the van into first gear and pulled away.

Chapter 37 – The Corona Borealis

It was almost midday when Shona caught up with Fortescue in an Edinburgh coffee house. She had warmed to him considerably during their stay in the Scottish capital as indeed Fortescue's infatuation towards her had grown. He was much more civil since she had shown him a firm hand!

'How are we this morning, then?' asked Shona, but before Fortescue could reply her smart phoned buzzed and in came a message from the Duchessa – lunch half past one?

*

Gus was sitting with Oliver in the reception hall of the Charleston Hotel when the Duchessa strode in. No Luigi in tow. He had served his usefulness and been packed off home, that morning, on the nine-thirty flight to Marco Polo Airport. Luigi had cried, in fact sobbed. Heartbroken was the young grocer who had been swept up on a wave of uncontrollable passion of courgettes, marrows and melons only for the fruit that he now so craved to be denied him. And when it came to it, the Duchessa had been equally tearful, emotions running amok; she had found it harder than expected when it came to say goodbye. But Luigi was young, and she knew only too well that a young heart heals quickly and once back in Venice within his old haunts with his old friends, the irresistible sparkle of his tender young eyes would return. It wouldn't be long before he would have a new *bella ragazza* on whom to spill his affections.

'Come, come,' said the Duchessa, airily breezing in and beckoning them to follow with her right index finger. They dutifully stood up. Down the corridor, through the solid oak door and into the fine old private dining room with access onto the small courtyard at the rear. Within a few minutes Shona and Fortescue arrived. Waiters bustled in, waiters bustled out, taking orders and replenishing drinks and soon there was a huddle at one end of the table. Hamish entered. There was silence; no one had been expecting the gnarled old auctioneer.

'Of course, I quite forgot,' said the Duchessa breaking the impasse, vaguely recalling inviting him for lunch at some point. 'Come, you're welcome to join us,' she continued, moving to greet him and allowing the old boy to peck her on the cheek. Ohhhh... what awful breath! The Duchessa reeled backwards from the ferrety face and stinky fumes.

'Come on, sit down then,' she said, pulling out a seat and placing Hamish at the far end of the table before taking her rightful place at the head. A gazpacho soup starter arrived. Gus felt his phone vibrate and then ring.

'Do you mind if I take this?' he said, seeing Professor Zinbottle's name flash up on the screen.

*

'I think I've found something.'

'Yes?' replied Gus.

'The circle of images. I had them scanned electronically and then did a comparison from our database of constellations... I got a match – The Corona Borealis!' There was quiet and contemplation while Gus tried to weigh up the implications.

'The Corona what?'

'Borealis,' replied the Professor. 'An interesting little constellation, Northern Crown, small but well formed. Ptolemy discovered it in the second century. Wonderful man was Ptolemy. Greek by birth although lived in Alexandria, Egypt; not sure why, but there we are.'

'Bbbbut, what does it mean?' stuttered Gus in excitement.

'Haven't a clue. That's your job,' replied Zinbottle, matter-of-factly.

Gus was in a spin, not at all sure what the Corona Borealis meant and if it would help in their quest to find long lost treasures.

'I will email the results,' said the Professor before hanging up.

*

'Who was that?' asked Oliver, wiping his chin with a napkin when Gus arrived back in the dining room. The Duchessa looked on expectantly while he took his place at the table and reached for a sherry glass. In one continuous motion Gus gulped the contents while everyone stared and then puffed out his chest to make the announcement.

'That was Professor Zinbottle and he's found a match… The Corona Borealis!' Fortescue stopped playing with Shona's thigh and started to take a keen interest in where the conversation was going.

'Corona what?' repeated Oliver.

'Borealis. It's a circular constellation in the northern latitudes.'

'And what does it all mean?' asked the Duchessa. There was quiet. No one had an inkling because no one had a clue what the Corona Borealis was and how the stars would lead them to the treasures they had all convinced themselves lay within Lusieri's wonderful painting.

'It's a start,' blurted Oliver. Once we have Professor Zinbottle's full report and results we can give it some thought and see where it takes us. Hamish was all ears, interested to find out what they were all up to.

Chapter 38 – The Greek Bureau of Culture

Mercifully, the heat wave in Athens had abated in recent weeks and life was returning to normal. Fatima Fatiakos was now venturing outside to tend to her sunburnt garden and sit under the cherry tree while enjoying the shade and devouring the ripe fruits. Gladios had been away for almost a fortnight now, cavorting around Scotland in search of relics from the Parthenon Temple. Oh, that wretched temple and the goddess Athena. Forty years he had been at the Bureau, forty years he had been in love with the Acropolis and for forty years it had felt like there had been another person within their marriage – dear old Phidias and his wonderful sculptures... which, of course, now lived in the British Museum!

'Shoo, shoo,' Fatima shouted, raising herself from the rickety old wooden bench at the sight of a feral goat jumping over the wall and making its way to the orchard at the bottom of the garden. The goat stopped, turning its head to see the spherical shape waddling down the garden with their apron blowing in the breeze and brandishing an old broom. Where was Gladios when she needed him?

*

Prodius was also missing Gladios and their regular chats in the Sarcophagus Tavern. The chef's specialities changed from week to week and the owners' pet octopus seemed to grow bigger and bigger with the passing days. It would soon outgrow the tank. He had been called into the Finance Department, only that morning, to answer questions about the expenses Gladios had run up.

'Four-star hotel! Does he really need to stay in a four-star hotel?' Prodius had calmed the manager but it was only a matter of time before he would have to call his colleague and ask him to return. Another wild goose chase, another false dawn, another hole in their budget with nothing to show for it. With that in mind he pulled out his smart phone and dialled his friend's number.

*

Gladios and Helena were getting off the train at Thurso when the call came through. Looking down at his phone he ignored it. Gladios knew it would be a difficult conversation and if the worst came to the worst, he had a secret stash of American dollars tucked away in an offshore account which Mrs Fatiakos knew nothing about. It would be painful to dip into his lifetime savings, but he felt they were getting close to unearthing long lost treasures, relics from their ancient past. Dragging suitcases, they made their way to the bus station for onward transition to the ferry terminal at Scrabster. Brialto and Bruno hailed a taxi.

*

'Crisps?' offered Kenny, opening a packet in the back of the van and thrusting it forward between the front seats towards Elspeth who had taken a hundred miles to calm down. So hot had been her tongue, on finding out Iona had left her sister in charge of the gallery, it had felt like a sauna in the car as Ranald and Kenny had tried to smooth things down. But now that Elspeth had phoned Megan and discussed everything she was beginning to feel that her shop would be in good hands. They were on the A9 within a few miles of Inverness and contemplating where to stop for lunch.

*

The Duchessa was checking out of the Charleston Hotel and what a hullabaloo she was making of proceedings. Footmen scurried here and porters scurried there. Suitcases were loaded into the waiting taxi, not an ordinary cab, good heavens no! That would never have done and would never have been half big enough to take her wardrobes of clothes, most of which she had not even worn. The people carrier was full to the brim by the time they had finished. Brialto had already settled the account and all that remained was to say goodbye to the exceedingly patient staff, who were lined up on the front steps ready to bid their farewells. It was like royalty leaving. They smiled and cheered her departure, reminiscent of the time the Sultan of Brunei had stayed. The manager smiled. It had been a profitable although trying stay.

On the people carrier motored to the ring road and Edinburgh Airport, where a privately chartered jet was being fuelled ready for the hour-long trip to Kirkwall on the Orkney archipelago. Brialto had previously arranged the travel after Bruno's tip off from the helpful receptionist at the Hotel.

*

Hannah knocked on the Chief Superintendent's door while waiting patiently with Donald to be called in for their regular de-briefing.

'Enter,' barked the overweight Superintendent who was already getting psyched up to give them a ruddy good rollocking, come what may. He always felt better after giving someone a thorough dressing down, a scolding of immense proportions; hell hath no fury like the Chief Superintendent when he was in one of his moods. And he was in one of his moods; he was always in one of his moods. The cannon fodder took a seat in front of the baboon of a man. He swivelled to face them, slowly raising his arms and hooking his hands together behind his head, revealing putrid yellow sweat stains under his arm pits.

'Well?' the baboon barked with the faint hint of a snarl creeping into his terse facial features. 'Do you have any leads yet?'

Donald, who had been in the force for many years, had seen the likes of the present incumbent come and go with the changing times. Egocentric, narcissist, tyrannical regimes which usually always culminated in failure in the end. It was just a question of time before the untouchable ego strayed too far; a pinched bottom, lavish expenses, an harassment charge and the so-called ivory tower would prove to be little more than a pack of cards and come tumbling down.

'Nothing to report,' said Donald quickly before Hannah had time to answer. The baboon's eyes narrowed with spite while moving his grande derrière and leaning forward, placing his hands on the desk and squaring up to the impertinent detective who was siting before him. His hands rotated, knuckles down, helping to lift his fat bottom off the chair and propel his ugly face forwards. The buttons of his white shirt were straining to keep his gut covered up. 'Apart from the tracking device we fitted to the Forbes and McKillop van. It was last seen heading towards Inverness,' said Donald quickly.

'Just north, on the road to Thurso, now,' interjected Hannah with her smart phone in her hands. The baboon paused, slightly thrown off track by the information he had just received.

'Presume it's alright for us to follow?' asked Donald, buoyed that he had something to report. Sitting back down the baboon reclined in his seat and again placed his hands behind his head. Hannah winced.

'Go and follow then, although no fancy hotels or extravagant expenses and keep me informed,' snarled the Chief Superintendent. Donald and Hannah stood up and left.

Chapter 39 – The Ring of Brodgar

It was almost five o'clock, late afternoon, when the Forbes and McKillop van rolled off the ferry at Stromness on the Isles of Orkney and drove the short distance to the Central Hotel which was situated close to the marina. They entered to find Gladios and Helena waiting in reception, only too pleased to help with suitcases and luggage while they checked in. Unsurprisingly, the hotel was packed with foreign tourists, milling around the hallway, checking out pamphlets and working out which attraction they should visit next. Elspeth was feeling weary after the ferry ride; the swell of the sea, the gentle rolling of the boat had not really agreed with her current condition and the final stages of pregnancy were beginning to tell. Helena was surprised to see Iona whom she had only met briefly at the gallery in Glasgow. To see her around Kenny caused a tinge of regret and a pang of jealousy, even though she knew their time together had reached the end. The lift pinged, announcing its arrival, ready to take them to their various rooms.

*

There was pandemonium at the Orkneyjar Hotel, which overlooked the attractive harbour in the centre of Kirkwall, just a few miles north of Stromness.

'It's the best room we have madam,' said the receptionist politely when the Duchessa returned after viewing the accommodation.

'I always have a suite of rooms. I like a bedroom, a bathroom, a dressing room and a reception area.'

'Money is not a problem,' added Brialto, who took out a roll of notes and placed them on the desk. 'Just shift some of the other guests.' The receptionist went to find the manager and after some toing and froing and a heated exchange of opinions the message started to get through. Ten thousand pounds was paid into the hotel's bank account and a number of guests were moved to a charming bed and breakfast for no charge. The Duchessa had the top floor, hers to do with as she pleased.

'We have more guests arriving tomorrow,' said Brialto as the fraught receptionists flicked through the computer screens to see what bookings they had.

'Is that the party from the British Museum?' Brialto nodded, pleased they had received his message and reserved some rooms.

*

Donald and Hannah arrived at Thurso and realising they had missed the last ferry to the Isles had managed to find a cheap hotel for the night. After unpacking they met in the bar for a pre-supper drink, taking a seat at the round table next to the fireplace and waiting to be served. The hotel was quiet apart from a couple of die-hard locals who were sipping pints after their round of golf.

'Tell me a bit about yourself,' pressed Hannah who was enjoying the trip and the excitement of the investigation, even though it all seemed rather pointless. She had warmed to Donald during the time they had worked together. Always considerate and polite, Hannah had found him quite intriguing; his nuances and his mannerisms, harking back to a different era. And of course, she was eternally grateful for the gallantry Donald had shown when that mad man had entered the house in Prestonpans armed with a machete. 'Never married?' Hannah asked, going straight in at the deep end. Donald huffed and puffed, in between nervous sips of wine; visibly squirming under interrogation while answering her probing questions and revealing he still lived at home with his parents. Hannah smiled kindly. Donald had a second glass, loosening his tongue, and by the time they went through to the dining room she even knew where he had been at school.

'They're on the move,' said Hannah feeling her smart phone vibrate. Switching on the police tracking app, she watched the little dot continue along the main road out of Stromness

*

The Forbes and McKillop van was riding low to the ground with Gladios wedged in the back beside Helena, Iona and Kenny. Elspeth had offered her place in the front although the congenial Greek was having none of it and instead squeezed in beside his colleagues on the rear seat. The van gently motored along the road towards Kirkwall, slowing when it neared the junction at Stennes. Ranald flicked the left-hand indicator and took the turn towards the Ring of Brodgar.

'There they are,' shouted Elspeth, in excitement, stretching her hand across Ranald and pointing towards the standing stones. They were clearly visible to his right.

'Keep going,' said Iona. 'Those are the Stones of Stennes. It's over the water and they are on the left.' On Ranald went across the bridge which separated the Loch of Harray and the Loch of Stennes, while Elspeth gazed out over the huge expanse of flat water and barren desolate landscape beyond. Within a minute the Ring of Brodgar came into view.

'There's a car park close by,' shouted Iona from the rear of the van, recalling her geography field trip many years ago. Within a short distance Ranald had pulled up. Excitedly, they all got. 'Follow me,' said Iona, like an eager schoolgirl who had been let out on her own. She started striding down the pathway towards the stones. Kenny was alongside, keen to reach their journeys end. Within a couple of minutes Gladios trundled into the ring and made his way to the centre where his colleagues had congregated, surveying the Neolithic earth works and circular shape of the towering stones. The sun was beginning to set on the horizon and the light starting to fade. Despite the warmer mid-summer weather, they had been experiencing of late, there was suddenly a faint chill in the air as the breeze rolled in off the water's edge. There was something spiritual, something moving about where they now stood, all alone, without the background chatter of other tourists; on a site which man had built almost twelve thousand years ago, an ancient civilisation established before even Christ had set foot on earth.

'What does it all mean?' asked Gladios, suddenly overawed by the place in which he found himself, dating back to a dynasty far older than his own ancient Greek times.

'And where do we even start to look?' questioned Elspeth, surprised by the scale of the site and the magnitude of the task which lay ahead of them in seeking lost treasures within this gargantuan ring.

'I've been thinking,' replied Ranald, as all looked on in expectation. 'The verse from The Curse of Minerva... it must hold a clue. What was it again Kenny?'

'Yet still the Gods are just, and crimes are crossed: See here what Elgin won and Elgin lost,' he recited. Everyone looked perplexed not sure where his ramblings were leading and how it would help.

'It has to mean something?' Ranald suggested. All were quiet taking in the atmosphere of this sacred place, absorbed within the moment and the wild landscape. In truth they were daunted by the task ahead of them!

Chapter 40 – Surveillance Time

Bruno was up at the crack of dawn. After a strong coffee and a couple of cigarettes he left the hotel to collect a hire car which had been arranged the previous evening – an immaculately clean Ford Focus!

'NO, NO, NO,' he vented to the apprehensive trainee, spitting on the windscreen to show his distaste for anything other than Italian cars. 'Alfa Romeo,' he insisted. 'Fiat, you must have a Fiat,' Bruno pressed. But after a cursory look at the handheld screen the trainee shook his head and handed him the keys to the brand new Ford. Good heavens, Bruno was livid at having to drive an American car. Slamming the door shut with ferocity he crunched the gear stick into reverse and floored the accelerator. The Pirelli tyres squealed, laying down rubber, before he clattered into the curb and hit the brakes. Off went Bruno in a ball of rage the car a torrent of noise with smoke drifting up from the wheel arches. He was heading in the direction of Stromness and within five and a half minutes he screeched to a halt close to the marina. Abandoning the car on the roadside, he didn't even bother to lock the doors. Bruno was there to stake out the Central Hotel where he knew Helena and Gladios were staying. But first he needed more caffeine. Off he marched, in search of a coffee house from where he could keep an eye on the hotel.

*

Hannah and Donald had boarded the first ferry out of Scrabster and were now standing on the foredeck looking out to sea. A strong wind swept over their faces, blowing Hannah's hair and making Donald's cheeks glow. His hand slipped on the polystyrene cup, spilling tea over his arm. Hannah giggled. She had enjoyed their evening last night, unearthing Donald's inner being and discovering a warm and kind-hearted man. There was more to him than instantly met the eye and

Hannah was very happy to be working in the Criminal Art Department with her newfound mentor.

'Come, let's go inside,' said Donald, when the boat was cast from the harbour side and the diesel engines began to roar propelling the ferry towards the Port of Stromness, the gateway into the Orkney archipelago.

*

It was almost nine in the morning when the early flight touched down on the tarmac of Kirkwall Airport and taxied to the terminal. Fortescue and Shona were sitting beside each other with Oliver and Gus in the row behind. All were intrigued by the Duchessa's summons although they had little idea why they were required on the Northern Isles. Even big Don had been surprised by the turn of events but after internal discussions with the Museum Principal he agreed to the request and extension of time. Into the taxi they all bundled for the five-minute journey to the Orkneyjar Hotel where they would have plenty of time to check in and freshen up prior to their midday lunch appointment with the Duchessa.

*

Gladios had risen earlier than normal and was sitting on his own at a table within the generous bay window of the dining room. The waitress had poured him a coffee which he sipped in between scrolling down the breakfast menu. It reminded him of life at the Sarcophagus Tavern where he would share a table with Prodius whilst waiting for his dear wife, Fatima, to arrive for dinner. And like his favourite Greek tavern, the breakfast menu also had Chef's Specialities made from locally sourced eggs, free range pigs and freshly caught haggis! Haggis... hadn't he had that before when staying in Edinburgh? It rang a bell as his memory cast back, recalling a pudding type dish of mainly grains and peppery spices. It was not an unpleasant recollection. His appetite began to grow and his mouth salivate.

'Full Scottish breakfast with freshly caught haggis, please,' ordered Gladios. The young waitress smiled.

Iona arrived, fresh faced and eager for the day, quickly followed by Kenny, Helena and then Ranald who looked dishevelled after a broken night's sleep. Elspeth had snored continuously. Polite chatter flowed within the eclectic group while tea and coffees were served and orders were taken. Elspeth arrived to a full breakfast which she quickly devoured and within half an hour they were gathered outside the front of the hotel loitering on the steps. Ranald pulled up in the Forbes and McKillop van to collect them and return to the Ring of Brodgar to continue their quest. Off the van set, gently accelerating along the main road leading out of Stromness.

*

Bruno placed a ten-pound note on the table, stood up and marched out of the coffee shop without so much a bye your leave or cursory glance at the pleasant middle-aged lady who had served him.

'You've forgotten your change,' she shouted, poking her head out of the doorway and watching Bruno's muscular physique striding towards the marina. He had seen Gladios in the hotel window, earlier, and watched the bumbling lump squeeze into the back seat of the Forbes and McKillop van, like a pig being taken to market. '*Il porco,*' he had mumbled with a smile when the doors had been shut and the van pulled away. With the grunter in the rear they were going nowhere fast.

Arriving at the irritating hire car he spat on the windscreen, again showing his displeasure, then jumped inside and screeched out of town.

On the distant horizon the ferry from Scrabster was coming into view.

*

It was almost midday and there was an air of expectation in the private dining room of the Hotel as all waited for the Duchessa to arrive. She had grown more demanding without the affections of young Luigi to distract her and Brialto was wondering if it had been such a good idea to pack him off, back to Venice. Shona placed her hand on Fortescue's knee and he returned the affection by stroking her arm. Oliver sipped sherry which Brialto had insisted they all have while he watched the coming and goings within the car park. A Ford Focus shot into view.

'Lunatico,' said Brialto, knowing full well who was driving. The little car bounced off the curb before being awkwardly parked in the disabled spaces. Suddenly, the door opened and in walked the Duchessa.

'Please sit down,' she said, as everyone stood as if to attention. 'Lovely to see you all,' the Duchessa continued, wafting around the table in a flowing silk dress before sitting down close to Brialto and holding out a sherry glass. He filled it. 'So good you could all make it: Oliver, Gus and the rest of you.' It was patronising the tone in which the Duchessa addressed everyone, but she was titled and an heiress to a billionaire's fortune through the biggest industrial wallpaper makers in Europe. To be frank, she could be rather self-righteous, on occasions, and tended to treat people however her whim directed.

Bruno clattered into the meeting room, wild eyed and angry with a cigarette hanging from his mouth. Without waiting to be asked he helped himself to a whisky from the decanter on the side table before sitting down.

'Brodgar,' he said in his monosyllabic tone before taking a generous swig of the undiluted malt. Phwooarr - he loved the raw, rasping taste. Not as good as the whisky he had drunk at the National Gallery, that time. Yes, that time when he had taken on the guards, that time when the lights had dazzled him and his demons had come calling, that time when he had seen the pretty water colour reveal all. He had been lucky the police never pressed charges.

'Brodgar?' questioned the Duchessa, amused by Bruno's sudden outburst.

'Brodgar,' repeated Bruno, before taking another gulp. Phoarr - the whisky burned the back of his throat, the warn sensation slipping down into his empty stomach. 'The Ring of Brodgar,' he continued, as everyone looked on not really sure what he was going on about. 'I followed *il Porco* – the fat Greek - and his chums straight to it this morning. A ring of stones.' Everyone started to pay attention.

'Where is it?' asked Fortescue while Gus picked up his smart phone and did a google search.

'Just down the road,' said Bruno, taking yet another slug of whisky.

'Neolithic site,' interjected Gus, who had now found it on the internet. 'A circular ring!'

Everyone was suddenly silenced, their brains switching into gear. *Circular* had caught their attention although no one was really sure why... until Shona enlightened them.

'Circular, like the pentimento?' Yes, that was it. That was the missing link which they had all been racking their thoughts for. Something buried deep within their sub-consciousness, teasing their minds and now a light which had been switched on. Oliver was rifling through his briefcase to get the images which they had uncovered while Gus switched his phone onto maps to get an aerial view.

'Here, what do you think?' Oliver examined the google image on Gus's phone. The Duchessa arose and made her way around the table to where they were all huddled, scrutinising the likeness. Fortescue wasted no time in making his assessment.

'Twenty-seven dots.'

'He's right,' said Gus, who had also done the mental arithmetic. A wave of excitement rippled through the room.

'Let me see,' demanded the Duchessa. The group parted to allow her in for a closer look. Oliver used his pencil to point out the similarities and she quickly recognised the correlation. But the instant euphoria was gradually replaced by uncertainty – what did it all mean? A distant star constellation, the Corona Borealis, a Neolithic site and an ancient stone circle. And then, there was Byron's poem – The Curse of Minerva. Crikey, what a riddle when all mixed together.

'I'll take you there this afternoon,' said Bruno, who didn't seem particularly interested in everyone's wild musings. He lounged in his chair and sipped whisky.

The doors clattered open and in came the waiter with a trolley full of starters. He was surprised to find everyone on their feet, examining the papers which were strewn across the table.

'Are you ready for lunch?' he asked politely. The Duchessa nodded. The sommelier arrived to take the wine order.

Chapter 41 – Back at the Ring

The site had been deserted when the Forbes and McKillop van arrived at the Ring earlier that morning. Not a car in the parking area, not a soul to be seen, just the wild landscape with some sheep grazing in a nearby field and the occasional gull gliding overhead. Kenny was excited to be there with his brother's old metal detector which he had brought on the trip. Gladios trundled and others ran and within a short time they had dispersed around the Neolithic earth works to search for clues. Clues! They had not an inkling what they were looking for.

Backwards and forwards, to and fro paced Kenny with his detector humming, emitting the occasional beep; a coke can found, an old key ring and other metallic trash of equal insignificance. Elspeth had visited Kirkwall to collect lunch and now that she had returned, they were lounging around the back of the van with the doors wide open, eating sandwiches, munching crisps and swigging dandelion and burdock pop. However, the mood was flat. Flat, at the gradual realisation of the enormity of their task.

'We need a strategy,' piped up Iona, the enthusiasm of youth not yet curbed and likewise Kenny was buoyed by his new-found friendship with the charming young archaeological student. Gladios sighed, his were legs tired from the morning's exertions.

'Iona's right,' said Elspeth. Rather surprisingly her feud seemed to have been forgotten. Helena nodded, realising their morning had been wasted with no clear direction.

'Let's look at the clues again,' said Ranald, 'and see if we can make any sense of them.'

*

Donald and Hannah had collected a hire car and checked into a bed and breakfast at Stennes. Keen to find out what the suspects were up to they followed the phone app which took them towards the Brodgar Ring. The Forbes and McKillop van could clearly be seen, parked at the side, with the rear doors wide open and everyone milling around.

'Keep driving,' hissed Hannah, sinking into the passenger's seat and ducking so she could not be seen. Obligingly, Donald sped up and continued along the road. 'They were all there,' said Hannah, poking her head up and peering out of the window. Donald slowed once they were out of view and parked in a lay-by.

*

The Duchessa walked out of the Hotel into the car park, took one look at Bruno's Ford Focus and sniffed haughtily.

'Get me a taxi,' she instructed Brialto.

'Make it two,' said Oliver, 'in fact, Gus can go and sort it out,' sending his assistant back to reception to make the arrangements.

'Come,' said Bruno staring at Shona and catching her eye. Fortescue braced himself as he instantly felt protective of his new-found love. But there was something about Bruno which made him difficult to refuse. Shona took hold of Fortescue's hand and dragged him towards the car. Within a couple of minutes they were sitting in the rear seat gunning it towards the Ring of Brodgar, along the coast road, travelling at full pelt.

*

'I'm sure there's something in the poem,' said Ranald, trying to generate a little enthusiasm for the afternoon's endeavours. Gladios nodded in agreement although he was unsure what. Kenny took up the cudgel.

'There's three hundred and twelve lines, twenty verses and - *yet still the Gods are just...you know* – is within the eighth verse. And we've got the Ring of Brodgar.'

'There's clearly something missing,' said Helena. 'It's a riddle of some sort. The painting of the Parthenon Temple on a Scottish Island, the secret images and the verse from the poem. What was Lusieri trying to tell us, what did he want encrypted and saved for later times?' Their musings were disturbed by the sound of a car approaching; not a normal engine note but a whining, strained wail of desperation.

The rev counter hit the red as Bruno kept his foot to the metal. The little car rocketed into view. It was soon upon them and once closer the occupants could clearly be seen when it began to slow.

Dark wavy hair and a big bulbous moustache, there was something about that face which registered with Kenny, an unmistakable look. Now where had he seen it before? And then it came to him in a flash, like a bolt of electricity conducting through his veins and tingling his extremities. Adrenalin began to flow and fear descended.

'It's the Machete Man,' he whispered, no one hearing him at first, but as the implications of the new arrival dawned, he panicked and shouted out, 'IT'S THE MACHETE MAN!' Everyone stared in surprise. 'It's the man who attacked us in Prestonpans!'

*

Bruno parked further along the road and left the car.

'Follow me,' he said, directing his comments at Shona and then set off at his usual, controlled and monotonous gait with the British Museum sidekicks following on behind.

Ranald looked at his pregnant wife and his paternal instincts took hold. He ushered Elspeth into the van.

'Come on let's go.' Gladios quickly devoured the remnants of his sandwich before scrambling into the back and once the door was shut, Ranald slipped the old van in to first gear and quickly pulled out, passing close to Bruno who was oblivious to the havoc his presence had caused.

'That's the British Museum people,' said Elspeth, recognising Shona whom she had briefly met at the auction when Lusieri's painting made a record price. Up the road they fled, as fast as the van would go, and after quarter of mile they pulled into a lay-by to breathe a collective sigh of relief.

*

The Duchessa arrived at the Ring escorted by Oliver and Gus with Brialto trailing along behind. He found the air bracing and was distracted by the wonderful panorama across the loch and the windswept landscape beyond. There was warmth in the mid-summer sun so he stopped to enjoy the moment and take in the views.

Shona and Fortescue were now standing in the centre with Bruno prowling the perimeter, stalking the earth bund like a caged tiger in a zoo enclosure. Within a short time they all congregated to discuss what to do.

'We've a number of clues,' said Oliver, naturally taking command. 'The pentimento looks to be a map of the stone circle. Certainly the same shape, correct number of stones and even in roughly the same position. It seems to correlate. And then there's the poem. Did you find anything else about that?' he asked, looking towards Fortescue who let go of Shona's hand.

'It was never formally published. Byron was highly critical about the looting of the Parthenon Temple which, as we know, remains controversial to this day.'

'And any ideas why Lusieri inscribed a verse on the back of his water colour?' asked Gus, who was equally mystified by the conundrum. Fortescue shrugged.

'I've done some research on Lusieri who was a talented artist in his own right. The *View of the Bay of Naples* hangs in the Getty Museum and there are a number of other works in National Galleries around the world. No idea how he became involved with Elgin though, other than, I suppose money. Making a living as an artist has never been easy, even in those days.' The Duchessa listened with interest, delighted to learn more of her distant ancestor.

'But reading between the lines,' continued Fortescue... he paused, while everyone looked in expectation. 'I get the feeling, just a hunch really, but I sense that Lusieri wasn't wholly approving of Elgin's work. Of course the Turks were looting the Temple at that time so it probably made little difference, but I suspect that he would have preferred to leave the Parthenon's sculptures and statutes where they stood.' It was insightful but difficult to fathom how all of this had led them to the Isles of Orkney and an ancient Neolithic earth work, where they now stood, surrounded by stones more ancient than the Greek treasures they had come in search of.

'And then there's the Corona Borealis,' added Oliver to further muddy the waters. 'A distant constellation within the northern latitudes so far away that it is barely visible.' Brialto sighed, wondering if they would ever piece together the jigsaw and find the treasure.

*

Donald and Hannah were sitting in their hire car when the Forbes and McKillop van parked in front of them. Hannah checked the App on her smart phone and, yes, it was the same vehicle they had tagged and followed to Orkney. The doors opened and out stepped Elspeth who needed some fresh air. She breathed in, she breathed out and then bent resting her hand on her knees. She felt the twins move inside. Ranald had now joined his wife and placed a reassuring hand on her shoulder. He heard car's doors being shut.

'What are you doing here?' asked Donald, getting straight to the point. Ranald stared in silence. He was lost for words. Elspeth stood up and rubbed her bump. Kenny's head was sticking out of the window.

'The lunatic with the machete is at the circle,' he shouted with desperation creeping into his voice. Donald shuddered, recalling the traumatic evening in Prestonpans; wild eyes, brutal force and uncontrollable violence unleashed by the psychopathic man in a whirlwind of destruction at number 9 Heysham Drive. 'Why don't you go and arrest him?' continued Kenny, now quite agitated and keen to get moving.

Donald and Hannah looked flustered, not really sure what they should do but before they could blink, Ranald and Elspeth were back in the van with the motor running.

'I'll catch up with you later,' shouted Donald. Ranald waved from the car window as the Forbes and McKillop van pulled out of the lay-by. Hannah looked at Donald.

'What now?' Thrown by events he shrugged his shoulders and appeared blank. Hannah led the way back to their car.

'I suppose we had better have a drive by,' and with that they set off in the direction of the Brodgar Ring.

Chapter 42 – Beowulf the Pagan

Beowulf was in the vegetable garden of his pretty, stone cottage in the hamlet of Twatt just a few miles north of Brodgar. He moved sedately with his hoe, down the lines, grubbing up organic carrots which his wife, Ezrulie, would collect when she returned. It was a warm afternoon and he was sweating under the brow of his sunhat. Where was Ezrulie the voodoo goddess he pondered before wiping his face and leaving the hoe propped against the fence. He entered the fruit cage to collect some tayberries.

'Wulfy, Wulfy?' he heard his wife cry as she walked across the lawn in her bare feet, holding a tray with homemade elderflower cordial resting between her saggy breasts. Her stomach wobbled and her bare thighs flexed while making her way to the bottom of the garden. 'Wulfy?' she called again.

Beowulf stood up and stepping backwards reversed into a gooseberry bush.

'OUCH,' he yelped like a young pup, pricking his bare bottom and drawing a pin head of blood from his saggy buttocks.

Ezrulie placed the tray on the table and sat down on the hard bench, her bare cheeks enveloping the wooden plank, worn smooth by their naked flesh over the years. Beowulf appeared from the fruit cage, resplendent in his leather sandals and straw hat. He was old, worn, wrinkled, saggy and smelly. Very smelly, like a rancid billy goat but so was Ezrulie who honked like an old sow and not surprising really since they only bathed twice a year at the Spring and Autumn equinox. Of course, they were both nudists, devoted to the cause, a life less complicated by material belongings and clothes.

'Cordial?' asked Ezrulie, holding out a glass towards Beowulf and revealing a hairy armpit. Parking his bare cheeks on the smooth wooden bench he accepted gratefully and started guzzling from the glass to quench his thirst. 'Should be a good turnout, this year,' continued Ezrulie. 'We've received e mails from pagans and druids from all over the country, confirming their visit.' Beowulf nodded while thinking of the summer solstice festival which they had run for over thirty-five years.

They had been quiet in the early days, just Beowulf and Ezrulie at the start of their relationship. Him in no more than a flowing woollen shawl held up by a cheap copper brooch and Ezrulie in a druid cape tied around her waist with some hessian string. They drank, they smoked, and they danced to celebrate the longest day, acting out their rituals under a starlit sky, playing out courtship and symbolic gestures of fecundity and fertility. Although it wasn't symbolic in the spring of 1986 was it? Beowulf had roared and Ezrulie had pulled him to the ground in the centre of the Ring, ripping his cape open and feasting on his bounty. It had worked though, oh yes it had worked, their decadent behaviour on that mid-summer night rewarded by the fertility goddess, Eostre, when only nine months later a bonny little girl, Bronwen, their only child, was born.

And as time went on the summer solstice festival grew in popularity not only on the isles but also further afield on the Scottish mainland where long rooted pagan beliefs flourished. Beowulf was their leader, the self-proclaimed King, the master of ceremonies and fount of all knowledge on ancient Scottish celebrations, even though he had been born in deepest Wales, somewhere near Caerphilly.

'I've heard from Cerunnos,' said Ezrulie. 'He sent a WhatsApp earlier to let us know that the Lochaber Pagans will be setting off tomorrow and should arrive in time.' Beowulf placed his glass on the table and belched heartily before shifting his weight onto his left buttock cheek and farting.

'Good,' he replied, 'good, good. We have big numbers this year, the usual from the north of Scotland and I had an email, a day or so ago, from the Goole Pagans in Yorkshire. They're coming as well.'

'And what are you intending to sacrifice, my darling?' enquired Ezrulie. 'Something tender, something succulent?' Beowulf began to think. The excitement of the Mabon and sacrificial ceremony started to whet his appetite. How he enjoyed reciting the verses, his homage to the deities before the pinnacle of the evenings worship when he would scream to the heavens, plunging his knife downwards, spilling the entrails of their sacrificial offering onto the stone. Fires would rage and pagans would dance, sing and make merry while consuming intoxicating substances and enjoying each other in an orgy of excess.

'I thought a marrow this year,' said Beowulf. 'Yes, a marrow. They've done rather well on the compost heap at the bottom of the garden.

'Two marrows,' said Ezrulie. 'Two great big orbs of... indulgence.'

'Two marrows it is then my little sorceress,' replied Beowulf. With a sparkle in his eye, he took Ezrulie by the hand and led her through the fruit cage to the compost pile!

*

Donald and Hannah had driven back along the road towards the Brodgar Ring where they parked and apprehensively got out. They were on tenterhooks. Breathing in, they tentatively set off on the path to the circle. Ahead were a couple of figures on the horizon and what looked to be children running up and down the earth trench and hiding behind the stones. Nothing instantly looked like the towering figure of the mad machete man so they continued on the trail and soon reached the Ring. The parents and children were now clearly visible to the left. And scanning elsewhere they were puzzled to find the rest of the site deserted; well, that was until a head appeared from the trench on their right, looming into view. A tall figure with long hair... Donald momentarily gulped.

'No moustache,' said Hannah, trying to alleviate their fears.

'Might have shaved it off,' replied Donald, not pacified by her comments.

In truth, neither of them could remember exactly what the mad machete wielding lunatic looked like, not from this distance, and not without seeing those wild dilated eyes. They stood transfixed like lemmings, not sure whether to run or stay put as the looming figure approached.

'They've got sandals on,' pointed out Hannah. Donald remained stumm and suddenly the stranger was within ten yards and coming upon them fast.

'Afternoon. You here for the festival?

'Festival?'

'Mabon,' replied the man in a Yorkshire accent. 'The summer solstice – it's a pagan celebration.' Donald sighed and Hannah looked relieved as they realised this was not the lunatic who had tormented then in Prestonpans.

*

Bruno had returned to the hotel and was in the conference room which the Duchessa had booked for their brain storming session to see if they could unlock Lusieri's mystery and solve the puzzle. Not that he was contributing much, slouched in a seat, ignoring the *no smoking signs* while drawing on his cigarette. No one seemed brave enough to mention this, but in any event, the Duchessa enjoyed the smell of the Italian cigarettes. It reminded her of the Duca who had been an avid smoker in his day. Professor Zinbottle was on speakerphone and they all huddled around the central console, listening to his description of the Corona Borealis.

'It's only visible with the naked eye between the spring and autumn equinox and even then, it's usually only the Alphecca star which can be seen between latitudes 50 and 90 degrees. You should still be able to see it at this time of year… just.'

'But what does it signify, what does it mean?' asked Oliver who had the most rudimentary knowledge of the solar systems. The Professor was silent, not really sure where they were going with their questions, what they hoped to prove and how it was going to help them find lost artefacts from the Parthenon Temple. He was fairly sure they wouldn't be in space.

'It's the Northern Crown situated between the Vega and Arcturus stars. I think it's linked to the legend of Theseus and the Minotaur – can't remember exactly what it was about.'

'What's a Minotaur?' asked the Duchessa, innocently.

'Half man, half bull,' replied Fortescue. Best known in Greek mythology when Athenian hero, Theseus, slayed the Minotaur.'

'Is that all?' asked Zinbottle, realising he had contributed as much as he could to their discussions.

'Thanks,' replied Oliver before hanging up.

'What now?' asked Brialto who had not an inkling where the clues indicated they should look. Oh, there was apathy in the room, listless apathy with no energy or drive as to what they should do next. Bruno stood up and without attempting to find an ash tray, stubbed out his cigarette on the table. He was uncouth, slovenly, a darn right disgrace to the Corolla family, according to his mother. But the Duchessa had a soft spot for dear Bruno, looking up at his fine chiselled features and bushy moustache.

'It's simple,' he said. 'We let *Il Porco* find the treasure and then we take it from him. No clues, no mystery, no effort, no bother. That's the way us Corollas work and that is the best way to get the bounty.' He lit another cigarette while continuing to stand.

'*Il Porco?*' asked Shona. Bruno smiled.

'*Il Porco,*' he repeated.

'And who is *Il Porco?*' enquired the Duchessa.

'*Il Porco,* snorttttt, snorttttt,' repeated Bruno with a grin on his face, finding the confusion rather amusing. '*Il Porco* is the fat Greek pig from the Mediterranean. Let his snout do the work, let *Il Porco* smell out the loot and let *Il Porco* lead us to it and then… Kaput - *Il Porco* gets it.' Bruno swiped his finger over his neck in a cutting motion. There was no doubt what he had in mind.

'It's a good plan, no?' said Brialto. There was quiet, everyone glancing uneasily at each other not sure how to react to Bruno's appalling suggestion. Oliver swivelled in his chair, catching Gus's attention and rolling his eyes skywards. He hadn't warmed to the Italians who he thought were a couple of thugs.

'We can spare *Il Porco,*' said the Duchessa, taking command of the situation. 'Although, unless anyone else has any better suggestions then Bruno can keep tabs on the Greek and see what he can find out.'

Bruno smiled delighted his idea was gaining some traction. *Il Porco* would get it, come what may!

Chapter 43 – Il Porco goes Snouting

Gladios was awake in bed mulling things over. They hadn't made much progress with finding long lost Parthenon treasures and the Bureau was beginning to lose patience with their Scottish adventure. It had been ambitious from the outset and after nearly a month of expenses, with no visible return, there were rumblings that they should return to Greece. Too early for breakfast, Gladios went for a walk to the marina which was close by. He stopped, resting against a bollard while looking across the rows of boats and the sea beyond.

'Hallo there,' he heard from below and looking down saw a pretty turquoise ketch bobbing up and down. Sticking out of the hatch was a blue Breton cap beneath which was a well-tanned, bearded face. 'Too much rum last night?' the old sea dog continued, jokingly. Gladios realised he was an unruly sight perched on the quay.

'I like your boat,' he replied, changing the subject and genuinely admiring the clean lines and classical shape.

'She's Matilda. Come and have a look if you like.' Gladios shifted from the bollard and made his way down to the floating pontoons. 'Come aboard,' suggested his new-found friend. 'I'm Terence, by the way.' Lumbering forward, Gladios took a big step onto the deck and then nimbly dropped into the cockpit. 'You've been on boats before,' commented Terence, rather surprised by the big man's agility. The boat rocked as Gladios sat down.

'Hellenic Navy. Only for a couple of years National Service but they were happy days roaming the high seas and travelling the world.' And with that introduction they settled down for a good natter.

*

'Where's Gladios?' asked Helena, pulling up a seat at the dining table. Kenny was sitting beside Ranald and they were making plans for the day. The metal detector had run its course and in any event was not going to detect ancient stone artefacts. It had been wishful thinking to bring it in the first place. Iona entered with a wholesome smile, full of the joys of youth, and after collecting an orange juice and bowl of muesli from the buffet table appeared to hesitate before sitting down next to Kenny. Helena felt a pang strike through her heart, realising Kenny's new relationship was beginning to blossom. Gladios stumbled in to join them and sat down at the head of the table.

'Tea or coffee?' asked the waitress. Gladios shook his head. He had had his fill on Matilda. Elspeth arrived and they started to make a plan.

'We could split the ring into quadrants,' suggested Iona, who had been on digs before. Everyone takes a section and examines the landform closely, looking for any changes which may indicate a disturbance of the soil; you know, sudden differences in vegetation or a mound, that sort of thing.'

'Then what?' questioned Elspeth.

'Well,'... Iona hesitated, 'the usual practice is to dig.'

'Dig,' repeated Elspeth. 'It's a UNESCO World Heritage Site!'

'Yes, I know,' replied Iona, falling silent with no obvious solution.

'We could dig at night,' suggested Kenny, optimistically. Elspeth raised her eyebrows. The twins kicked. What was she doing here? Two weeks from her due date and here she was on a wild goose chase on the Isles of Orkney in search of relics from the Parthenon

Temple. It was ridiculous, beyond comprehension that they should have embarked on this adventure at all. Her body language conveyed her feelings as the mood palpably fell within the room and their shoulders sagged. But Helena still had fire in her belly and remained committed to the cause. She was convinced that Greek treasures lay buried in that ring and after seven years of working for the Greek Bureau of Culture, seeking artefacts of their heritage, she was in no mood to give up, just yet.

'Night-time dig it will be then.' It was said with purpose, it was said with conviction and it was said in a manner not to be trifled with. Elspeth felt the womanhood of a lady scorned. In fact, everyone around the table knew that they had come too far to give up now. Gladios stood to rally the troops and indicate he was ready to depart and return to the Ring. Ranald felt his smart phone vibrate and on looking at the screen saw a message from Hamish – *can you give me a call?*

*

The Duchessa was last to arrive in the hotel conference room which they had now taken over along with her suite of rooms. She met a table strewn with papers, surrounded by laptops as her makeshift team busied themselves, trying to unlock the vital clues and work out Lusieri's secret. Shona seemed to be in charge, directing operations while she scurried around, moving from station to station and seeing what was coming in. There was no sign of Bruno who was staking out the Brodgar Ring. He was sitting in the long grasses beside the Loch of Harray with a set of binoculars waiting for his friends to return. And return they did, shortly after ten o'clock, whereupon they methodically split the site up and started to search. Bruno smoked his ganja and then lay back, watching the clouds drift slowly overhead while entering his happy land where he was no longer tortured by his ever-persistent demons. *Il Porco* would find the treasure and then he would simply walk to the Ring and collect it.

*

Oliver stood up and went to replenish his coffee cup from the cafetière on the sideboard. He was immersed in deep thought about what they should do next and after filling his cup returned to the central table.

'I've been thinking,' he announced. Everyone turned to see what he was going to say. 'We've been through these clues trying to decipher their true meaning for some time now and I don't think we are any closer to solving the riddle.' It was true, as much as they racked their brains, did internet searches and make enquiries they had in fact made no meaningful progress.

'Go on,' said the Duchessa. Oliver took a deep breath.

'We need to dig! The Ecografia Scanner is still in Scotland, we could get it here on a low loader in a day or two.'

The ruddy Ecografia Scanner, thought Shona, remembering the great promise it held on its last outing at Loch Leven, only for the expectations to be cruelly dashed when it found an old Zanussi fridge. The Scottish press had had a field day with their headlines, trumpeting in delight, knocking the establishment and portraying the British Museum as a bunch of cheap skate Sassenach prospectors.

'Is that a good idea?' asked Fortescue, a little unsure of the wisdom of a second dig.

'I know what you are thinking, and I know things didn't go as we hoped in Fife but realistically we are unlikely to pin point exactly where there may be buried treasure without scanning,' replied Oliver. 'We've done well to get this far and narrow our search down to the Brodgar Ring.'

'It's a Historic Scotland site,' protested Shona, dreading another conversation with Laura Patterson. Her Irish charm had worked once but it would be a difficult sell the second time around.

'And what is the Ecografia Scanner?' enquired the Duchessa.

'Lovely bit of kit,' said Gus, who had been rather taken with the machine and enjoyed its workings and sorting out the reams and reams of data it produced. The Duchessa looked around the table and saw the hesitancy within the faces.

'Tell me more about the Eco...what was it? scanner?' Gus looked at Oliver for moral support and sensing his approval he began to speak.

'Latest technology, state of the art scanner and there is only a handful in the world. It's been accredited with some excellent results in the Middle East, particularly Palmyra. Not a lot else to say really, other than... it's made in Milan.'

'So, it's Milanese,' observed the Duchessa. 'The last time I was in Milan I went to La Scala to see Cosi fan Tutt... very good, of course. Most things from Milan are very good, their cooking, their clothes, even the industries there are rather efficient. We have a factory on the outskirts.' No one spoke, no one wished to interrupt her train of thought. Silenced descended apart from the Duchessa tapping her pen on the table until she caught Gus's eye and smiled. 'Send for the Eco... whatever it is called.'

Shona sighed; she was not looking forward to her discussions with Laura Patterson.

*

Donald and Hannah arrived at the Brodgar Ring around eleven in the morning and found the Forbes and McKillop van in the car park. They were hesitant about trekking along the hard path to the stones circle, after they had been warned that the mad machete man had been sighted in the vicinity. But reasoning, that the Greek cohort were as much a target as them they plucked up courage and started on the track to the Ring.

*

Ranald and co had been searching for almost an hour. Iona had provided some useful tips while demonstrating, on all fours, how to scour the ground thoroughly; backwards and forwards, looking for the smallest of details. With a quadrant each, she had left them to it, a most peculiar sight, as they shifted around on hands and knees. Poor old Gladios was not accustomed to such exertions and finding it particularly tiring he had resorted to lying on the ground to save his knees. Looking out across the horizon he felt his smart phone vibrate as a text came in. It was Prodius – *Can you give me a call? The Bureau would like you to return* – It was the message he had been dreading, the call to come home. He pressed delete. They had come too far to give up, just yet. His government credit card would be cancelled soon, although he had his secret stash of dollars, squirreled away, which he fully intended to use. Mrs Fatiakos wouldn't approve… but then, she wouldn't know!

'Hello, hello, hello,' he heard and looking up he found Donald standing over him with Hannah at his side. 'I suppose the rest of your gang are here?' Gladios remained prostrate, lying on the ground and without saying a word waved his hand in the general direction of his newfound friends.

*

Bruno had smoked a pouch of weed and was on his back fast asleep with a gentle breeze occasionally ruffling his hair. But he awoke with a start when he became aware of something crawling over his face. Sitting up with a jolt, he watched the bumble bee lazily drift off and discovered he was surrounded by a flock of sheep who were methodically making their way across the field. An old blackface ewe gazed at him inquisitively while chewing some grass, perplexed why there should be an interloper within their midst.

'Shoo,' shouted Bruno, waving his hands to send the flock on their way and then he reached for his binoculars to see what he could spy.

*

'What do you want?' asked Elspeth, standing up, her back aching from bending over and searching the ground.

'I could ask you the same question,' replied Donald with little idea why they should all be here on Isle of Orkney. Ranald arrived.

'I'm not sure why you are still pursuing us,' continued Elspeth. 'The painting was found long ago.' Her comments instantly deflated Donald who was also unsure why they were still compelled to investigate the matter. Hannah was quiet and for once her boss seemed unsure of himself. Hesitating, he looked around at Ranald as Kenny arrived.

'If you want to do something useful why don't you find that lunatic who attached us with the machete,' the young Hibernian supporter suggested. Donald felt a cold shiver, recalling that fateful evening in Prestonpans when he saw his life pass before him as he remembered the fear that wild man had instilled into them. Poor Hannah had been cowering when he went to her aid, and he was sure they would have been mincemeat but for the timely intervention of the disfigured accomplice with the handgun.

Iona and Helena arrived to see what the huddle was about and this was the cue for Gladios to get to his feet. He raised his substantial bulk from the turf and was now standing up.

*

Bruno could see the gathering through his binoculars. He thought he recognised the faces, although his brain was fuddled from the baccy he had just smoked and he wasn't too sure. He picked himself up and began walking towards the Ring for a better look.

*

'I see your point,' replied Donald, now on the back foot. 'Although a crime was committed when the painting went missing and we're still looking to solve it. You remain the chief suspects.'

'Surely not,' said Gladios, appealing to his better nature. Hannah could see the futility of their quest in hounding these people the length of the country with nothing more than circumstantial evidence to connect them. Yet even her suspicions had been raised. It seemed odd that they continued together in their shared goal, although exactly what that was remained a mystery.

'There's someone looking at us,' said Kenny who had spotted Bruno beside the boundary fence, peering through his binoculars. He was circling in an anti-clockwise direction not quite close enough to be identified with the naked eye, although his towering muscular frame looked familiar and began to haunt them. There was something instantly recognisable, something which reminded them of a darker time, something they would rather not get involved with again. The chilling thought of the machete attack was foremost in their thoughts.

'Come, let's go,' said Hannah, setting off in the direction of the path as all began to follow, picking up pace, faster and faster they strode until they began to flee. Even Elspeth broke out into a jog while Gladios showed a surprising turn of pace bringing up the rear.

Bruno smiled to see then running like wild animals. Within a couple of minutes he saw the large rear of *Il Porco* scrambling into the back of the van and the vehicle pull away.

Chapter 44 – Shona works her Charm

'Hello Laura,' said Shona in an upbeat and friendly manner.

'Hello,' replied Laura, rather apprehensively, instantly recognising the voice and recalling the dig on Loch Leven Island; the hype, the publicity, the press articles, the TV coverage all for a... Zanussi Fridge! The British Museum had been apologetic and made good the site, even offering to pay for a new walkway, but it had tarnished their reputation and had taken some explaining to the management committee. 'What can we do for you this time?' she said, sensing Shona would have a request.

'We're in Orkney.'

'Lovely,' replied Laura not giving anything away.

'We're at the Brodgar Ring.'

'NO!' said Laura emphatically. 'It's a UNESCO world heritage site.'

'I know,' replied Shona, realising she was likely to be on the phone for some time.

*

Donald had instinctively followed the Forbes and McKillop van back to Stromness and parked alongside in the hotel car park. The thought of another machete attack had instantly bought them together. Elspeth was still recovering from her earlier exertions and was again questioning why she had ever embarked on this crazy adventure in her current condition. They all congregated in the dining room and ordered some tea and scones. Ranald felt his phone buzz and decided to take the call from Hamish.

*

Bruno screeched to a halt outside the main entrance of the Orkneyjar Hotel. Striding into reception he tossed the keys to the receptionist who would arrange for the battered, little car to be parked elsewhere. On he went, barging into the meeting room without even knocking or a cursorily hello. Instead, he helped himself to a whisky from the decanter on the sideboard and sat down.

The Duchessa smiled at her truculent adviser, amused by his wayward manner.

Shona re-entered the room and everyone looked up in expectation as she began to speak.

'Apparently part of the site has been excavated before but nothing was found; certainly no clues indicating there may be treasures from the Parthenon Temple. Not surprisingly, they are pretty sceptical. However, I've managed to get permission for us to run the Ecografia Scanner over the site although no digging until they are sure there is something worth excavating. It's a start.'

The Duchessa nodded, pleased with her efforts. Oliver caught Gus's attention and, with a thumbs up, indicated he should arrange the transport.

'We should be able to get it here late tomorrow afternoon. It's packed up ready to leave,' announced Gus.

'Oh yes, that reminds me,' said Shona. 'We are not allowed on site until after the summer solstice celebration. Apparently, druids and pagans come from all over Scotland and beyond for the longest day.' Brialto called to Bruno who was nursing his whisky.

'And you, boy. How's your man doing? Is he likely to find us anything before then?' Bruno ignored his father, not even bothering to acknowledge his comments. He calmly lit a cigarette before replying.

'*Il Porco* will take us to the treasures, soon enough. You're wasting your time with the scanner. My way is best.'

'I'll organise the transport anyway,' said Gus, being as diplomatic as ever.

*

Beowulf and Ezrulie arrived at the Ring in the middle of the afternoon with the sacrificial stone in a wheelbarrow. They had permission to host the Mabon although it had come with conditions: bins were to be provided, portaloos too, only picnic foods and strictly no alcohol on site. It was the same every year and, just like all previous years Beowulf ignored the diktat. Yes, there would be a few token ladies' cubicles, but nowhere near enough to service the hundred or so pagans who were expected tomorrow night. They much preferred to crap in the Loch of Harray, as pagans and druids had done since time immemorial, rather than queue for a chemical closet. And then there was the alcohol and homemade hooch; bottles, even barrels of the stuff, sold illegally from the back of camper vans and clapped-out estate cars. There would be more than enough grog to carry them through the solstice in their usual intoxicated and debauched way.

'Comet Stone?' enquired Ezrulie while lolloping alongside her husband in her cork sandals and hessian robe. She found herself scratching again.

'I thought we would try something different this year,' Beowulf replied. 'How about the centre of the Ring; you know, just like we did in 1986? Remember, it was the year we… Errr… Bronwen! Ezrulie didn't remember a great deal, certainly not the immaculate conception of their only daughter, just the grass stains on her back and sore knees the following day.

'We're expecting a lot more druids and pagans than in 1986. It was just the two of us then,' replied Ezrulie, cruelly dousing her husband's fond memories.

*

It was just after lunch when Hamish heard his phone ring.

'Where is it he muttered?' looking towards the bedside table and then recalling he had left it in the back pocket of his trousers which were strewn across the floor.

'Get that for me, will you my dear?' barked the old rogue as Agnes returned to the bedroom with a pot of tea and plate of macaroons. Dressed in a silk camisole, barely decent for women of a certain age, Agnes delicately placed the tray on the bed before retrieving the phone and climbing between the sheets. It had stopped ringing but Hamish was pleased to see that Ranald had returned his call. He pressed the redial button.

'Hello, how are you keeping?'

'Fine,' replied Ranald, interested to hear what Hamish had to say. They spoke about this and they spoke about that while the old auctioneer tried to winkle out of Ranald where he was and what he was up to. But he was being distracted by dear Agnes who was gently massaging his chest and offering him a nibble of macaroon! Hamish was suddenly keen to resume their *business meeting* so decided to get on and tell Ranald what he knew.

'The Corona Borealis.'

'The Corona what?' repeated Ranald.

'Borealis,' said Hamish, feeling his blood pressure begin to rise. 'I had lunch with the Duchessa a day or so ago and whatever you are embroiled in, apparently, the Corona Borealis has some relevance'

'What is it?'

'Come on you nit-wit, use your noggin,' snapped Hamish rather impatiently. 'It's a star constellation,' and with that he hung up. Agnes slipped a chocolate macaroon into his mouth. My, she was a tease!

*

Elspeth was lying on the double bed with her legs outstretched in a star shape. She was breathing heavily.

'You all right?' asked Ranald on entering the room. Elspeth nodded.

'Just recovering from the morning's exertions.' She hesitated momentarily and that was sufficient for Ranald to broach the subject they had both been meaning to discuss.

'We will leave late tomorrow. Let's give it another day and then we can go.' Elspeth smiled, glad their adventure was about to come to an end. It had been a whimsical notion, in the midst of summer, and in more normal circumstances would have been a heavenly treat. But Mrs Milngavie was now within ten days of giving birth and even her nonsensical husband had come to realise it would be best to be at home, close to a hospital, where at least there would be chance of following their birthing plan.

*

Dinner that evening in the Stromness Hotel was quiet. The set menu was all the kitchen could muster for their group; polenta, ragout and an ice cream dessert. Gladios hoovered up the leftovers, even the vast helping of stodgy polenta, which no one else seemed willing to eat. The fresh Scottish air had done little to diminish his healthy appetite.

'I had a call from Hamish today,' said Ranald, directing his comments towards Kenny who was sitting in between Iona and Helena, making polite conversation.

'The Corona Borealis.' Kenny looked blank while momentarily distracted from his attractive companions.

'It's a star constellation seen during the summer months,' continued Ranald. 'Represents a crown according to the internet.'

It resonated with Kenny as indeed it had done with Ranald. Both had seen the wild images that Lusieri's magical water colour revealed, after a good helping of Kawatachi ten-year-old malt whisky, and both had been drawn to the star-like configuration which appeared on the Temple floor. Helena had also seen these images and like Ranald and Kenny was perplexed as to what message they conveyed.

Gladios scraped the bottom of his bowl collecting the remnants of the melted ice cream and wafer biscuits which he had crumbled on top. Methodical in his movement, from right to left and left to right, until he placed the spoon in the centre of the bowl, indicating he was finished. He could sense that morale was flagging. Two days they had been on the Isles and for two days they had drawn a blank, no closer to finding Parthenon treasures than when they had first left Greece on a whim, a false dawn of hope and a promise to be dashed yet again, if they were to return empty handed. The money had run out and Gladios was now dipping into to his secret stash of dollars to keep their hopes alive. He was aware the sands of time were slipping away although he remained resolute they should have one last try.

'Helena, search the internet and find all you can about the Corona… whatever it is called.'

'Borealis,' chipped in Ranald, not sure why no one could remember the name.

'The Corona Borealis,' repeated Gladios, 'and then let's all get together for an early breakfast tomorrow morning for one last brain-storming session.' He seemed to have roused everyone sufficiently to gain their co-operation. Placing his napkin on the table he stood to ease his digestion and then decided to take a walk.

*

Out of the front door and down the steps trudged Gladios, smelling the sea air as gulls squawked overhead. On he went, step after step, panting like a dog while his stomach churned and gurgled, sounding like an old washing machine on a hot cycle. He was in search of his newfound friend and his charming turquoise ketch.

'Ahoy there,' he heard from the distance as Gladios saw the familiar Breton cap bobble up from behind a row of boats. It was Terence and after a closer look he saw Matilda tied up.

'Hello,' said Gladios, arriving alongside the boat.

'Coffee?' asked Terence, sticking his head out of the cabin while the kettle boiled. He filled the cafetière and the smell of freshly ground beans awakened Gladios' senses. Suddenly his indigestion began to subside.

'Come on, make yourself comfortable,' insisted Terence, placing a cushion on the cockpit seat so Gladios could sit down. And down he sat, the little ketch rocking in the water when he parked his great derrière. Lovely, thought Gladios, to be on the waterside in this pretty old wooden boat on this pleasant summer's evening. He was quickly regaining his appetite and when Terence thrust a packet of chocolate digestives in his direction, he instinctively reached out and helped himself.

'Milk?' Gladios nodded and within a flash Terence handed him a mug and joined him in the cockpit where they soon became engrossed in idle chatter. It made a welcome respite.

'And what about your mystery, your conundrum; any bright ideas, yet?' Gladios shrugged his shoulders.

'Nothing of any substance. We've all the clues but, we just can't seem to work out what links them together.' Terence smiled sympathetically as he knew this frustrated his new friend.

'Remind me what you have again?' Gladios breathed in and sighed before speaking.

'The Brodgar Ring, a verse from a Byron poem and as of tonight a distant constellation; the Corona Borealis, ever heard of it?' Terence shook his head. Gladios felt his stomach churn and gurgle, making an audible noise. He realised he needed the loo.

'Alright if I go below?' Terence instantly knew what was required.

'Within the bow of the boat,' he directed as Gladios started to climb through the hatch and down the steep steps leading to the WC; rather a bucket vaguely concealed by a shabby curtain! And as Gladios squatted in a sumo stance, taking his full weight while hovering above the target and waiting for his bowels to evacuate he looked up and saw a sextant mounted on the wall and recalled his early navigational training in the Greek Navy, plotting his route from the stars in the sky. Stars, why did that suddenly excite him, tickling his train of thought when suddenly... the CORONA BOREALIS sprang to mind! HOLY MOSES! Was this it? The divine intervention, the stroke of luck, the chance discovery which would set them on their way – a sextant!

There was a shudder and Gladios' bowels began to clear with a *whoosh!* Standing, he collected the bucket before returning to the cockpit.

'I'll empty it.' Terence nodded. It was only polite.

Chapter 45 – Gladios the Great

As the early morning sun streamed in through the window Fortescue lay in Shona's arms, pleased with how things had developed between them. Of course, his mother wouldn't approve; he could hear her words - *hot tempered Irish bint.* She had been longing for him to settle down with Miranda who was much more to her liking. Not that Fortescue cared a jot. Shona had shown a firm, but caring side, one which took him back to his early childhood and his Hungarian nanny, Henast Itsnigel. He felt a warm shiver run down his spine.

'What are we to do today?' he asked when Shona stirred.

'Nothing just yet,' she replied, pulling the duvet over them and squeezing his bum.

*

Donald and Hannah were having breakfast at the quaint Bed and Breakfast, where they were staying, reflecting on the previous day's events and what on earth they were doing here. A video call with the Chief Superintendent was scheduled for ten o'clock when they hoped the pig-headed baboon would change his mind, close the investigation and allow them to return to Edinburgh. The sighting of the wild machete man had heightened their senses and put them on alert, although their concerns were not shared with their superiors who appeared ambivalent to the threat.

'If he still wants us to continue, then I think we simply observe from a distance,' suggested Donald who was fed up pursuing a crime which had already been resolved.

Hannah smiled over her bowl of muesli and nodded.

*

Bruno was sitting in the coffee house, keeping an eye on the hotel, although was surprised to see *Il Porco* trundling back from the harbour with an instrument tucked under his arm. He quickly raised his binoculars and, peering through the glass window, zoomed in for a closer look at the unusual semi-circular shaped object that *Il Porco* was holding. It meant nothing to Bruno, it was too technical by half, but even he thought it worthy of comment so he sent Brialto a text, letting him know what he had seen.

*

Brialto was having breakfast when the message arrived, lighting up his phone which lay on the dining table beside his expresso. Oliver and Gus sat close by, all quiet and calm, but they were interested to hear what Bruno had found out on his early morning recce.

'Instrument, semi-circular instrument. Any ideas what it may be?'

Oliver shrugged.

*

Gladios was out of breath by the time he reached the dining room where his friends were already seated at their usual table in the bay window. Quiet, they were all quiet with little conversation, just a tinkle of cutlery as they buttered toast and poured tea.

'I may have the missing link!' blurted Gladios, sitting down next to Helena and placing the sextant on the table. Everyone stared in silence not really sure what to say.

'Do you know what this is?' he asked, brimming with excitement. His mood was effervescent. Still there was quiet from the dining table. Everyone appeared baffled by the semi-circular instrument with little idea what it may be.

'It's a SEXTANT,' boomed Gladios, 'used in bygone times to navigate the seas from the sun and the stars.'

'And how's it going to assist us?' enquired Helena who felt obliged to say something. Otherwise, the faces remained blank.

'It works off refraction, aligning a planet, usually the sun, and the horizon gives a precise location at a certain time of day.' Everyone looked perplexed, as rightly they should have been, because navigation with a sextant is no easy thing. Gladios realised that his audience were not in tune so he decided to spare them the technical details and cut to the chase.

'In short we have some numbers from the Byron poem and a constellation of stars and perhaps, just perhaps the sextant is the link which pulls these together and unravels the mystery which has baffled us so far.' It was a tantalising proposition, by a long way the best idea they had yet, but the technicalities bamboozled all, apart from Gladios. However, the big Greek gave them a little inspiration and with an air of trepidation and the begins of hope they all congregated outside of the Stromness Hotel, waiting for Ranald to pull up in the Forbes and McKillop van. It was back to the Ring for one last hurrah.

Bruno ambled out of the coffee house after watching them depart and then made his way back to the Orkneyjar Hotel for a debrief with the Duchessa.

*

Beowulf was in the garden shed, rifling through the storage cupboard looking for his costume and muttering to himself.

'Must be here somewhere.' he chortled, opening drawer after drawer, removing old summer hats and garden gloves, racking his brain as to where he had left the suit which he had used only last year. What's that? he thought looking up at the cardboard box on top of the cupboard. He managed to grasp it with the aid of an upturned bucket and garden hoe. Cripes, it was dusty. Sneezing uncontrollably while brushing it clean, he ripped open the top and found what he had been searching for - his minotaur suit - half man and half bull! And there beneath were garlands of artificial flowers which he would wrap around Ezrulie, his devoted helper, to add to the theatre and sense of occasion. Beowulf felt himself getting into the mood, into the zone to perform his demented dance to the hordes of onlookers who would be gathered there tonight to cheer him on.

'ROOOAAARRRR,' Beowulf shouted in preparation for what was to follow later that day.

*

Bruno was in the conference room waiting for the Duchessa to arrive. She had missed breakfast, instead preferring to visit the hotel spa and sit in the sauna for ten minutes before a dip in the pool. Scotland was beginning to bore her. She felt the tug of Venice calling; hot dreamy summer days, stifling heat and choking pollution. Of course, their ancient city would be clogged with ocean cruisers, brimming with chavvy tourists who would congregate in St Mark's Square, but she always managed to avoid the hoi polloi; instead, the Duchessa visited the exclusive haunts of Venetian society with dinner, drinks and cocktail parties galore. It reminded her of the early days with the Duca when she first burst onto Venice's social scene as his second and much younger wife. She even missed Luigi, recalling his well-rounded cabbages and firm courgette.

'Good of you to join us,' said Brialto with a hint of sarcasm as the Duchessa sat down. She smiled distastefully at her lackey and poured herself a coffee from the cafetière before speaking.

'Well, what's on the cards for today?' Bruno caught the Duchessa's attention. He always did; tall, brooding, temperamental - there was something edgy about Bruno that excited the Duchessa. Raising an eyebrow, she signalled for him to speak.

'I saw *Il Porco* this morning, making his way back to the hotel. He had visited the marina to see his new buddy in the pretty little sailing boat.' Bruno paused to draw on his cigarette.

'Go on,' said the Duchessa, trying to winkle out the information.

'He had an instrument.'

'A semi-circular instrument,' said Brialto.

'Yes, a semi-circular instrument,' repeated Bruno with the air of annoyance. He didn't like being patronised by his father.

'Can you to tell us any more about this instrument?' persisted Brialto. Bruno drew on his cigarette again whilst pausing for thought.

'Can you draw it?' asked Fortescue, realising progress was not fast. Shona pushed her notebook and pen forwards.

'Yes, draw it,' insisted Brialto who was becoming fed up with his son's truculent behaviour. Bruno blew smoke rings, appearing to ignore everyone.

'Draw it,' said Brialto, pulling out his Beretta and casually pointing it at his son.

Shona gasped while everyone looked on with apprehension not sure how events would unfold. The Duchessa was used to the Corollas' shenanigans, although on seeing the startled faces around the room she placed her hand on the pistol and pushed it down so it was pointing at the floor.

'Just draw it Bruno… Please.' Within a few seconds he pushed the sketch into the middle of the table for all to see.

'Any ideas?' asked the Duchessa. Fortescue shrugged his shoulders and Gus looked equally blank. However, Oliver was taking a keen interest, peering at the paper closely.

'And was this an eye piece?' he asked, pointing at the image. Bruno shrugged his shoulders and Oliver looked again as the sketch. 'I think, I have it. I think I know what it is.'

'What?' everyone shouted in unison.

'It's a sextant… I think!'

Chapter 46 – With Hope

By the time the Forbes and McKillop van arrived at the Brodgar Ring there were already camper vans and all sorts of clapped-out cars in the parking area including a bus emblazoned with mythical figures. The windows had curtains and from the roof protruded a metal chimney from which faint wisps of smoke drifted. Inside, Rowan and Ceridwen were sitting cross legged beside the stove, drinking nettle tea. They had travelled from North Wales and were looking forward to the solstice celebration and catching up with Beowulf and Ezrulie, their old friends. Yet more cars and vans were being parked, haphazardly, along the public road as the masses continued to arrive.

'Excuse me, why so many people here?' asked Ranald, directing his comment to a young lady with braided hair and a ring through her nose.

'Litha – summer solstice, you not been before?' Ranald shook his head not really sure what Litha entailed although before he could enquire further the young lady furnished some more details. 'Fire, song, dance, you'll like it. And of course... the sacrifice!' Letting out a witches cackle she was gone in a flash. However, Ranald and his merry band were too pre-occupied with Gladios' discovery to be concerned with the impending festival. Like school children they raced to the centre of the Ring.

'We are probably too early,' announced Gladios when he arrived. 'Midday is likely to be the best time to try. Now what were the figures from the poem?'

'Three hundred and twelve lines, twenty verses and the immortal words, what were they Kenny?' asked Ranald.

'Yet still the Gods are just, and crimes are crossed: See here what Elgin won and Elgin lost,' Kenny recited like clockwork.'

'Well, they are within the eighth verse.'

Gladios pondered. He had been so excited by his discovery that he hadn't really considered the measurements and if they would work. He held the sextant to the sun and aligned the eyepiece with the horizon and then looked down at the scales to see what they revealed.

*

Oliver dialled Professor Zinbottle and waited for him to pick up.

'Hello.'

'Hello.' They chatted about this and that, polite preamble, until they got down to the reason behind Oliver's call.

'A sextant! Do you think a sextant may help?' Zinbottle was quiet; he had been caught off guard, bowled by a loose ball which he was not sure how to play.

'A sextant, you say? And what has led you to that?'

'Oh, just a whim,' replied Oliver nonchalantly, not really wanting to go into the detail of where the idea had sprung from.

'Well, they are used to navigate by the stars but it's usually the sun which is the focal point not the Corona…umm… Borealis.'

'Right,' said Oliver not sure what to say next. 'But it's not impossible that it could help in some way?'

'In theory it might, but if you are taking a point off the Corona Borealis then it's not visible until night and even then it's not easy to see.'

'Thanks,' replied Oliver before quickly hanging up.

'We need a sextant.' Fortescue was already onto it, racking his brains and searching the internet on his smart phone.

'Let's try at the sailing club. If they don't have one then they may be able to point us in the right direction.' The Duchessa smiled, pleased there was at last some action. Bruno sulked off to find his little car. He was going back to the Ring to see if *Il Porco* had found anything, yet.

*

It was nearing midday and Gladios was in the centre of the Ring, lining up the sextant and checking the measurements – one hundred and twenty by the arc and forty-eight on the drum. Crikey, it was not even close to the figures they had, not by a long way. He looked at his watch to see that noon was almost upon them.

'Any good?' asked Helena, hopefully. Gladios shook his head and sighed. This wasn't how he imagined it would work. Rather optimistically, he had expected to find the precise location where relics from the Parthenon Temple had been buried, although how he intended to excavate them was not clear, particularly with a crowd of pagans moving in ready for the solstice celebrations. Gladios sat down on the earth bank of the ancient Neolithic circle.

'What about the Corona Borealis?' asked Iona who had been excited by the morning's developments.

'I've got an app,' said Kenny, 'which can locate the stars. Look.' He held up his smart phone so everyone could see. 'It works off satellite navigation.' Gladios glanced at Kenny's phone and the star gazers app.

'It may help, although let's not forget it will be barely dark tonight so it won't be easy to see.' In truth the big Greek was slightly downcast with his great idea. The sextant hadn't even been close to producing figures around the numbers they had. The place was like a circus with druids and pagans everywhere and to escape it all Gladios decided to take a walk along the banks of the Loch of Stenness. He knew he should phone Prodius to update him on events.

*

Fortescue had been to the yacht haven and by the slimmest of chances was redirected to O'Flanagan's Pub in the centre of town. It was open for lunch and there, as he had been advised, beside the gentlemen's loo, hung a peculiar half-moon instrument wired to the wall. The bar man sent him to Kelly O'Flanagan's office where a clean-cut girl with a mischievous twinkle in her eye was sitting. Fortescue was determined, very determined to get hold of that instrument, come what may, although Kelly O'Flanagan was enjoying the tease.

'It belonged to my great uncle. I really don't want to let it go.'

'£500,' snapped Fortescue, keen to close out a deal. Kelly paused, as if she was giving the matter serious thought, but it was a smokescreen because she knew fine well what she was going to do.

£1,000?'

'Deal,' barked Fortescue, holding out his hand although the wise publican wasn't finished, just yet.

'Plus the £200 removal fee.'

'Removal fee?' retorted Fortescue, realising he was being ripped off. Kelly nodded with glee.

'We'll have to repair the wall once it's been taken down.'

'I can hardly believe…' Fortescue stopped mid-sentence and took out his wallet. 'Do you take cards?' Kelly nodded with a triumphant smile. Within a couple of minutes the sale was complete and Fortescue was out of the door. He was soon back at the hotel with his new acquisition.

*

'Excellent,' said Oliver who had just had another chat with Professor Zinbottle on how to work the ancient navigational tool. He held it to the window and looked for the sun, aligning it on the horizon; crikey, he was enjoying himself! The Duchessa was also excited that at last they seemed to be getting closer to whatever her great, great, great uncle may have squirreled away.

'Come on, no time to delay,' said Oliver, indicating to Gus to order some taxis. It was time to visit the Ring to see what they could find with the help of the sextant.

*

Bruno had already arrived in his usual tempestuous manner, parking on the raised verge and cracking the engine sump. Oil started dribbling onto the road. He was surprised by the theatre and atmosphere of the place as pagans and druids congregated everywhere. Tying a handkerchief around his forehead he put on his denim jacket and instantly blended into the crowd. Then meeting some revellers, who were squatting around a fire, Bruno managed to cadge some ganja in exchange for a rolled-up wad of notes.

'Join us bruv!' suggested a bearded man who was pleased with the deal. Bruno accepted and sat down with the little group beside a woman breast-feeding her baby. He rolled a smoke.

*

Beowulf and Ezrulie emerged from the mythical bus, dressed in capes. On they wandered, greeting friends while making their way to the centre of the Ring to check the sacrificial stone was still in place.

*

The Duchessa and her group climbed out of the taxis and were surprised by the sizeable number of straggly and unkempt bodies ambling around. Remarkably, she found the vibe quite uplifting. The Duchessa had never come across anything quite like it in Venice, recalling the non-stop circuit of cocktail parties, evenings at the opera and fine dining on the sun-drenched terraces of the best restaurants. But there was something earthy about these nomadic people with their dogs and feral children, something which took her back to ancient times and her primeval instincts. She felt a whim to join the masses, dress in a sack and let her hair down.

Despite his bandana, the Duchessa spotted Bruno sitting with his new friends, smoking a spliff and enjoying some tea. Brazenly, she strode over and sat down beside her henchman who offered her a drag on his home-made smoke. Inhaling, the Duchessa began to relax into her new surrounds.

Brialto shook his head. What would the Duca think of such behaviour, he mused, remembering the tall, elegant and sophisticated man who was always immaculately dressed in the best Egyptian poplin cotton shirts, neatly fitting trousers and shiny shoes. Otherwise, the rest of the team were delighted that the Duchessa and Bruno were amusing themselves, leaving them to try out the sextant and see what it would reveal.

Oliver had taken charge of the technical side while Gus peered through the eyepiece and aligned it with the sun. Fortescue and Shona stood by, waiting with pen and paper for the readings to see if they could make sense of the riddle.

*

Gladios spoke with Prodius for almost an hour. Surprisingly, he had been understanding and wanted to help once he learned where they were and what they had been up to.

'Let me speak with the Secretary of State for Culture and see if they can offer any assistance.' For Gladios this had been a morale boosting chat and he was now much more upbeat about their prospects and chances of success. With renewed energy he walked back to the Ring in search of the others.

*

Elspeth was in the back of the Forbes and McKillop van, resting on some cushions and breathing heavily. It felt like something was stirring from the depths of within, but… she was not particularly sure. Ranald was at hand although a fat lot of good he was, tending to her with soothing words and the offer of a stale sandwich and a swig of coke. Otherwise, the rest of the motley crew were roaming the site, looking for clues but it was futile with the ongoing pandemonium of the mid-summer celebrations.

'Helena,' shouted Gladios when he spotted her near the Comet Stone to the east of the Ring. A small party of druids were close by, enjoying their lunch of barbequed offerings stuffed between cheap bread rolls and smothered in tomato sauce.

'HELENA,' Gladios wheezed, now out of breath. She looked up to see her colleague trundling towards her as fast as he could. 'I've spoken with Prodius and… he's onside! In fact he's going to speak with the Government to see what support they can provide. And…' he coughed, still catching his breath, 'they're going to look into the star configuration, the Corona Borealis, and help us locate it.' Helena was spell-bound, completely taken by surprise.

'Come on, let's go and tell the others,' she eventually said, leading Gladios through the melee towards the van.

Chapter 47 – The Summer Solstice

When Gladios and Helena arrived at the van they found Elspeth standing up. She felt much better after stretching her legs and things seemed to have settled down. Iona and Kenny were queuing for ice creams which some enterprising druid was selling from the back of an old estate car. Within a couple of minutes they had been served and returned with their cones in hand and by the time they reached the van, Gladios was sitting in the rear with his legs hanging over the bumper. They all clustered around.

'I've spoken with the Bureau,' he said with confidence, 'and they are going to help out. Currently there is someone investigating the Corona Borealis to give us a hand locating it with the sextant and they are also looking into how else they can assist.' Helena smiled, delighted that her nation had taken it upon itself to step up. A proud Greek, she was fed up with austerity, fed up with their standing in the world and fed up with the doomsters and the naysayers for doubting the Bureau's ability to find lost relics from their ancient past. Iona and Kenny smiled at each other while holding their cones with ice cream dripping down the sides. They were torn between a fast-growing infatuation towards each other and the exciting news. Oh, but Elspeth was pragmatic and much more down to earth, not blinded by the fervour; she kept her feet firmly on the ground.

'We haven't found anything yet,' she reminded her boisterous friends, the voice of reason and a steadying hand. Gladios begrudgingly acknowledged this truth, which he fully understood, but for a man who had spent his whole life devoted to the Parthenon Temple any hint of their heritage was just too tantalising not to pursue. He knew it was a long shot with only the slimmest of chances, but he was more determined than ever that his life's work would not be wasted. Instead, it would reap some reward. It was, of course, beyond comprehension and sensible thought, but for some unfathomable reason, Gladios felt he was being guided by the ghost of Phidias, directing him to long lost treasures. He was not to be swayed or put off his task for he knew they were closer than he had ever been before. He felt his smart phone vibrate and looking at the screen saw a message from Prodius.

*

It was almost four o'clock and the afternoon was starting to drift. Fires were being lit all around the Ring, although none on the sacred circle as convention prescribed. This was the mecca, the holy land, not a public picnic site; something the pagans and druids always respected.

Oliver and Gus had been all over the place with their sextant, aligning it to the sun, but however they approached the task they always ended up with readings that had no relevance to the numerical codes which Fortescue had deciphered from the poem. They had called Professor Zinbottle, on a couple of occasions, seeking help and guidance and he always obliged, but however congenial he was on the phone they could sense he was starting to find the whole escapade quite tiresome. Shona and Fortescue seemed pre-occupied with each other and looked to be losing interest by the hour. To all intents and purposes they could have passed for festival goers with their laid-back attitude and easy ways. Oliver was beginning to think that their only route, to whatever Lusieri's watercolour concealed, was as the mad Italian had suggested; let *Il Porco* do his work and then snatch the lolly. Crazy as it seemed, he was now thinking that Bruno had as good a chance as anyone of recovering the treasures, if indeed, any existed at all. And reminding himself of the crazy Italian, Oliver recalled he hadn't seen him for some time, nor for that matter, the Duchessa.

*

Bruno was still sitting cross-legged with his newfound friends, smoking gange and drinking cups of nettle tea. He had bought a round of hot dogs from the burger van, which was parked on the verge, and shared these with his posse of pagans who had been pleased with his offering. Cribbio! the smokes were good, raw and undiluted; Bruno puffed on them like a steam locomotive going up a hill. The Duchessa had left some time ago after working her way through a whole joint and feeling, well, how shall we put it... giddy! She had been helped to her feet by Brialto who had been standing close by. Within a couple of minutes he had organised a taxi to take them back to the hotel for afternoon tea. It seemed remarkably civilised after the earlier events but the Duchessa was adamant that she would return later.

*

Donald and Hannah approached the Ring with caution but with so many pagans and druids roaming around they now felt safer, merging into the crowds and not instantly recognisable. Once into the central throng, Donald threaded a route through the bodies while Hannah kept a look out for the mad machete man with his cold blade of steel. The mere thought of him made her pulse race and the hairs on the back of her neck stand. Backup had eventually been authorised by the Chief Superintendent and the local police force were on standby in case anything untoward occurred. However, nowhere to be seen was the big Italian who was still in his cluster of pagans smoking dope. On Donald and Hannah prowled while they started to enjoy the carnival atmosphere and the sense of occasion.

*

Gladios lay on the grass in an adjoining field adrift from the merry revellers so he could speak on the phone while Helena remained close by aimlessly picking meadow flowers to fill in the time. Ranald and Elspeth had gone back to the hotel for supper and Gladios suddenly felt a pang of guilt that he had dragged them to this far flung land in search of Greek treasures. Elspeth was in no condition to be travelling, not in her state, only a couple of weeks from her due date. It was just after six, eight o'clock Greek time, when Gladios' smart phone vibrated and he saw a message appear from Prodius. Must be working late he thought, delighted by the effort and diligence the Bureau were putting in. Gladios was proud of his countrymen who seemed to be rising to the challenge in their quest for success. He looked down at the screen - *The Corona Borealis should be visible tonight in a southerly direction at seventy-eight degrees. Hard to see with the naked eye, particularly at midsummer when it barely gets dark. You will need a telescope.*

A telescope thought Gladios. Lordy be, where was he going to get a telescope from in this god-forsaken place. He decided to call Prodius.

'Hello, I thought you might phone.' He had been expecting Gladios to ring. He always did when he was unsure and he guessed that his colleague would now be more confused than ever and not clear about what his next steps should be. 'We can get a telescope shipped out to you, but it will take a couple of days.'

'That may be too late,' replied Gladios with a hint of panic in his voice. His obsession with the Parthenon and the treasures she once held had become all consuming, enveloping him to the extent that he could barely think of anything else. He paused and reflected.

He had missed Fatima and their meals together at the Sarcophagus Tavern, the warmth of a Greek summer and drinking rosé wine on their terrace in the evening while watching the sun go down. He had been away from his homeland for a number of weeks, and he now found himself on a wild Scottish archipelago with only the slimmest of clues to help.

'Too late?' questioned Prodius, sensing alarm.

'Yes, too late,' replied Gladios, reinforcing the point. And then, deciding to furnish some more detail, explained to his long-standing friend that other factions were also on the hunt for their prized treasure. Yes, their treasure, Greek treasures which other nations had plundered over the years. This instilled a little urgency into Prodius who now seemed to understand their predicament.

'Leave it with me; I'll see what I can do.'

*

Gladios knocked on the door to room number sixteen at the Central Hotel in Stromness and after a couple of seconds he heard footsteps and the door lock jangle. Ranald's head appeared around the side.

'I just wanted to check Elspeth is okay,' blurted out the big man. Ranald nodded, opening the door to allow Gladios in. He was relieved to see her stretched out on the double bed watching TV. Elspeth smiled.

'You don't mind if I don't get up?' Gladios nodded, delighted that she was alright and then, after updating them on events, he made his way back to reception where Helena was waiting.

'Come, I've had an idea,' she said with that eternal optimism that only youth can bring. Too young to know failure, her eyes were alight, brimming with excitement; this was a young lady who was far from done. On Helena marched with hardly a word said, out of the hotel and across the road towards the marina. Of course, Gladios thought, his brain kicking into gear as he guessed where he was being led.

'Where's the boat moored… Matilda, is it?' asked Helena. Gladios smiled.

'Second pontoon on the left,' he replied while quickening his pace; he was jogging, no running as they hurried along to see if his newfound friend could help out, again.

'Terence, Terence?' called Gladios before jumping on board, causing the wee boat to bobble and roll as it had done before.

'Anyone in?' he shouted, poking his head down the hatch to see if he could find Terence in the galley. The curtain in the bow of the boat twitched and Gladios instantly knew that he was otherwise engaged.

'He'll be up in a minute,' he said, reversing back into the cockpit and sitting down. They waited.

'Hallo,' said Terence coming up through the hatch, holding the bucket with an old towel draped over the top. 'What can I do for you? How can I help this time?' he asked while jumping onto the pontoon and leaving his cargo by the bollard to be emptied later.

'Telescope,' boomed Gladios, too excited to say anything else.

'A telescope?' repeated Terence.

'Yes, a telescope,' intervened Helena as impetuous as ever. 'We need a telescope to locate the stars tonight - the Corona Borealis.'

'Ah, the Corona… yes, the Corona, whatever it's called. The constellation which is going to lead you to your long-lost treasures.' Terence was smiling, plainly not convinced by their tale.

'Well, do you have one?' pushed Helena.

'What, a telescope?' replied Terence.

'YES, A TELESCOPE!' re-asserted Gladios and Helena in unison, with a trace of desperation creeping into their voices. There was quiet, an air of anticipation.

'Of course,' said Terence with a smirk and a smile. 'What good sea-faring captain would be without one? I take it you want to borrow my telescope?' Gladios nodded, relieved that his friend had, yet again, come to the rescue and helped them out. He sagged into his frame, his shoulders sagging with the relief that they had located a scope, the next piece of the jigsaw on their voyage of hope.

'Fancy some supper?' he asked.

Terence nodded and after collecting the telescope they stepped onto the pontoon to make their way into town and find a suitable place to dine. Helpfully, Gladios picked up the bucket and off they strode.

Chapter 48 – The Festival gets Underway

Beowulf was dressed in a fur cape, tied at the waist with a leather rope. It stretched down to his knees and had been given to him as a present by the Yukon Druid and Pagan Society when they visited in 1991.

'Pass me my staff,' he commanded of Ezrulie, brusque in his manner while starting to slip into character – King Beowulf of Twatt – Chief Pagan of the Northern Isles and master of the surrounding seas. And Ezrulie was his loyal Queen, maiden of his heart's desire and mother to their only child, Bronwen, conceived in this very ring almost thirty-six years ago.

'Come,' said Beowulf, beckoning Ezrulie forward and onto the path leading to the Ring. He was bearded and unkempt with shaggy long hair and looked a majestic sight, marching with his followers to cheers and applause. Beowulf was the Alpha dominant of all gathered here, the chieftain, the great one, the one who must be obeyed. Up to the fire he strode to meet fellow druids and pagans who were waiting for the celebrations to begin.

*

It was quite a scene as the crowds began to converge, dressed for the occasion, almost Neolithic in their character from an ancient time. Adults led while children followed and dogs lolloped on behind, having left their camps and picnicking places where they had enjoyed barbeques, grog and song in readiness for what was to come.

Bruno was still with his ramshackle friends including a pretty, young druid, Calliope, who was barefooted and had come on her own. She had an enormous ring right through her nose and smouldering emerald eyes which Bruno found irresistible in his current state. He wished to impress her on this day of celebrations to the Sun and the Gods for which he now felt complete adulation. So, when Calliope suggested he should wear a smock, Bruno jumped at the chance and was now clad in a Harris Tweed drape, looking the part. But while the drape gave an innocence to this towering man it concealed his machete blade, sharpened, lethal and ready to surprise.

'Follow me,' beckoned Calliope, holding out her hand and encouraging him to join the procession snaking to the centre of the Ring. Up he stood in his new garb and followed this earth woman towards the crowd.

*

'Beowulf, Beowulf, Beowulf,' chanted the masses while he stood at the centre of the Ring, close to the fire with Ezrulie at his side. He recited poems to the Wiccan Gods, full of love and cheer, and the crowds roared him on while drinking beer. Bruno was dragged forward by this wicked girl who danced provocatively as she began to twirl and the large Italian, all muscle and brawn, swayed his hips; he was ready to jive until dawn. Crumbs, it was only half past eight and the crowd were already feverish with excitement, enjoying themselves on this mid-summer night.

*

On the outskirts of the crowd not far from the Ring, Donald and Hannah were gazing in at the hordes of wild, drunken pagans getting into the spirit of things. They had eaten at the burger van but been wary to keep their distance in case they should stumble into the machete man. Otherwise, they had kept tabs on the group, observing them leave just after six and tracking their movements on the police app saw that the van had returned to Stromness. The young couple, Kenny and his companion, had remained on site and were traipsing around hand in hand, appearing half smitten with one another.

'Shall we follow them?' Hannah had asked when the van first left. However, Donald had been firm and decided to remain put. He felt sure if anything was going to happen then it would do so at the Ring.

*

It was half past eight when the Duchessa returned. Dinner had been pleasant enough, in fact, she had quite enjoyed Brialto's company, sharing a bottle of wine together and reminiscing about the old days when the Duca was still alive.

'What would he have made of our trip?' she asked her trusty old adviser who shrugged his shoulders as he usually did. He was missing Venice and his old ways, extorting money out of hard-working Venetians and collecting ten percent from the interests he managed. The Duca, of course, would have thought what nonsense it was to have bought the painting for such an extortionate price, on some vague family connection, let alone go in search of treasures in deepest Scotland.

'I'm sure he would be proud of you,' replied Brialto, tactfully, not wishing to upset his longstanding client.

The Duchessa ignored the comments and started on the short walk along the hard track towards the Ring with all the waifs and strays, and riff raff which a summer solstice festival brings in. Brialto plodded on behind while looking menacingly at these unusual folk dressed in all sorts of bohemian wear. He instinctively felt the holster within his brushed wool jacket and the reassuring solid shape of his pistol.

*

It was almost nine thirty when Gladios, Helena and Terence stepped out of the harbour side bar with a stomach full of scampi and chips and plenty of beer. Helena was impatient that they should return to the Ring and had already called Ranald and Elspeth who were keen to re-join them. They had the telescope and after bidding Terence farewell made their way back to the hotel where the Forbes and Mackillop van was waiting. Within a few minutes they arrived at Brodgar where they could see the fires burning, smoke billowing upwards and being whisked away on the gentle evening breeze. Ranald dropped them off and then went to park further along the road.

'Are you sure you're okay?' asked Gladios as they walked down the track towards the stone circle. Elspeth nodded, although deep down she was not so sure - she was firmly in the drop zone, with all that may bring! But Elspeth was feisty and didn't like to miss out. She was determined to join them on the final leg of their outrageous quest. By the time Ranald had caught up, they had found Kenny and Iona and were already making a plan.

*

Bruno was unrecognisable from his usual self, apart from the suede cowboy boots which he was still wearing; otherwise, he looked bedraggled in his new druid's cape.

Calliope danced to the makeshift band, a man with some bongo drums and a flute-playing friend. And there was music elsewhere, drifting on the breeze, the strum of a banjo, the jangle of bells while the wail of some bag pipes kept everyone attention upheld. It was a haphazard shuffle which Bruno and Calliope performed, her bare feet moving neatly between his cumbersome boots. The audience applauded, clapping to the beat of the thunderous Italian who danced like an ape with two left feet.

'Here, have a smoke, big man,' offered a pagan, thrusting a joint towards the dancing couple. Calliope snatched it with eager delight and after inhaling on the wicked weed, snogged dear Bruno while exhaling her smoke and making the Italian nearly choke. But Bruno was strong, as strong as an ox, gulping in air he was not going to detox. On roared the crowd as they created a scene; as a warmup act they were almost obscene!

Beowulf watched, pleased with the sight. It gave him a break from entertaining the masses for he knew when midnight arrived, he would have to step forward for the sacrificial ceremony. A present to the gods for the bounty of summer and fertility of mankind.

*

Fortescue and Shona had enjoyed a dalliance on the banks of the Loch of Harray away from the crowds in a quiet bay. He had whimpered, as he always did, the seemingly peerless arrogance evaporating and revealing his true self. Tenderly, he took hold of Shona's hand and led her back towards the Ring to find the rest of their team. Up the field, through the fluttering summer grasses, swaying in the breeze, and within ten minutes they neared the parking area where they found Oliver and Gus sitting on the verge eating fish and chips. They were hungry, not having eaten since midday and were ravenously devouring their supper.

'Where is the Duchessa?' asked Fortescue. There was no response as Oliver finished his mouthful, almost gasping for breath, he was eating so fast. He pointed to the Ring and then after swallowing was able to speak.

'Gone with Brialto for a walk.' Shona, no longer distracted by the attentions of her lover, realised she was also hungry and keen for some food. The burger van was close by and looking at Fortescue she cursorily nodded towards the queuing diners. His eyes were bright, almost defiant in their illumination, although it was futile to resist. With a wag of her finger, he did not disobey.

'Ketchup?' Shona nodded and Fortescue scuttled off.

'Where is Bruno?' she asked Gus who was washing down his supper with a can of ginger beer. In reality they were keen to catch up with the big man because they were all coming around to his great idea that it would be simplest to *COMMANDEER* whatever treasures were found!

Commandeer? What a fine old word, far better than stealing, pilfering or just plain old theft which had been hard to come to terms with for such upstanding folk. Fortescue had helped out though, and put their minds at rest, when unintentionally he mentioned – *commandeering* - a much better phrase. It gave a sense of necessity, the greater good, even public spirited. If all else failed, Bruno would *commandeer* as he saw fit. This now seemed respectable and above board but for the essential piece within this great masterplan and that was the big Italian. No one had heard from him since the morning when he had left the hotel. They had texted and called, left repeated voice messages which yielded nothing despite their endeavours. In fact, his battery was flat; he was pre-occupied with Calliope and smashed out of his head. He barely knew where he was while dancing in the middle of the Ring to continued cheer.

*

Helena had the telescope wedged in her bag while Gladios held the sextant firmly as they walked briskly down the track towards the Ring. It was still pleasantly warm, despite nearing ten o'clock, and the sun could still be seen beyond Loch Stromness on the distant horizon.

Gladios knew they needed a darker night sky if they were to have any chance of seeing the stars, particularly the Corona Borealis which is distant and not easy to find. He hoped Prodius had some decent pointers to help out, or he feared they would never manage to locate it.

The fire in the centre blazed, fuelled with tinder-dry wood and the occasional old tyre, sending black waves of smoke billowing into the sky. The druids and pagans knew how to enjoy themselves with the revelry excelling and the tempo increasing. Beowulf was still holding court, beside the sacrificial stone, discussing the order of offerings and what would be first to fall under his sword.

On Gladios scuttled with Ranald and Elspeth bringing up the rear until they were at the far side of the Ring where it was a little quieter, apart from the odd frolicking druid who had drunk too much. The sun was now setting and looked ready to disappear below the horizon, allowing twilight to descend. They were unsure how easy it would be to find the Corona Borealis in the heavens above as doubt crept into their grand plan. Gladios decided to give Prodius a call to find out if his team of experts had any suggestions which might help.

Chapter 49 – The Minotaur Arrives

Beowulf and Ezrulie had returned to their camper van where the ageing pagan was butt naked and struggling to get into his Minotaur suit.

'Gently,' he shouted, as Ezrulie pulled up the rear zip, giving his buttocks a playful squeeze, before zipping the suit up to the neck. 'I don't know why I do it,' Beowulf muttered, already starting to feel hot and clammy in the cheap plastic suit.

'They love it,' Ezrulie reminded her husband who instantly recalled the loud cheers elicited every year when he would slice the sacrificial offering in two. Beowulf smiled laconically, accepting his fate. After a sip of nettle tea, laced with home-made gin, he picked up the bull's head hood, with its pointed horns, and slipped it on. Stepping out of the van he looked resplendent - half bull and half man! Ezrulie held out her hand and together they set off on the track back to the Ring.

Prayers to the Gods would begin at eleven with his sword being unsheathed from half-past the hour ready for the sacrifice just before midnight. The inebriated followers would be raucous, dancing around to great cheer and egging him on. Beowulf was getting into the mood and the right frame of mind to whip up the crowd into a storm.

*

'We just can't see it,' said Gladios into his handset while Kenny held the telescope to his right eye where he could barely make out the more obvious constellations.

'Find Hercules!' said Prodius who was still in the office with the astronomical experts at well after midnight. They were desperate for success and determined to throw everything at this tender lead, the delicate thread which Gladios had unearthed. He looked down at his smart phone and the plan of the northern hemisphere stars.

Kenny heard the directions bellowing through the audio which was on loudspeaker, although, try as he did, he just couldn't find Hercules in the twilight. The sun may have disappeared below the horizon, but it was hardly nightfall as they had hoped. It was the *simmer dim* when it never truly became dark in the Northern Isles.

'It's in between Bootes and Hercules,' continued Prodius who was barking out commands to his long-standing friend. It meant little to Gladios, though, while he peered at the brightly lit sky of the midsummer night. He sighed, they had been on the phone for over an hour and were no closer to finding the Corona Borealis, let alone any clues it held, than when they first started. It frustrated Gladios that they had not made the progress he had hoped for and, fed up with the discussions, he bade farewell to his dear old friend.

*

Resorting to espionage Fortescue had divided the team up and was ready to send them in different directions to search for the Greek contingent and find out what they were up to. No sign of Bruno anywhere, despite the numerous calls and messages they had left on his phone. He seemed to have disappeared, much to the annoyance of Brialto and the Duchessa. Without the big man no one had an inkling what the Greek party looked like.

'Show some initiative,' Fortescue insisted. 'We know one of them is quite large - *Il Porco.* Look for anything suspicious.' With hundreds of pagans and druids roaming all over the place the odds appeared to be stacked against them, but devoid of any other ideas they left in pairs to see what they could find.

*

Ranald was sitting with Elspeth, close to the Comet Stone on the southeast side of the Ring. It was isolated, situated on its own circular earth plinth and an impressive sight, towering over them, a fatherly figure within this barren land. Kenny and Iona seemed to have given up on their quest and were now joining in and enjoying the celebrations. They had found an elderly man selling home-made beer from a trestle table which they sipped from plastic cups while watching the festivities unfold.

'I think Gladios is struggling,' said Ranald, realising that they still hadn't found the Corona Borealis. Looking towards the sky and the simmer dim it appeared unlikely to make a showing tonight.

'There must be something else which can help us,' said Elspeth who despite her condition had become wrapped up in the whole adventure - their search for ancient Greek treasure on these wild Scottish Isles. 'I've re-read the poem a couple of times and as much as I have racked my brains, I can't find any more clues.'

'I know,' said Ranald who had also been back through the text again and again.

Gladios and Helena who had been traipsing around the site to collect their thoughts joined them. They sat down in a huddle on the grassy knoll.

'We've just been running through everything,' said Elspeth, 'to see if we can approach the conundrum in another way.' Gladios nodded, grateful for their help. However, it was pointless to deny that their efforts, to date, hadn't reaped the rewards they had hoped for. Prodius had been helpful and no one could fault his endeavours in their time of need. Although despite the hours they had put in the fruit of the Corona Borealis seemed but a distant dream.

'Let's start from the beginning,' said Helena who still had passion and refused to give up. 'We know roughly when the marbles were shipped to Britain between 1801 and 1805 and that Lord Elgin's intention was to house them in Scotland at his home in Fife. One ship sank and the records indicate they docked in London, although, as we have previously thought, an assignment could have been diverted to Scotland.

'And we think this was the hand of Lusieri?' interrupted Elspeth. Helena nodded.

'What if the Corona Borealis has nothing to do with the map?' said Ranald suddenly. 'It barely fits the pentimento and the only reason we latched onto it was because of some eavesdropping old Hamish picked up on.' He had always been a bit sceptical about the merits, or otherwise, of these distant stars. There was quiet while everyone paused not sure what to say until Helena broke the impasse.

'What if the numbers from the poem mean something else?'

'Well, what?' asked Gladios who felt they were about to go around in a big loop.

*

Fortescue and Shona stood some distance away and observed the little posse close to the Comet Stone. The rotund dark-haired man seemed to fit the description of *Il Porco;* and, nor was he dressed as a pagan just like the rest of the group. Fortescue reached for his smart phone to send a text - *Positive I.D. in the southeast corner near the large stone.*

*

The Duchessa who had become bored of being chaperoned by Brialto and had given him the slip, ignored Fortescue's text and instead mingled with the crowds, deciding to learn a little more about the pagan way of life.

*

Bruno had been subdued by the wacky smokes and was now sitting with Calliope watching from the side while Beowulf, dressed as a Minotaur, stood in the centre of the Ring with Ezrulie close by. It was approaching midnight and the time had come for his act to begin. The fires roared with smoke billowing skywards as Beowulf began his well-rehearsed routine - stomping to and fro around the sacrificial stone, reciting his verses and waving his sword to the heavens, whipping the crowd into a frenzy. Rowan arrived carrying a sack containing the bountiful offerings to be served to the gods!

*

Gladios was lying on his side, close to the Comet Stone while lining up the sextant with the head stone beside the northwest causeway. Ranald had a copy of the badly scrawled images they had seen within Lusieri's painting and was providing a narrative as best he could.

247

'Try aligning it with the stone beside the south-eastern entrance.' These appeared the most significant landmarks within the ring and with little else to guide them they had decided to use the sextant in a different way, searching for the point which coincided with the measurements they had deduced from the poem; the eighth verse of twenty.

Slowly Gladios moved the lower arm, bringing the stone downwards until it aligned with its counterpart on the eastern entrance and then without bothering to finely adjust the drum, he looked at the measurement - twenty degrees!

'I think you may be onto something,' said Gladios, brimming with excitement as his hand began to shake. With the sextant repositioned he turned the drum to determine the minutes and once delicately adjusted he looked at the reading.

'Eight – EUREKA!'

*

Beowulf reached inside the sack and pulled out the first offering – a cucumber. It still had the ruddy Tesco sticker on but too late to be bothered by such minor details, he quickly slapped it on the sacrificial stone.

'WHOARRRR,' roared the crowd, stamping their feet on the ground and egging him on. Hot air could be seen snorting from the bull's nose. Bruno started giggling.

'It's a cucumber,' he shouted with glee while standing up and pointing at the long green vegetable.

'WHOARRR,' bellowed Beowulf, bringing his old sword downwards and neatly cutting it in two. The crowd roared with excitement as Bruno began to snigger. He had smoked too much baccy and barely knew where he was let alone understand the importance of the sacred act.

Again Beowulf raised his hands to the heavens while reciting prayers to the deities above and getting ready for the next offering. Ezrulie handed him a melon which he held above his head before placing it on the stone and grasping his sword with both hands.

'WHOARR...' the crowd cheered. Beowulf raised his sword above his head, but, before he could dispatch the next piece of fruit Bruno shoved him out the way. With his machete in hand, he started mutilating the tacky, yellow melon; flailing his sharp blade up and down, backwards and forwards and from side to side, slashing the orb into a hundred pieces!

*

Hannah stood transfixed on the edge of the Ring her eyes wide open. She felt her palms go clammy as adrenalin began to flow. Tugging Donald on the sleeve of his jacket she managed to speak.

'It's him!' No more needed to be said because Donald also recognised the psychopathic thug and the brutality of how he used his weapon. He reached for his phone and called the emergency number for Kirkwall Police Station.

*

Kenny and Iona received a text from Ranald informing them of their great discovery and on hearing the news they raced back to the van to collect the spade and metal detector. Around the crowds they jogged with their equipment, making their way to the Comet Stone.

*

Beowulf was angry, incandescent with rage. Who was this interloper who had stolen the stage, his evening of celebration and his moment of fame? Holding his sword flat, WHACK, he slapped Bruno around the head with venom. The big Italian swayed from the force of the strike. He momentarily saw a bright flash of light while staggering on his feet, moving left then right. But before he could regain his composure he heard a wailing scream and turning around saw the head of a bull coming his way!

Beowulf was old and a little overweight, although despite the odds being stacked against him he connected with his full weight into Bruno's midriff and sent him spiralling to the ground. Ezrulie, looking to capitalise on events, brought a sacrificial turnip down on to his head, splitting it in two. This appeared to be the cue for widespread participation as Bruno's newfound friends joined in the fray. Calliope jumped onto the back of the Minotaur which ignited the two sides and stoked the fires of a drunken brawl!

*

Kenny switched on the metal detector and it instantly bleeped!

'It's just a test,' he reassured and then moved off, circling the stone to see what his machine would reveal. Around he went in a clockwise direction slowly swinging the detector, backwards and forwards, as he held it a few inches above the ground. Then, after a couple of ever decreasing circuits, green lights started flashing on the screen and everyone froze… BLEEEEPPPPP!!!

Chapter 50 – Athena Parthenos

Fortescue was standing beside Shona when Oliver and Gus arrived at the edge of the Ring. Blue flashing lights could be seen in the distance, approaching from Kirkwall, and the unmistakeable wail of a police siren was growing ever louder. Tapping Oliver on the arm, Fortescue pointed towards the stone where they could just make out industrious bodies taking it in turn to dig.

'They're onto something,' he said.

Oliver looked at Gus and he nodded. They had witnessed the debacle, break out earlier, and had chatted at some length while half-heartedly searching their area. The whole adventure had seemed fun to start with. Paid for by the Duchessa they'd nothing to lose in joining her bespoke team and decamping to Scotland for what had been the best part of a month. However, they were good folk at heart, decent upstanding people and the presence of Brialto and Bruno had unnerved them. Fortescue and Shona seemed blinded by ambition and, to cut to the chase, they weren't struck on stealing whatever treasures were found.

'It's not for us,' said Oliver hastily. Fortescue paused, not sure what to say. 'We've discussed it and we think it's best to let the authorities sort it out,' continued Oliver. Gus nodded in agreement.

'I doubt the authorities, whoever they are, will get anywhere near the treasure let alone sort it out,' snapped Shona. 'If we don't act now it will disappear and probably never be seen again.' Brialto arrived after becoming fed up searching for the Duchessa. He had watched Bruno flailing around in the mass brawl and for once decided not to intervene. The Minotaur seemed to have plenty of support and, along with his fellow pagans, Beowulf appeared to be getting the upper hand.

'Found anything?' he asked. Fortescue nodded and pointed to the little huddle beside the Comet Stone who now seemed to be digging ever faster.

*

The police van arrived and out jumped a full complement of twelve officers. They met Donald and Hannah beside the hard track leading to the Ring and following a quick debrief and description of Bruno they set off, at a sharp pace, towards the fire. Donald and Hannah followed on behind, however, by the time they arrived things appeared to have settled down. Bruno was lying in the perimeter ditch, tied and gagged with a couple of hairy druids sitting on top.

Beowulf asked, 'Can I help you?'

*

Kenny had dug no more than a foot when he felt his spade hit something beneath the rocky soil. It was firm, although flexed on impact and made a hollow sound. Scraping he revealed a wooden surface.

'I've found something,' he exclaimed as everyone peered into the small hole to see what he had discovered. Kenny was now digging frantically at the edges, shovelling the dirt as fast as he could and within a couple of minutes had revealed a substantial wooden covering.

'Break it open,' said Helena, realising it would take some time to dig up, but before Kenny had a chance to act, Gladios stepped down onto the wooden panel. Everyone heard the splintering crack and within a flash… he had dropped out of sight!

*

'Follow me,' said Brialto, starting to walk towards the Comet Stone, slowly, methodically and with purpose. The picture belonged to the Duchessa and it was the picture which had helped find the treasure. And to Brialto's rather simplistic way of thinking, the treasure was the Duchessa's and therefore ten percent belonged to the Corolla's! It was time to collect his dues.

Helena saw them coming and instantly recognised the squat shape of the troublesome little Italian whom she had seen at the Charleston Hotel when they had stayed in Edinburgh.

'We've got visitors,' she said to the rest of the group who were still peering down the hole.

'You okay?' shouted Kenny, concerned for his Greek friend. Although when the dust cleared, he could see the top of Gladios' head move, just below ground level, as he heard him groan.

*

The big Greek could taste the dust which was gradually clearing. He shuffled his feet forwards then backwards, relieved nothing seemed to hurt. His back was grazed from the fall although, otherwise, he felt fine. Rotating his head left then right he took in the stone-lined walls which appeared to surround him. It looked like he had fallen into a small priest hole or something of that sort. Instinctively, he felt his new surrounds, allowing his hands to roam over the rough hued stones while feeling the dimensions of the small space where he now found himself. Sharp irregular edges apart from what felt like a gap to the front just below his belly line. In his hands went, like octopus tentacles, until something wobbled which he instinctively grasped before it fell to the ground. It was solid, reassuringly solid, intricate, angular and pointed in parts. Gladios lifted his find upwards until it was level with his eyes. He gasped, as there before him was… *Athena Pathenos!* Not the original, of course, good heavens no, the original was forty-four feet high the pride of the Parthenon Temple and a most distinguished piece of work, until it was stripped by Lachares to pay his troops. This was a miniature of, arguably, Greece's greatest chryselephantine sculpture, surely, created by the hand of none other than Phidias himself. Gladios felt his chest grow and his hands begin to tingle at the sudden realisation that his life at the Bureau had not been completely wasted. Far from it, the big man had his hands on their history. His place in the hearts of his nation would be immortalised forever. The sky suddenly went dark when Kenny slid some broken planks over the hole and his jacket on top.

*

Helena stood at the front of the little posse with her hands on her hips, majestic and defiant, like Athena herself. Whatever her bumbling colleague had stumbled into she wasn't for standing aside and letting this obnoxious little man through. Otherwise, Kenny and Iona lurked

253

behind, not sure what to do, while Ranald knelt beside Elspeth who just had to sit down. She was breathing heavily and had a look of concern.

Brialto was followed by Fortescue and Shona, and despite protesting, Oliver and Gus had also been dragged along. The squat Italian stopped in front of Helena and held her stare. The scar over his right eye flickering as if afflicted by a nervous twitch. Brialto said nothing and neither did Helena while standing her ground and not giving way. He grinned sarcastically, scorning this young woman who blocked his path, and then stepped to the left. Helena stepped to her right and squared up to this evil little man who reached inside his jacket and pulled out the Beretta. He signalled with the barrel for her to move aside, but Helena had fire in her belly and on occasions, air in her head. She stayed put. It was dangerous to defy this nasty little villain with a loaded pistol pointing in her direction, but defy him she did, not shifting an inch.

CRACK! … Brialto caught her with the handle of his gun, knocking Helena to the ground and leaving this young maiden clutching her head. Kenny left Iona's side and leapt to her defence, but after a couple of steps forward, Brialto squeezed his trigger finger, unloading a couple of shots into the sky. Kenny stopped in his tracks. He instinctively raised his arms.

Ranald was shielding Elspeth who was breathing hard as her cheeks became redder and her brow started to glow. She felt there was movement afoot.

Pushing Kenny to one side Brialto continued towards the hole which was not very well concealed under the jacket. Fortescue was soon at his side and bent down to remove the coat and reveal the opening. Gladios felt some soil spill from above.

*

But the gunshots had raised the alarm. The police, who were already on site, began running towards the Comet Stone to see what was going on and suddenly there was a stampede of pagans and druids sprinting in from all directions to find out what the commotion was about. Bruno was left on his own and without the weight of the hefty druids holding him down he soon managed to loosen the rope shackles and free himself. There was his machete lying in the grass, only a few yards away, and once reunited with his trusty weapon he started ambling towards the stone.

*

'I think my waters have broken,' said Elspeth, feeling a warm surge run down her inside leg. Gentle contractions were starting to wave through her lower body and she instantly knew that childbirth had begun.

'I'll phphphone for an ambulance,' stuttered Ranald, grasping his handset and pulling it from his pocket. But before he could scroll to the keypad…KERRBOOM. Brialto unloaded a bullet into the ground at his feet. He shook his head and Ranald let his phone drop and raised his arms.

*

The shot stopped the police in their tracks, bringing them to an abrupt halt about a hundred yards from the Comet Stone. But while the men in blue wished to go no further there was a surge from behind as the crowds concertinaed. Beowulf, still dressed in his Minotaur suit, pushed his way to the front.

'Hold it there sir,' ordered the police sergeant.

'Hold it where?' questioned Beowulf, in a muffled tone, through his costume. Looking around the sergeant jumped, startled by the appearance of the bull's head! Ezrulie arrived and stood by her husband.

*

'*Il Porco,*' shouted Brialto, looking down at the jet-black mop of hair within the hole. Gladios said nothing, instead, he clutched the statue of Athena held below his belly line well out of view.

'What have you found, fat man?' continued Brialto, enjoying the torment and power he wielded from above while he pointed his pistol. 'You not going to answer me, fatso?' he persisted. Still no reply. 'Then I will have to shoot you!'

Gladios heard the click as the gun was cocked and he knew that his time was nigh. Yet, despite the dire situation he found himself in, he was at peace, clutching the miniature *Athena Parthenos* which he felt was surely the work of Phidias's hand. He could feel it through his palms. Fatima would be upset, of course, although his state pension would keep her in the manner to which she had become accustomed. And then there was his dear friend, Prodius, and all of his other colleagues at the Greek Bureau of Culture. Nearly forty years of dedicated service, the trials and tribulations, their successes (none), their disasters (quite a few) and the long suppers they had enjoyed at the Sarcophagus Tavern. He would miss the Aegean Sea, long hot summer days basking in the sunshine in a quiet cove, he would miss the feral goats in the Kolkonos Hills and he would miss Greece and all things Greek.

*

'I can feel a head coming,' shouted Elspeth who had quickly dilated and was fast moving through the stages of childbirth. 'AAARRRGGGHHH,' she yelled with venom while clutching Ranald's hand. Iona was staring at her and quickly realised she needed to get Elspeth's trousers off.

'Look away,' she shouted to the small group gathered at the hole.

'AAARRGGHHH,' bellowed Elspeth, as the contractions got underway.

Ezrulie heard the screams and she instantly recognised the pitch and tone.

'There's a woman giving birth over there,' she said to the policeman who along with his colleagues had their hands outstretched keeping everyone back.

'We need to do a risk assessment before approaching,' the officer replied.

'Risk assessment,' protested Ezrulie, suddenly inflamed by the response.

'OOOWWWHHH,' shouted Elspeth again. The womanhood was too strong. Ezrulie knew what that poor kindred spirit was going through and she had no intention of standing by.

'F _ _ k your risk assessment,' she said before ducking under the policeman's arm and starting to run. Beowulf was startled by his wife's sudden intervention, but he wasn't about to let her run on her own. Shoving the officer to one side he set off after Ezrulie at a terrific pace. And where the Minotaur goes others follow. There was a surge and a shout as over a hundred pagans and druids started on the hundred-yard dash towards the Comet Stone.

*

Brialto had been unsettled by the shouts and the screams. Hesitating, he had turned to see what the commotion was about and was presented with a horde of savages, stampeding forwards, shouting and bellowing while covering the ground.

CRACK, CRACK - he fired a couple of shots into the air as those close to him took cover, diving to the floor. Ezrulie was within forty yards and proving rather spritely for a lady of a certain age! Beowulf was closing in on his agile wife and suddenly the Minotaur was leading the charge with his horns to the fore. Brialto lowered his pistol settling the open sights on the bull's head ready to squeeze the trigger when suddenly... he felt a hand grab his right leg which was pulled from beneath him as he fell to the ground, unloading a bullet into the earth. Gladios had summoned enough strength to shuffle up the hole and timely intervene. He slipped back into his dark dungeon.

Brialto managed to get back on his feet but by the time he had recovered his poise the pagans were getting mightily close and nearly upon him. He squeezed the trigger while pointing at the oncoming crowd only to hear a solitary… CLICK. His magazine was empty. Turning, he fled.

Ezrulie arrived and took charge of Elspeth and within a short time there was a cordon of women surrounding her, allowing some dignity in her time of need.

'Remember to breathe,' said Ezrulie while Elspeth panted between contractions. 'Now push!'

*

Darkness returned to Gladios' world when Kenny replaced the wooden planks over the hole laying jackets and various articles of clothes on top to hide their workings.

*

'One more push,' said Ezrulie who had now moved to the business end of proceedings and was helping out.

Fortescue and Shona were slinking off, following Oliver and Gus who had left as soon as Brialto fled. They had decided that there would be repercussions after the mad Italian's interventions and despite being so close to the treasure they felt now was an opportune time to make themselves scarce.

'Almost there,' said Ezrulie, placing her hands lovingly on the slimy little head. One more shove from Elspeth and whoosh… Ezrulie was cradling the precious cargo which began to cry. Placing the newborn on her mother she cut the umbilical cord with Beowulf's old penknife and tied it up. An ambulance could be heard in the background.

But Elspeth hadn't stopped panting and was still breathing hard. She passed her newborn to Iona and directed Ezrulie back to her workstation.

'Twins,' she managed to blurt out in between deep breaths.

'F _ _ K,' said Ezrulie for the second time that night.

*

The crowds were dispersed by the time the paramedics arrived to help mother and babies to the waiting ambulance. There was a procession including Helena whom the medics insisted was checked out at A & E and by the time they were all bundled into the back of the ambulance, Iona decided that Kenny should drive the van to the hospital so she could be with her cousin in her time of need. Within ten minutes they were gone and the small site close to the Comet Stone was deserted apart from a couple of random jackets left loosely over the dig.

On hearing the quiet above, Gladios shouted out, 'Anyone there?'

His call was met with silence. Sensing he had been left alone and not sure how he had survived his close encounter, Gladios began to work out how he was going to climb out of his little den.

*

Within Scapa Flow HMS Katsonis, a Papanikolis Class submarine, surfaced!

Chapter 51 – Il Porco the Great

With his back to the wall Gladios managed to get his right toe into a nook and push himself upwards. He kept a firm hold of *Athena*. Then, placing his left toe on a small ledge, he pushed again and ever so slowly, like a cork being pulled from a bottle, he scrambled higher until he could push the old boards, covering the entrance, to one side and haul himself out. Lying on his back, looking up at the twilight sky with his legs still dangling downwards, he kissed *Athena Parthenos*. Even in this murky light Gladios could see the clarity of shape and intricate design, an exact replica of the full size chryselephantine sculpture. He was sure it was an original created by dear Phidias. Priceless! His smart phone vibrated and he saw a message come in from Prodius.

'Go to the banks of the Loch of Stenness and we will collect you.' Oh, how he smiled with glee, not really believing that their outrageous quest was now looking like it might well pay great dividends, if he could just get this priceless treasure back to mother Greece and return it to its rightful place within the Temple of Parthenon. Athens would be grateful; the whole of Greece would be joyous and celebrate their wonderful feat.

He stood up, dusting down his trousers and then, after a quick check on Google Earth, set off towards the Loch of Stenness, bypassing the Brodgar Ring. The fire still burned in the centre, although, other than a few die-hard druids who were still drinking ale, the place was much quieter than earlier. He was buoyed, almost jubilant with the situation he now found himself in. He moved with haste across the rough-cut grass.

*

Stavros de-throttled the outboard motor and the inflatable craft slowed as they approached the small bridge over the thin strip of water which connected the Loch of Stenness to the sea beyond. The four Greek

Special Forces soldiers, darkened with camo and well-armed, ducked when passing beneath before the boat accelerated towards the distant bank and their rendezvous.

*

'*Il Porco, Il Porco.*' Gladios hesitated, not sure what he had heard or where the call had come from. He looked around, back towards the stones, but couldn't see anything other than the distant goings-on within the Ring. '*Il Porco,*' he heard it again, coming from some long grass to his right and on squinting through the hazy light saw a small crimson dot and instantly recognised a cigarette glow! He stopped in his tracks. 'Where are you going, *Il Porco?*'

Gladios remained still, not sure what the implications were while staring towards the distant glow which seemed to be getting brighter and then suddenly went out! And from the long grass a large hulk appeared, standing tall and silhouetted against the clear night sky. Ever so slowly it started walking towards Gladios.

Run! The big Greek decided to run and even though he could now see the inflatable craft approaching the banks of the Loch of Stenness it was a race he was never likely to win. Within fifty yards the tall Italian had caught *Il Porco*, tripping him up with a well-judged kick!

Gladios ploughed into the ground, headfirst, and then rolled to one side, managing to prevent *Athena* from being damaged. Coming to a halt he gently placed the exquisite statute on a soft piece of grass. However, by the time he looked up Bruno's menacing figure was towering over him with the heel of his cowboy boot resting on his fat stomach. He withdrew the machete from the inside of his cape and Gladios instantly recognised the glint of steel.

All Bruno saw was a fat pig carcass, a weaner ready to be butchered, severed limb from limb and hung up ready for sale, just like he had seen many a carcass at the butchers in Venice. But there was no rush. None whatsoever, he mused, smiling with glee while pointing the machete at the throat of *Il Porco.* He was teasing and mocking the big Greek, knowing it would be futile for him to resist.

And all Gladios saw was a vision of evil and unpleasantness, a bully at work. Indignant that his life had come to this; to be slaughtered upon some foreign land, not Greece, not his home, not with the people he loved. No, he was to be sacrificed by a despot Italian lunatic. In both hands Bruno raised the machete above his head ready to dispatch *Il Porco.*

But Gladios didn't see himself as a defenceless pig at the abattoir. He was a wild boar who had been cornered and like all wild animals in such circumstances, there was only one thing left to do - turn and fight!

Bruno's eye's narrowed and his moustache curled with a sarcastic grin. Gladios could see the veins in his arms begin to bulge, flexing his muscles in readiness to swing the machete downwards and that split second advantage was enough for *Il Porco* to seize the initiative. Like a coiled spring he curled forward and head butted the Italian firmly in the groin, causing Bruno to miss his target as the machete blade sank into the soft earth, before he crumpled up and fell to the ground. And this is where the wild boar suddenly had the upper hand, scraping at close quarters. Bruno was strong, mightily strong, but Gladios was heavy, very heavy and after felling the big Italian he shuffled on top of the brutal man, using his whole weight to pin him down and then… sank his teeth into his arm. And boy, did Bruno squeal - like a wounded animal!

*

The inflatable craft beached on the shore and the Special Forces soldiers could clearly see the scrap unfolding in front of their eyes. But their orders were clear and unequivocal in their terms – under no circumstances set foot on dry land.

'Can you get a clean shot?' barked Stavros to his colleagues in front and while the soldiers raised their assault rifles to the fore there was no chance of shooting the big Italian while Gladios was on top.

*

Of course, Bruno was angry at being held in this way and after rolling a little to his left he was able to free his right arm and punch *Il Porco.* And my! could he punch, even from this restricted angle. His club-like fists starting to reign blows onto the head of the old snouter who was locked onto his arm. Gladios' eyes became glazed and started to swell and then with a firm right blow he was caught on the side of his chin with such force it fractured his jaw. No longer could he hold the mad Italian between his teeth in a vice-like grip as Bruno's left fist sprang into action. He hit *Il Porco* squarely on the face from the other side. Suddenly punches were being thrown from all angles, battering this dear old Greek. The only course of action left was to wrap his arms around his head to afford some protection from the vicious onslaught. Gladios' vision became blurred and then shards of light flashed through his head. Within a nanosecond Bruno had leapt to his feet and retrieved the machete, which was lying close by, and for the second time raised it in two hands above his head ready to finish off the fat Greek.

*

'Shoot him!' ordered Stavros to the soldier at the front of the boat.

*

Bruno was sneering with delight, flexing his back, ready to put all his strength into bringing the machete downwards onto *Il Porco,* but, before he could decapitate Gladios, Bruno was hit from the side by a solid object which caught him off balance and knocked him to the ground. There was a CRACK and a bullet whizzed above. The soldier shook his head.

*

Donald Mackenzie had initially approached with care, but on seeing the dire situation unfold he had been haunted by his earlier encounter in Prestonpans, only a month ago. His fear tuned to anger. He was livid; furious that this lunatic should attack once again and recalling the fright be had seen in Hannah's eyes he sprinted into the fray as if it were a P.E. training session on the Meadows in Edinburgh. Knees high and arms pumping he launched himself at the tall Italian with such pace he knocked him clean off his feet and the blade out of his hand. A scissor kick to the face, as Bruno staggered, not once but twice and then a forward roll, diving beneath the big Italian who lunged forward to catch him. Donald neatly slipped out of his reach. Squat thrust; ducking to miss a well-aimed punch and then instinctively a burpee, jumping upwards and inadvertently catching Bruno under the jaw with his head which left him reeling. Two more sharp scissor kicks and Goliath was felled, banging his head on a rock when he hit the ground. Hannah was on hand, in a flash, and had a set of hand cuffs secured and his legs bound.

*

Gladios was now sitting up in the long grass. Both eyes were swollen and his head was throbbing from the pounding he had taken. He could feel a trickle of blood run down his cheek. He had seen Mackenzie's intervention, for which he owed him his life, and suddenly *Athena Parthenos,* which was lying close by, seemed less important. Hannah had picked up the statue and held it in awe, admiring the intricate carving before passing it to Donald who inquisitively took hold of the exquisite piece of art. This was his salvation, his reputation restored, his career properly rewarded after years of little recognition for the tireless service he had given. His face lit up with a beaming smile.

Gladios stood up with his head bowed in defeat. His race had been run and as always he had come off second best. But, despite the indignity of losing at the last, he owed this wiry Scotsman his heartfelt thanks for saving his life. If he could have swapped it for *Athena* he would gladly have done so, to return her to her rightful home on the Acropolis, the Temple of Parthenon and to the Greek people.

'Thank you,' he said holding out his right hand. Without thinking Donald took hold and nodded while looking into the fat swollen face and sallow dark eyes. Gladios turned and started slowly trudging towards the boat.

'Well done,' said Hannah all joy and smiles. She was delighted for Donald and that at last his endeavours would be recognised. And Donald was upbeat with his great success while he thought of the sickening look on the Chief Superintendent's face, that ruddy baboon, and how he would have to finally acknowledge his achievement.

But of course… the Chief Superintendent wouldn't trumpet his good work. Somehow that baboon of a man would turn it around, skew the truth and present it as his great masterplan and claim the credit. He knew only too well the infuriation he would feel. Donald was no longer smiling; his eyes were transfixed on the dejected, bear like, lumbering figure who was slowly crabbing his way towards the beach. He knew only too well how he would be feeling.

'WAIT,' he shouted in a firm, authoritative voice and then set off at a brisk walk towards the shore. 'Wait,' he repeated again when he was within a few yards of Gladios who was getting ready to enter the water and board the boat. He met the big Greek's gaze as he turned, seeing his red cheeks and blood shot eyes. They stared at one another while standing just a few yards apart. The moment was poignant. Donald stepped forward, holding out *Athena Parthenos.*

'Here… take it. Take it back to Greece where it belongs.' Gladios was overcome, unable to move and no longer transfixed on the statue. Instead, he stared into Donald's eyes as tears ran down his cheeks. He moved forward, grasping the Scotsman to give him a hug and flexing his big muscular biceps embraced him warmly before eventually letting go. Taking *Athena* he turned, climbed into the boat and waved goodbye.

'What did you do that for?' questioned Hannah who was now standing beside her colleague. Donald didn't answer straight away, preferring to stare seawards and watch the boat disappear until eventually he spoke.

'It felt right.'

Chapter 52 – Run Boy Run

The phone on the First Sea Lord's bedside table rang.

'Hello, yes, what? … unbelievable!'

*

Katsonis had steamed out of Scapa Flow and once in open water beyond the archipelago had dived for cover, heading back towards the North Sea where she had been on exercise in Norwegian waters. But Katsonis had been spotted by a routine reconnaissance flight on a test exercise around the coast. Now, locked onto the foreign vessel, the surveillance plane passed on its location to the Vanguard nuclear submarine which was able to pick up the acoustics despite being some distance away.

*

The telephone in the First Minister's bedroom rang at five-thirty in the morning.

'Fit what? Owh ga te bed will ye, yur pullin me leg.' The First Sea Lord explained the gravity of the situation, although it seemed to be lost on the Minister at this early hour. 'Fit, what do ya want me to do?' The Sea Lord paused, not sure how to broach the subject again. 'I'll tell yur what, whay don't you ask that blonde scarecrow from London what to do and then do the opposite. Do yur ken? That's what I always do,' and with that the First Minister hung up, slipped into her sheep-skin slippers and went to make a cup of tea. The phone rang in 10 Downing Street.

'Phwoarr, Phwoarr, Phwoarrrrrr!' The First Sea Lord put the phone down and decided to waste no more of his time. He radioed Captain Sterling who was in charge of the British Nuclear submarine and gave him his orders.

'Chase alien vessel down, but do not fire.' Sterling knew exactly what was expected of him, relaying the message to the engine room where the Chief Officer hit the burners and throttled up. If they could close the gap they ought to be able to recognise the craft from the acoustic signature and then they would let the Foreign Office take it up.

And HMS Vanguard did not disappoint; the behemoth of a submarine being swiftly propelled through the water at twenty-four knots. Katsonis could see on the radar that they were being pursued and realising they had been detected started to run towards Norway. But while Katsonis was seaworthy and a mighty fine craft she was much slower than the British vessel. Captain Prakatis knew it was likely to be a nuclear submarine on their tail and he also knew how fast they could travel!

'Are we going to make it?' he shouted across the floor to the Chief Navigator who was plotting their course on the large, illuminated screen in the control room. Without turning, he shook his head. Prakatis sucked in a deep breath of air. He could see the large flash on the monitor getting ever closer – 'o agapite mou!'

*

The Greek Prime Minister had been briefed and was up early having a coffee when the phone rang.

'Yes, yes, I see.' Within a couple of minutes he was on the doorsteps of the French Embassy where he was met by an attractive svelte lady. She ushered him towards the kitchen to meet Ambassador Lafette who was having breakfast.

'Croissant?' he offered. The Greek Prime Minister shook his head, having already eaten. Looking disgruntled the Ambassador went to the corner cupboard and retrieved a couple of glasses and a fine bottle of Champagne. 'Aperitif? he insisted and without waiting for a reply, popped the cork and half-filled the flutes before topping them up with Crème de Cassis. 'Comment ca va?' and then in a single motion they both sunk their drinks'. The Prime Minister knew it was futile to resist. He wanted a favour from his French friend and it wouldn't be discussed until they had finished the bottle and were at least halfway through a decent Beaujolais and a big slab of cheese. It looked like it was going to be a long morning!

*

Sterling was sitting on the bridge watching their progress on the digital screen. He could see they were making ground and he was confident they would intercept the alien craft while in British Waters. The intercom beside his seat flashed and bleeped and on picking up the handset, Sterling realised he was speaking with the First Sea Lord.

'How close to recognition?' the Admiral barked.

'Initial acoustic data indicates a diesel-powered vessel consistent with a Howaldtswerke-Duetsche Werft Craft.

'German? What on earth are they doing in our waters?'

'Not necessarily the German Navy, Sir. They build submarines for other countries.' The First Sea Lord paused while thinking. He was in his chauffeur driven car heading for Portsmouth and Navy Command Headquarters.

'Okay, keep streaming the data to Central Ops and let me know if there are any major developments. Otherwise, as soon as you are in range, get ready to fire a warning shot across their bow.'

'Aye, aye, Sir.'

'Load the Spearfish torpedoes,' shouted Sterling to his lieutenant who was standing close by. However, before he could contact the loading bay, they were distracted by the navigational team who were waving frantically, beckoning him over.

'We've got company.'

'Company?' questioned Sterling confused by the comment.

'Yes,' said the first navigational officer pointing to the monitor. There was another flashing light on the screen!

Chapter 53 – We've got Company

It was almost midday when the Greek Prime Minister left the French Embassy, stumbling down the steps before being helped into the back of his ministerial car.

'Damnnnn Monsieur Lafette,' he slurred while slouching in the back seat with his shirt half unbuttoned and his tie hanging loosely. The attentive under-secretary retrieved a can of coke from the drinks compartment and passed it to the PM. He knew how the French Ambassador worked. It was the price of co-operation.

*

Katsonis's captain had been delighted to see reinforcements arrive when the additional flashing light appeared on the screen and began to move towards them. The British submarine was still eating into their tender lead and with seventy miles to go before they reached the safety of Norway's waters, it still wasn't clear how events were likely to play out.

'Keep pushing,' he shouted down the handset to the engine room. The diesel engines purred ever faster.

*

The First Sea Lord was in the control room at Portsmouth HQ watching events develop on the large monitor in front of him. He was furious that another alien craft should have appeared from nowhere and when Sterling rang to seek orders of how to proceed he was unequivocal on what they should do.

'Fire a warning shot.'

*

The spearfish torpedo shot out of the hold amongst a storm of bubbles which were streaming towards the surface.

'TORPEDO!' screamed the Greek captain. His crew sprang into action and the submarine began to dive looking to avoid the fast-approaching threat. But, as all watched their screens in anticipation, they saw another torpedo, fired from the new vessels, travelling to intercept it.

*

The P-8 Poseidon left the runway at RAF Kinloss in the North of Scotland. It was seven minutes away from where the submarines had congregated and was fully armed ready to assist HMS Vanguard, if required.

*

KERBOOMMM!! the torpedoes collided two hundred and fifty yards from Katsonis, sending shock waves through the water which rocked the craft, causing the lights in the control room to flicker and knocking the captain to the floor. Jumping back to his feet, he was pleased to discover they had not been hit. Onwards Katsonis steamed as fast as she could.

*

'French,' shouted the Head of Intelligence at Navy HQ in Portsmouth.

'French?' repeated the First Sea Lord in surprise.

Nodding, the intelligence guru walked over and presented the acoustic readings.

'Rubis Class, we think.' The First Sea Lord was put through to the Secretary of State for Defence.

'Yes, yes, I see.' He put the phone down. 'Tell Sterling to back off.'

*

An aide was dispatched to the French Embassy in Knightsbridge.

*

HMS Vanguard de-throttled to a modest twelve knots sufficient to keep pace with Katsonis although they were no longer closing the gap. The little Greek vessel kept motoring full steam ahead.

*

The French weren't receptive to a visit from the British Civil Service so with little response the PM was wheeled out. Macron took the call.

'Bonjour.' The interpreters took over. The PM kerfuffled and kerfuddled while the P-8 Poseidon continued circling over-head. And the more they spoke through their respective translators the closer Katsonis got to Norwegian waters. Eventually the PM slammed down the phone in a pique of rage.

The Secretary of State for Defence arrived at 10 Downing Street in a chauffeur driven Jaguar and quickly scuttled inside.

'PHWOOAARR,' barked the PM, 'Phwooaarrr, Phwooaarrr, Phwooaarrr!'

271

'We have a plan,' replied the Secretary, trying to pacify the Prime Minister who took some time to calm down. But once sitting in their favourite wingback chair with a fresh cup of tea and a plate of digestives, the PM began to listen to the trusted cabinet minister who explained what he had been up to and what measures had been put in place. The Secretary of State for Defence spoke and the Prime Minister nodded while munching their way through half a packet of biscuits. Within twenty minutes it was all agreed. The First Sea Lord was put in the picture and Sterling was ordered back to base, leaving Katsonis to make her way across the North Sea and into Norwegian territory, unhindered. On she continued at a lightning pace and by late evening she surfaced in the Hardangerfjord south of Bergen where she remained overnight. However, when the sun arose over the fjords the following morning a Norwegian military patrol boat approached and docked alongside. They were made welcome by the Greek crew who were only too happy to let them on board and search their craft.

Chapter 54 – A Newborn's Cry

Elspeth had been rushed to the Balfour Hospital on the outskirt of Kirkwall following the timely birth of her twins at the Brodgar Ring. Checked over and now in the maternity ward, her babies were feeding well and lay asleep in the cot beside the bed while Ranald fussed around them like an old hen.

'Jock, how about Jock?' he suggested as he doted over the little boy. Elspeth raised her eyebrows. The midwife entered to check they were okay.

'Jock, what do you think about Jock?' she asked the stout nurse who was smiling coyly at the babies who lay contently on their backs.

'I like Emily for the wee girl. Oh, it's a dear name is Emily, I've always liked it,' she replied.

'And what about Jock?' persisted Ranald hoping for some moral support. The silence was awkward while the midwife thought on her feet.

'Err... Jockstrap?' she replied with a mischievous smirk. Elspeth smiled.

*

The debrief at the British Museum was scheduled for early next week. It would be chaired by the Principal, Professor Cordingwell, and there was likely be a lengthy investigation as to why they had spent the best part of a month in Scotland for no tangible return. But this didn't seem to bother Fortescue or Shona who were on route to his family seat in the depths of the Shires to meet his parents and spread the good news. Fortescue's obsession with the fiery Irish girl had reached epic proportions on their extended stay and in a moment of whimpering submission he had capitulated and asked Shona to become the next Lady Fortescue of Harthogs Hall. His mother would be disappointed that no blue blood had been landed, but Fortescue knew his father would understand the wild attractions this raven-haired Irish beauty held.

*

Kenny and Iona were taking it day by day as they began to get to know each other during date after date. Hibernian Supporters Club had not been a good idea but the innocence of youth and their zest for life seemed to nurture the blossoming romance.

*

'You want Luigi?' questioned the ageing grocer at the vegetable stall

'Yes, I want Luigi,' insisted the Duchessa. Without further ado the young lad was packed off on his delivery bike, heading towards Palazzo Toscano with a couple of melons and large courgette in his box!

Brialto had been quiet since returning to Venice. He was back to his old business of blackmail and extortion without his bruising right hand man. Dear old Bruno was in bother, in the soup as they say, and was still being held under lock and key at Peterhead Prison, awaiting trial and a custodial sentence. He would be out within twelve months, so the lawyers said, and until then he would have to learn to like porridge for the duration of his Scottish stay.

*

'Would you like some more potatoes?' asked Mrs Mackenzie. Donald's father moved tentatively around the table topping up the wine glasses before taking his seat at the head of the table. Hannah smiled sweetly while enjoying Sunday roast in the dining room of the semi-detached villa within the suburbs of Edinburgh.

'It's so lovely to meet one of Donald's work colleagues,' waxed his mother, gushing with inquisitiveness as she eyed up the pretty young police officer. Donald blushed while raising his eyebrows towards the ceiling. His Father kindly intervened.

'And do you have any idea who took the painting?' he asked, saving Hannah from his wife's exuberance. Not that she was concerned in the slightest; in fact Hannah had warmed to Donald's parents who clearly meant well.

'Not yet,' she replied, 'but we are still working on the case,' and then looking towards Donald smiled gently. The wine bottle was drained and the main course plates were cleared. Pudding followed with a sticky digestif for the constitution and then cheese and coffee. Despite the constant stream of questions, Hannah had enjoyed Sunday lunch but as the afternoon wore on, eventually, it was time to leave.

'Do come again,' insisted Mrs Mackenzie.

'I would love to,' replied Hannah with a smile. And after the parents retreated back to the kitchen Donald was left on the front steps of the stone villa. Looking down he caught Hannah's eye and held her gaze. She leant forward and kissed him on the lips, catching Donald off guard. A look of surprise spread across his face.

'Why did you do that?'

'… It felt right.'

*

The days passed while the main protagonists settled down to their humdrum lives and a semblance of normality as life returned to the day-in and day-out routine. A distant dot appeared on the horizon of the Aegean Sea, barely visible from Piraeus Harbour on the edge of Athens. It bobbed and bobbled, gradually getting closer and closer as its white sails flexed in the breeze. The delightful turquoise hull of the pretty wee boat could now be seen and within the hour she had entered a quiet cove not far from the harbour mouth and pulled up alongside a short pontoon.

'Thanks for the lift.'

'My pleasure dear friend,' replied Terence and within a couple of minutes Gladios, with his crew bag, was in the back of government car being introduced to the Greek Prime Minister!

Chapter 55 – A Greek Celebration!

There was quite a crowd outside the Sarcophagus Tavern when Gladios and Fatima arrived in a chauffeur driven car which dropped them off close to the main entrance. Cameras flashed and microphones were thrust forward in a media melee as the spherical couple were ushered in by security guards, into the depths of the tavern.

'HURRAH.' Everyone applauded the arrival of Greece's prodigal son, Gladios, who had become an overnight sensation with regular appearances on daytime television to talk about *Athena Parthenos* which had now been dated back to Phidias's time. Of course, the whereabouts of his great find was left a little murky and on more than one occasion Gladios had been slightly elusive about where the beautiful miniature chryselephantine sculpture had turned up. But while some were perplexed by the exact detail of the mysterious find the vast majority of Greeks were not bothered with the minutiae; they were delighted that part of their heritage had been discovered and returned to where it belonged - the Parthenon Temple.

Prodius was sitting at the head of the table with many of the bigwigs from the Greek Bureau of Culture who were riding high on their great success. Helena was wearing an elegant sequined evening dress, looking sophisticated and stunning while she chatted with the Minister of Arts who had been invited to the party. As everyone took a seat at the large circular table in the centre of the room, champagne corks popped and the starter arrived - polpo! Gladios glanced at the central fish tank noticing it was empty. The maître d' smiled when he saw his look of surprise.

Toasts were proposed and toasts were made while dish followed dish of the finest cuisine that the Tavern could offer. However, there was little time to dwell on this joyous evening because at eight o'clock they were due at the Acropolis and the Parthenon Temple where the Greek Prime Minister would unveil *Athena Parthenos* to the world. And make no mistake this was a big occasion with hundreds of thousands of people expected to turn up, accompanied by the media who would broadcast the event around the globe: from America to Australia, China to Chile, Bombay to Macclesfield... By the time they finished their merry soiree it was time to go to the Temple and introduce *Athena*.

*

The streets were gridlocked by the swell of spectators whose numbers were now fast approaching a million, all making their way to the open land beside the Acropolis from where they would view the spectacle. Young, old, rich, poor it was an event which brought the whole of Greece together. The chauffeur-driven car was redundant in the packed streets so they joined the throng and began the half-mile procession to their destination, amongst the crowds. Gladios was quickly recognised from his appearances on national TV and was instantly lifted and placed on the shoulders of some sturdy Greeks, enabling them to carry the Messiah to his place of destiny - the Parthenon Temple. And on seeing the big man raised above the masses the crowds began to cheer and chant.

'GLADIOS, GLADIOS, GLADIOS...' Ladies threw garlands of flowers around his neck, showering praise on their unsuspecting hero who had returned *Athena Parthenos* to her homeland, to Greece and to the Greeks. Onwards the tsunami of followers rumbled, chanting in tune like the constant beat of their motherland's heart. Within twenty minutes they ascended the steps and arrived in front of the Temple. The sturdy men helped Gladios to the ground as the Greek Prime Minister looked on bemused by the arrival of Greece's new darling. And on seeing the great man the crowds, within the open land below, erupted like Mount Vesuvius with smoke billowing upwards as the energy of the occasion electrified them. There was a roar of approval.

'GLADIOS, GLADIOS, GLADIOS…' they chanted. The Prime Minister took to the microphone to try and calm the occasion although his efforts were futile, like Canute trying to quell the tide.

'You getting this?' shouted the NCC director to a cameraman as the images were beamed into the homes of ordinary folk around the world. *Athena Parthenos* stood on the small table beside the lectern where the Prime Minister was due to speak, but his aides quickly realised that the mood of the occasion had consumed the event and there was only one person who the Greeks wanted to hear. Gladios was pushed forward, impromptu, and the microphone thrust into his hand. Waving his palms downwards he managed to quieten the crowds who stood transfixed waiting to hear what the great man had to say. Gladios took his time, like the statesman he had grown into over recent days. Once a veil of silence had descended across the Acropolis, the big man held the microphone to his lips and began to speak.

'FELLOW GRECIANS,' he bellowed, asserting his authority and instantly he captivated the crowd. He lowered his voice to a quieter level. 'We are gathered here today to celebrate the return of one of our great treasures,' and with that he pulled off the silk cover to reveal *Athena Parthenos* as a spotlight was turned on, illuminating the small statue which twinkled in the light. The crowd roared with joy while streamers were thrown and fireworks were ignited, lighting up the dark evening sky. Athens was alive, full of joy, the likes of which had never been seen before. Cameras rolled and reporters reported, and the images were caught for posterity.

Again the big man waved his hands downwards to dampen the crowd and abiding by the wish of their new hero, the spectators managed to suppress their excitement. A wave of quiet rippled all around. Gladios began to speak again.

'This is a great day for Greece. Our motherland is once again re-united with a child, the daughter of *Athena Parthenos* returned to where she rightly belongs, back to the womb of the Parthenon Temple.' Again the crowds were effervescent, roaring their approval and again Gladios managed to quieten the hordes with a wave of his hands before continuing.

'It has been a monumental effort to bring *Athena* back to Greece.' All looked on in wonder. 'We threw everything at it, no stone was left unturned and even our Prime Minister helped with our endeavours when required.' He hesitated while the crowd took in the detail of what Gladios was saying.

'Yet even then...' he paused allowing the emotion within him to swell, 'yet even then... it would not have been possible without a little help from our friends.'

Silence descended across the Acropolis and with the sudden hush a strange wailing sound began to radiate from within the Temple. Faint at first, unrecognisable to ordinary Greeks, the wail grew louder and louder and from between the colonnades stepped forth a Seaforth Highlander in full regimental attire. Tucked beneath his elbow were the ceremonial pipes which he was playing with vigour. And the crowd were transfixed by this strange intervention, unsure what to make of this most peculiar sight; a skirted man with a feather bonnet and white hackles. All hot and sweaty the piper walked onto the stage and paused his tune while he caught his breath and re-inflated his pipes. The crowd looked on. Gladios had stepped from behind the lectern and stood to the front with his government colleagues, their hands crossed and held together as the piper picked up the tempo and began to play some more. And as the joyous notes radiated far and wide, Gladios and his colleagues began shaking their hands upwards and downwards. They began to sing.

'Should auld acquaintance be forgot and never bought to mind?
Should auld acquaintance be forgot and days of auld land syne?

The Curse of Minerva

For auld land syne, my dear, for auld lang syne
We'll take a cup of kindness yet for days of auld lang syne...'

And with that Gladios led the line forwards towards the crowds who were in awe of the performance, erupting in joy and once again the whole of Greece celebrated, with fireworks lighting up the night sky, as millions of Greeks cheered.

*

At the pleasant little semi-detached villa in the suburbs of Edinburgh, close to the Meadows, Donald sat transfixed by the television, clutching his whisky while he watched the live screening. His shoulders started to shake and he began to tremble in front of his parents.

'Donald are you all right?' asked his mother, looking at her cherished son. He breathed out and with tears streaming down his cheeks managed to pull himself together sufficiently to speak.

'Mighty fine people are the Greeks.'

The End